Praise for *Josie and V*

"With an authentic sense of place and time, *Josie and Vic* pulls the reader into the emotional depths of familial relationships and the pain of generational secrets. Author Debra Thomas has created characters who illuminate the essentials of the human heart in this story of love, loss, and renewal."
> —Johnnie Bernhard, author of *Hannah and Ariela*

"Debra Thomas is a magician. Her artistry, empathy, and gentle humor allow *Josie and Vic*, a novel grounded in the deepest of grief, to shine with hope, with compassion, with the reminder that connection and service offer us paths toward healing. An unforgettable, heart-filled, heart-filling novel."
> —Gayle Brandeis, author of *The Book of Dead Birds*,
> winner of Barbara Kingsolver's Bellwether Prize

"There is so much hope and forgiveness laced throughout Debra Thomas's examination of a family that has drifted apart and finally learns how to come back together. These characters stayed with me long after the final page. Bravo!"
> —Mary Camarillo, author of *The Lockhart Women*

"Each member of this multigenerational family must seek forgiveness and reconciliation, as we too must do within ourselves, as well as across regions, countries, and continents. Thomas's storytelling gift is one of empathy for her characters, both human and animal, and love of family in all its complicated conditions."
> —Gretchen Cherington, award-winning author of *Poetic License*

"A clear-sighted, moving, contemporary story of the familial support it takes to bravely move forward, *Josie and Vic* explores what it takes to heal a shattered self in favor of joining a greater whole."

—Claire Fullerton, author of *Little Tea*

"Beautifully crafted and richly detailed, this is a novel with a conscience and something important to say."

—Jeannee Sacken, author of *Behind the Lens* and *Double Exposure*

"With tenderness and empathy, Debra Thomas weaves decades of family secrets, betrayals, and tragedies. How do you find your way back home after unimaginable loss?"

—Eileen Harrison Sanchez, *Freedom Lessons: A Novel*

"An amazing story of love and loss, love and family, love and hope, this heartwarming novel is a compassionate tale of connections and explorations, underlining well-known truths and providing new insights as to how we navigate our worlds."

—Romalyn Tilghman, author of *To the Stars Through Difficulties*

"*Josie and Vic* is about transcending tragedy and finding the way back, or the way forward, with the help of those you love. An incredibly touching, heartbreaking story, filled with heart and soul."

—Lorraine Devon Wilke, author of the
award-winning novel *The Alchemy of Noise*

Praise for *Luz: A Novel*

"*Luz* is a deeply generous novel, steeped through with compassion and written with an open, observant heart. Our narrator, Alma, is enamored with math, and this book becomes a beautiful equation in itself—pain and hope and love adding up to a timely, magnificent story."

—Gayle Brandeis, author of *The Book of Dead Birds*,
winner of Barbara Kingsolver's Bellwether Prize
for Fiction of Social Engagement

"This is a novel of great tenderness and great brutality—Debra is right inside of her character's minds, bodies, spirits, their souls, and doesn't spare the reader either tenderness or brutality."

—Alma Luz Villanueva, author of American Book
Award winner *The Ultraviolet Sky*

"Debra Thomas has deftly interwoven the horrors and indignities, as well as the triumphs, of the harrowing journey of Mexicans and Central Americans to the United States, 'bringing to light' the commonalities of what by appearances are insurmountable differences. With love there are no borders."

—Luis J. Rodriguez, author of *Always Running* and *It Calls You
Back: An Odyssey through Love, Addiction, Revolutions, and Healing*

"Debra Thomas has written a novel of beauty and the nobility of the human spirit in the face of brutality and overwhelming odds. It's an adventure as well, full of vivid characters, most notably Alma Cruz, as wise and courageous a heroine as you'll find anywhere in literature. *Luz* is a story we need to read now more than ever."

—Elizabeth McKenzie, author of *The Portable Veblen*
and *The Dog of the North*

Josie and Vic

A Novel

Debra Thomas

SHE WRITES PRESS

Published 2023
Printed in the United States of America
Print ISBN: 978-1-64742-393-3
E-ISBN: 978-1-64742-394-0
Library of Congress Control Number: 2022912255

For information, address:
She Writes Press
1569 Solano Ave #546
Berkeley, CA 94707

She Writes Press is a division of SparkPoint Studio, LLC.

For my husband,
Bruce

Humankind has not woven the web of life.
We are but one thread within it.
Whatever we do to the web, we do to ourselves.
All things are bound together.
All things connect.

—Chief Seattle

Because truly being here is so much;
because everything here apparently needs us,
this fleeting world,
which in some strange way keeps calling to us.
Us, the most fleeting of all.

—Rainer Maria Rilke

Pangaea: the Supercontinent
Pronounced "pan-jee-uh"

According to modern geology, millions of years ago all the world's land masses were joined together into one supercontinent, Pangaea, surrounded by a single sea, Panthalassa. Through what we now call plate tectonics, the shifting of the Earth's crust broke up this super-continent into several pieces that drifted over the Earth's mantle and, ultimately, formed our present-day continents.

City of Angels

January 2001

JOSIE

Vic had always been her hero. Before his work with immigrants and refugees—even long before Vietnam. Josie remembered well how her big brother, with his boisterous laugh and vibrant spirit, would bound into their tiny house in a cloud-covered corner of Upstate New York, and, within seconds, their mother would actually hum—quietly and only a few notes, but still, it was the promise of music.

Now, calla lilies in hand, Josie hurried through the maze of hospital corridors with the same case and sense of purpose as the medical staff she passed. Nodding to the ward clerk at the desk, she turned into the second room on the right and was relieved to find no other visitors. With a grateful sigh, she sank onto the bedside chair and reached for her brother's hand.

"Vic," she whispered, trying not to disturb this moment of peace, yet wanting him to know she was there. He didn't stir, so Josie sat for a moment with her nurse's eye noting that his color was good, his skin warm and dry, and the urine in his Foley bag a clear yellow. All good signs. Perhaps she could take him home by the weekend.

Home, she thought with a shudder. That word had changed for both of them with one chilling phone call. For Vic, home would never be the same, for he had just lost his entire family—his wife and two children—in a tragic accident. For Josie, home had always been the same town in Upstate New York for her entire forty-two years, but, at least for a while—several months, perhaps a year—she'd be living with Vic in Canoga Park, a small section of the sprawling metropolis of Los Angeles.

The bed beside Vic's was still empty. Josie wished she could stretch out on the cool white sheets and take a nap. She hadn't slept well in weeks, not since the funeral and then her dash home to pack up and get things in order. Clearly, it had been the right thing to do—move in with Vic, pack up her life and move across the country for however long it took. No questions. No hesitation. Her brother needed her, so that was where she belonged. Oddly though, despite the sadness that surrounded the situation, that hung heavy and leaden with pain, Josie had felt a strange lightness.

She felt it first right after the funeral, when the chaos abruptly ended and an empty void left them both stunned as they sat in Vic's brightly colored living room. Staring at his open hands, Vic had asked her, "Now what do I do? What in God's name do I do now, Jo?" Josie knew there was nothing she could say, but she could be there until he found an answer—if there was one. Vic refused to leave their little house, and she certainly couldn't leave him there alone. At that very moment, all conflict in Josie's life had lifted. No more wondering about what she should do next. Her own husband, Ben, had died four years before, and her nineteen-year-old daughter, Ellie, abruptly moved to Seattle the previous summer, leaving Josie rattling around her large house with only echoes of the past to keep her company. Sitting with Vic in his living room that day, every-thing was suddenly clear, like someone opened a door and simply said, "This way, Josie."

But that feeling of lightness had disappeared with a second shocking phone call—this time about Vic.

Josie had been home less than a week, making quick decisions about what to store in closets and what to bring. She'd managed to lease her house to a very grateful colleague—a cardiac resident at the hospital, who agreed to a six-month minimum, one-year possible verbal agreement. And her greatest worry—who would care for her three beloved horses—had just been solved. Josie was about to sit down and take a deep breath when Vic's friend Rodrigo called to say that Vic had overdosed on a combination of anti-depressants and sedatives—drugs prescribed to help him through his horrific ordeal.

Had Vic planned this from the start? Had his seeming strength been meant to send her on her way so he could neatly settle things before she had time to pack and move? Or was it just an unplanned, unbearable moment, a desperate attempt to end the gut-wrenching pain that accompanied such grief? Fortunately, Rodrigo had stopped by earlier than expected, giving the drugs just a short time to work their damage. Two days in intensive care had everyone holding their breath, but Vic had finally stabilized.

Sitting at his bedside now, Josie slowly released Vic's hand and stood to replace the drooping roses beside his bed with the calla lilies. She first saw the white trumpet-like flowers in two framed prints on Vic's living room wall—bursting from a sack on a man's back and engulfed in the embrace of a brown-skinned girl. Diego Rivera prints, she learned. That morning at the market, these same flowers caught her eye—four white calla lilies, leaning separately in a large plastic container. As she arranged them now in the slender vase, they stood together, tall and proud.

Tossing the roses into the trash can, Josie sat back down and stretched her legs. Vic moaned softly and rolled to his side. His dark curls were now threaded with gray, but his sleep-softened face was still youthful despite its forty-eight years. Before the accident, Vic had barely a line on his face, except for a few when he laughed or smiled, but since December 18th, the lines were becoming more defined and dark circles were deepening under his eyes.

To lose your spouse was one thing—Josie knew that pain—but to lose both of your children as well was asking too much of any human being. How could anyone expect to recover from that? People at the funeral had murmured comments about Vic being young enough to start again, but Josie couldn't help but feel that it meant he had a longer road ahead of him to carry that burden. While Josie still woke some mornings to an emptiness so profound that she could barely push herself out of bed, Vic had lost so much more—wife, little son and daughter —all at once, as a car careened out of control and crashed into the tiny space where the three stood waiting at a bus stop.

Josie cringed at the thought of comments made about God's plan or His reasons for taking them all. Josie had given up looking for reasons long ago—reasons why her dad left, why her mom and Ben died too soon, and now Irma and the kids. No answer would make it any easier to bear, so why ask? The way she saw it, you sought comfort in the loved ones left and in those loved ones you hadn't yet met.

Josie wished her daughter Ellie could see that, instead of running away. Ellie wouldn't even come to their funeral; she just wept hysterically on the phone, saying there was *no way*, for she couldn't imagine seeing Isabel and Miguel in little coffins, not after spending two weeks with them in the fall. All those vivid memories. Painting Isa's little toe nails; blowing raspberries on Miguel's bare belly just to hear that infectious giggle. Ellie just couldn't do it. Vic had tried to soothe her, but lost it himself. In the end, Ellie stayed in Seattle.

While Josie had been furious and profoundly disappointed, she'd also been relieved. She needed all of her energy for Vic.

"Good morning, Jo." Rae, the head nurse from the ICU, stepped softly into the room. Though a large woman, she always spoke just above a whisper and moved with the grace of a dancer. Josie had first met her after the accident, when Vic's wife, Irma, was in the critical care unit. A registered nurse herself, Josie had been impressed not just with Rae's competence, but also with the depth of her compassion. The two of them together had walked Vic through the whole medical nightmare of Irma's last days. Weeks later, when Josie had rushed into the same unit for Vic, Rae had been waiting for her despite the fact that her shift had ended. Once he was moved out of the ICU to the medical floor, Rae continued to check in frequently.

"How are you today?" Rae asked, her eyes kindly probing.

"Okay—I guess. How's Vic's blood work?" Josie presumed that the chart she was holding was Vic's, so she approached and stood beside her, looking at the open page.

"His lytes and BUN look great. White blood count down. Liver panel good. Vital signs all normal. Looks like they're taking the Foley out today. I saw Dr. Wolfe this morning, and he said he'd be talking to you about taking him home soon. What do you think? Are you ready?"

Josie focused on Rae's long French-tipped nails, striking against her dark brown skin. "Yes, I think so. I've stocked the cupboards and fridge with everything Mom used to make. I plan to fatten him up with lasagna as soon as possible." She tried to suppress a nervous laugh, but it came out like a squawk. Vic stirred in the bed. They were silent a moment, watching him; then Rae looped an arm around Josie's shoulder and guided her out the door.

Once they were seated on a bench at the end of the hall, Rae squeezed Josie's arm. "Honey, you're gonna be fine. He's come out of this beautifully. And he'll continue to see the psychiatrist, so . . ." She paused, left the rest unsaid, then whispered, "You're gonna be okay."

"Oh, Rae, can you imagine what he's going through?" Josie shook her head.

"Sweetie, he's lucky to have you. Some folks don't have anyone, but he's got you. That's a blessing."

Some blessing, Josie thought, frantically searching in her pocket for a tissue. Wiping her nose, she sighed. "To think I almost lost him, my big brother. Took care of me after my dad left us and my mom had to work extra shifts. Helped me when Ben died. I don't know what I'd do without him."

Rae nodded her head with each statement, but when Josie stopped to blow her nose, she said gently, "Josie, Vic's still here. You haven't lost him. He may have been knocked down hard, but he'll get up. He just needs time—and you." She squeezed her hand again.

It was true she hadn't lost him, but something in Vic was gone—extinguished like a streetlight that abruptly loses power, leaving a startling darkness. Josie felt that loss acutely.

They both looked up as the ward clerk approached and said, "Sorry to interrupt, Rae, but ICU's on the line."

Rae stood, giving Josie's shoulder a squeeze as she rose. "I'll check back later. Let me know what Dr. Wolfe says. And Josie, I'd like to give you my phone number, to keep in touch. See how's he's doing. Maybe visit, if you like?"

Josie smiled up at her. "I'd love that. Have you over for lasagna?"

"Sounds wonderful," Rae said, starting down the hall. "I'll just have to check my Weight Watchers guide for points," she added over her shoulder with a slight laugh.

Josie watched her round the corner until Rae was out of sight.

Releasing her thick dark hair from its clip, she twisted it into a knot and fastened it again. Glancing at her watch, she caught herself computing the time in Seattle by subtracting three hours, something she'd been doing for months. It was a habit she had to break, now that she and Ellie were in the same time zone. 11 a.m. in LA, 11 a.m. in Seattle, too. Leaning back against the wall, Josie closed her eyes and wondered what Ellie was doing. Probably sleeping in after a gig last night—her musician daughter who always dressed in black. Like most musicians, Ellie was a night owl, the opposite of Josie, who loved the early morning and considered it a sacred time.

They hadn't always been so different; in fact, they used to be the best of friends, doing everything together: trail-riding, hiking, even baking. Josie was exhausted trying to figure out when or why things went south between them. Was it after Ben's death, or was it before, when Ellie declared she'd been abandoned both by her biological father—which to some degree was true—and by Josie when Ben got sick—which wasn't *exactly* true. Or was it? At least that's what Ellie had said, right before taking off on a band tour of sorts that ended in Seattle. According to Ellie, Seattle was a great place to be a struggling musician, so she and another bandmate decided to stay. Frantic with worry, Josie had been relieved when Ellie stopped to visit Vic on her way up the coast, and Vic convinced Josie that Ellie had a head on her shoulders and to let her find her way. If it hadn't been for Vic, Josie would have been on a plane to chase her down, which might have strained their relationship even further.

"Oh, Ellie," Josie said aloud, then, shook her head in frustration and tried to push her daughter from her mind. Glancing out the window beyond the hospital parking lot, Josie saw a peaked cloud in the shape of a mountain—a mountain graced with snow—and immediately heard her daughter's voice. *Mom, you should see the mountains here. You'd love it!*

That had been the closest connection she'd felt with Ellie in ages. Ellie's brief phone message left shortly after arriving in Seattle: "Uh, hi Mom. It's me. I'm in Seattle. I'll let you know when I get a place. Uh . . . oh yeah: *Mom, you should see the mountains here. You'd love it!*" That last part played over and over in Josie's mind, how Ellie's voice came alive in those two sentences, perked up and spoke directly to her. For a brief moment, they'd connected.

Josie stood up and stretched. She felt stiff and out of shape. It had been weeks since she'd worked out or hiked. Her usually toned body was beginning to feel flabby and soft. Maybe she'd hit the exercise bike she saw in Vic's garage or go for a hike. After a few side bends and toe touches, she headed back toward Vic's room.

Since he was still asleep, Josie settled into her chair again, stretching her legs out on the foot of his bed. Closing her eyes, she tried to picture something peaceful—a cluster of birch trees shimmering in the midday sun, a swaying palm tree beside the ocean, a rugged coastline at sunset. Hearing movement, Josie opened her eyes.

Lying on his side, Vic was watching her, his lips turned up slightly, the closest he could come to a smile. "You were snoring," he said, his voice flat.

She wondered if he was trying to tease her, but his eyes looked deeply sad. She leaned forward and tried to make sharp snoring sounds in his face, but it came out more like a grunting pig.

A flash of a grin appeared briefly on his face. Vic rolled onto his back and pushed the button to elevate the head of his bed. Josie jumped up to help, but he shook his head and waved her to sit back down. "I've got it!" he said, then added, "Sorry."

Once he was settled, he ran his hand through his hair and let out a long exhale. Turning a weary face to her, he said, "Josie, I'm sorry about all of . . ."

"Don't go there," she interrupted, reaching out and touching his arm. "Enough of that. You have nothing to apologize for. Let's just focus on now, on getting you better. I just want to get you home."

She saw him wince. *Home.*

Delicately, she broached the topic. "Would it be better if we found a place to stay for a while, maybe by the ocean or in the mountains? Just for a few weeks?" She paused, then added, "It can't be good for you . . . to be . . . there." She thought of the small pink shoe she had found under the sofa that morning.

His face softened, and when he spoke, his words were as gentle as a prayer. "But everything about them is there. It's the only place I want to be."

Josie remembered the smell and feel of Ben's flannel shirt that she slept with every night for months, even sought out, like a toddler's blanket, to nap with briefly on the sofa. She nodded. "Okay."

Vic closed his eyes. They sat in silence for a few minutes.

Josie thought he was asleep until he whispered something, so she leaned in closer and asked, "What did you say?"

He repeated it again, but she couldn't quite make it out. Was it, "I see you, Jo" or "I need you, Jo"? Didn't matter, for they both touched her deeply.

Early the next morning, Josie woke feeling energized. Not only was Vic to be discharged the next day, but things back home had settled into place. Amir, the cardiac resident, had finished moving in, so Josie's house was being cared for. But most importantly, she received a phone message that her horses had been safely trailered to their destination and were adjusting well.

From the moment Josie considered moving west to help Vic, the three horses that she kept on her property had been her main concern. Her greatest worry had been Fire Mountain, her oldest at almost thirty, for he was battling Cushing's disease and suffering from ringbone and arthritis. Her miniature horse, Luke, had a stubborn streak and could be difficult to handle, and her quarter horse, Jack, panicked whenever either of his herdmates was out of sight. Trying to find someone to care for all three on short notice had been a challenge.

Amir was too busy at the hospital and inexperienced with anything horse related, so she knew she couldn't ask him. She had called several friends, but even the most experienced horse people were overwhelmed at the prospect of taking on all three in the midst of a harsh Upstate New York winter. Farming them out to separate places could have devastating effects, considering how long they'd been together. When her equine veterinarian, Doc Lucas, finally returned her call and offered to keep all three at his place, Josie had actually broken down, sobbing with gratitude and relief. Once she pulled herself together, she thanked him repeatedly and started rattling off a list of instructions, including the fact that Jack was difficult to load into a trailer. Doc Lucas had stopped her firmly mid-sentence, saying, "Just go. Email me specifics. I have your cell. I can handle Jack." He was terse and to the point, a trait that used to annoy Josie in the past, but which now brought such comfort.

But there had been another reason for her immense relief. The horses had clearly felt the loss of Ben, and then Ellie, from their daily lives, and now Josie herself was leaving, too. How might that affect them, especially her old horse, Fire? It tore Josie up inside to imagine their confusion. So having Doc Lucas agree to take them all in was more than a prayer answered, and not just because he was a veterinarian. Many times Josie had noticed, as Doc was handling them, how each horse would drop its head and let out that long sigh. They didn't need words. They needed a certain touch, a strong and confident presence. That was certainly Doc Lucas—and that was why it had been less difficult to leave them.

So last evening, after talking with Amir and then listening to the phone message from Doc Lucas that the horses were safe and settled, Josie had fallen deep asleep—her first full night's sleep in many weeks. Waking to birdsong, she had felt the first inklings of hope.

Easing out of Isa's twin bed, Josie smoothed out the new ivory sheets and burgundy comforter that she recently bought to replace her niece's Strawberry Shortcake bed-in-a-bag set, a gift Josie had sent for Isa's last birthday. Rodrigo had moved Isa's clothes and toys into Miguel's room so Josie could unpack. He'd also removed posters from the walls, but had left, above the bed, a colorful wall-hanging made by Irma. It was an elaborately embroidered tree surrounded by pink and yellow flowers. Tiny cloth figures were attached throughout the scene. Called worry dolls, they were meant to take on Isa's problems so she could sleep peacefully each night. He'd also left on one wall a few framed photos of Isa with family and friends. But the most striking reminder was the scent of strawberry that still lingered—Isa's obsession with Strawberry ChapStick. Josie had found a few in the bedstand drawer.

As Josie made her way to the kitchen, she heard the gurgling sounds of Vic's coffee maker, which she'd set for 6:30. Sliding open the glass door, she stepped out onto the patio. Glancing at the brightly painted yellow and green metal swing set, Josie choked up at the sight of the two empty swings moving gently with the slight breeze.

Scanning the small yard, she saw that the redwood fencing looked sturdy and well-maintained, but the flower beds beneath were wilted and brown. The grass was fading as well. Josie made a mental note to talk to Rodrigo about a watering system and to ask about the nearest nursery. She couldn't wait to plant some flowers, maybe even a tree in the empty corner.

After a few stretches, Josie took a deep breath. The air was cool and crisp. Perfect morning for a hike, something she rarely got to do in January back home. She decided to see if she could find that stunning trail that Vic had taken her to the summer after Ben died.

It took a few wrong turns, but she finally found Chatsworth Park South and the trail that led to the Simi Hills. When she had first heard the name years before, she'd thought of them aptly as the "See Me" Hills, so different from anything she'd hiked before. Sky-scraping sedimentary formations dating back sixty to eighty million years ago, reddish-orange sandstone outcroppings, and magnificent boulders transported from another place and time—now at peace above the turbulent city of angels.

As Josie trudged up the steep trails and scrambled over rocks, she remembered that last time she had been here. After months of being tossed about in the sea of Ben's illness and Ellie's rage, and then swallowed up by Ben's death, Josie had pushed herself further and further up the trail until Vic made her stop and take a few breaths. In fact, Josie now realized, that's what he'd always done. Helped her slow down, catch her breath, and then move forward. Could she do the same for Vic? Was it even possible for him to move forward?

Hoisting herself up atop a smooth weathered boulder, Josie sat cross-legged and gazed up at the cloudless blue sky. A red-tailed hawk circled above. Closing her eyes, she took a few deep breaths and paused. At that moment, she felt calm and comforted, whole and self-contained, like no one's daughter, wife, or mother, simply Josie Serafini, which was how she always felt when she was with Vic.

Pangaea

Binghamton 1971

The light hit her bedroom wall and fell seemingly through the floor. Josie tried to focus on the light and not the image of a car descending the hill beyond their house. It could be like counting sheep, she thought, kicking off the sheet and turning her face toward the small fan beside her bed. Warm air tickled her cheeks and blew about the few strands of hair that weren't soaked with sweat. Another dash of light. "One," she began, closing her eyes, but she couldn't stop her ears from hearing the motor as it descended and approached the house. If it started to slow, as cars often did to take the dip in the road, she'd be tempted to jump out of bed and run to the window. It was a habit she couldn't shake, not since her father left eight years before, and she and her brother, Vic, then five and eleven, would lie side by side on her bed, watching the wall for that flash of light and then listening hard. The cars never stopped; they only left a silence that was filled, some nights, by their mother's muffled sobs beyond the wall that caught the light.

This car was noisy, pulling Josie up and out of bed. The linoleum felt cool to her feet as she hurried to the window in time to see a pickup roar by. She watched the taillights bounce in the distance. "Damn," Josie said out loud. "Now I'm wide awake." She'd known it was too early to be Vic. When he finished working on cars at the service station, he often met up with friends at Thirsty's Tavern. Plus, that motor wasn't anything like the coughing of his old Mustang, despite all the work he'd put into it. She knew the sound of his car, just like she knew the sounds of her mother coming home from the hospital at night—her heavy sighs, the hiss of a match as she lit up another cigarette and settled into the darkened living room. Josie had learned long ago not to interrupt that moment; it was her mother's special time to be alone. When she woke at the sound of her mother's keys, she never came down, but lay back and listened, wondering what her mother was thinking.

Josie pressed her forehead against the well-worn bulge in the screen. She didn't have to wonder tonight. Though they chose not to talk about it much, the air was thick with one fact: Vic would be leaving for basic training, the army, and—most likely—Vietnam.

Two weeks before, on August 5th, Josie and Vic had listened together to the draft lottery on the radio. Since Vic had turned eighteen the previous year, his August 10th birthday was randomly assigned the draft number twenty-five, which meant he was certain to be drafted. After much thought, Vic had made the decision to enlist in the army, a four-year stint instead of two as a draftee, but it meant he'd have a better chance of applying for and getting a specialty training assignment as a helicopter mechanic. This way he could avoid direct combat and add to his skills as a mechanic. "Kinda like goin' off to college," Vic had joked. "Just four years." So, on his unlucky birthday, he had officially enlisted and was set to leave in a couple of months.

Josie couldn't imagine this house without his presence. Even when Vic wasn't home, there was always the anticipation of when he'd sweep in. What he'd done. Where he'd been. He could make an aimless three-hour drive down to New York City sound exciting, even though he had simply driven around Yankee Stadium, stopped for gas, and come back. Josie swallowed hard at the thought of his leaving and pushed herself away from the window toward the door and the dull rays of light beyond the stairway.

Switching on the eleven o'clock news, Josie flopped onto the green sofa in front of the large fan. That's where she would spend most of the day, devouring a stack of old *National Geographic* magazines that Vic had picked up for her at a garage sale the week before. He had come home early that day and stopped at the kitchen doorway, beaming like a boy with a secret, then stepped aside to reveal the two large boxes filled with magazines and said, "Ought to keep you out of trouble this summer." He'd looked younger than his nineteen years, his bushy dark curls tousled and his cheeks flushed. Josie had wanted to fly at him and wrap her arms around him tight. Instead, she'd said, "Cool!" and bent down to look through the boxes as he walked away, whistling.

Her mother wanted Josie to be a nurse. The local hospital, where her mother worked evenings as a nurse's aide, had a reputable school of nursing, and that's where she saw Josie's future. But Vic had always scoffed at that. "Josie's no nurse. She's a doctor," he'd say. "Hell, she's too smart to be just one of the crew; she's gonna be the captain." He'd make his usual comments and little jokes. But one night, just last winter, when he'd teasingly asked what book she was buried in this time, instead of answering with a wrinkled nose and continuing to read, Josie had taken a deep breath and said, "I'm reading about Pangaea, the super-continent." Vic had stopped and looked at her for what seemed like a long time, until she started to talk and he sat down beside her.

She told him how the mountains were formed by constantly

moving plates of earth. How scientists were uncovering facts every day that supported this theory called continental drift. Josie pulled out a map and showed him how the continents had once fit together like a puzzle. "Pangaea," she said again. "That's what they call it. But it all broke apart, over millions of years. And it's still moving, still changing."

Vic had bent over the books and maps with the same concentration he used under the hood of a car, so she'd kept talking. She showed him the articles that her science teacher had given her, and the ones she'd found on her own.

"What kills me," Josie said, "what just kills me is that it's always been there. All these rocks, and mountains, and these ocean trenches, all the secrets of our earth's past just waiting to be uncovered and made sense of."

When she finally paused to catch her breath, she saw that Vic was slowly flipping through pages until he stopped and asked, "Who's this? With the hammer?"

He pointed to a picture of a thin young woman standing by a cliff. Her smile was slight, and forced at that, but Josie noticed how sure her footing was on the rocks, and how firm her grasp of the tool.

"You mean her name?" she asked.

"No. No," Vic said impatiently. "*What* is she?"

"I don't know. A geologist? Maybe a paleontologist?" Josie leaned forward to read the caption beneath, but her eyes blurred when she heard Vic say firmly in her ear, "Then that's what you're gonna be."

Now stretched out on the sofa, too tired to read, but too hot to sleep, Josie stared at the bright TV screen. The drone of the fan blocked out the words of the newscaster, but his face was hypnotizing just the same. His eyes seemed to smile, though his brow was creased and his lips settled into a slight frown. Then scenes of the Vietnam

War filled the screen. Soldiers in sweat-soaked fatigues, an old man peering up from under a large brimmed hat, the somber dirty face of a child. Josie shuddered. She just couldn't see Vic there. Not at all.

Startled at the sound of the door and her mother's raspy cough, Josie sat up. She watched as her mother walked wearily to the front of the fan, where she stopped, let the air blow on her face and neck, then leaned forward and let it billow down the front of her white uniform. Her short dark hair was tucked behind her ears. Her uniform, damp under the armpits, hung loosely on her ever-thinning frame. Her mother ate so little, Josie worried she'd waste away. Coffee and cigarettes were her main staple. When she did have time to make Josie and Vic a meal, she'd take one or two bites, scoot back her chair, and then light up another cigarette.

Turning slightly, her mother glanced at the TV and said in one long sigh, "Turn that off, Josie, for chrissakes. I don't want to hear about that place."

Josie jumped up and turned the knob on their beige console TV. Her mother looked at her expectantly, then with a slight, sad smile, she ran her fingers through Josie's long dark hair.

"You too, huh?" she said. "All the patients were restless again tonight. Too hot to sleep, too hot to breathe. You should tie this up in a ponytail." She gathered Josie's hair up off of her neck, then let it fall gently over her shoulders.

Josie shrugged. "I did. Took it out 'cause it was giving me a headache."

Her mother turned toward the kitchen. "Vic not home yet?" she asked.

"No," Josie answered. Then she heard herself say, "Maybe he won't go."

"Go where? Where'd he go?" Her mother stopped.

"To Vietnam, I mean. Maybe he won't go."

Her mother's face filled with color as she turned back and said in a hushed tone, "What'd he tell you?"

That was one way to get her attention, Josie thought. Where'd he go? What'd he say? Who's he seeing? Sometimes she told and sometimes she didn't.

"Is he planning to run? Go to Canada or something?" Her mother was holding Josie by the arms now, looking hard into her face.

"No," Josie said. "That's not what I mean. He didn't say anything. I just keep thinking that maybe he won't have to go."

Her mother grunted and let go, then heading toward the kitchen, she said, "Oh Josie . . . I thought . . . oh, Christ."

Josie considered following her and telling her what little she did know, but the most Vic had actually said on the subject was, "What the hell else am I gonna do?" and there wasn't any comfort in that. So Josie settled back on the sofa and tried to make out the blades of the fan as they whirled.

She was dreaming of children running down a long tunnel that began to turn, first slowly, then faster and faster until the children's laughter became shrieks of terror. When Josie opened her eyes, she couldn't be sure if she'd been one of the kids or just a spectator watching.

A high-pitched squeal filled her ears again, followed by her mother's uncharacteristically cheerful voice saying, "Now Vic, cut that out. You're embarrassing me."

"Well, you are, you know," Vic was saying. "The foxy lady of my life. She is, Jay, and a great dancer, too. Come on Mom, dance with me. Come on."

"That's enough, Vittorio." Her voice was firm now. "You've had a bit too much to drink tonight, and you know my feelings on that. Now if you boys'll excuse me, I'm going on up to bed."

Josie sat up. *Boys? Who was here?* she wondered, then lay back down when her mother's shadow filled the doorway. "Jay, in case my son doesn't follow through on his hospitality, there are towels in the closet at the top of the stairs . . . Vic, stop it, for chrissakes, I swear."

Josie smiled at the giggle of her brother's otherwise deep voice, then closed her eyes and feigned sleep as her mother passed by, stopping to linger for a moment beside the sofa. *Thinking what?* Josie wondered. Then she felt something laid over her legs, heard her mother's slow panting as she climbed the stairs, then the water running in the bathroom.

Kicking off the afghan, Josie stood up and smoothed out the oversized T-shirt that she slept in. It covered the gym shorts she wore underneath and was longer than most of her miniskirts, but when she edged to the doorway, the stranger's dark eyes that met hers swept down to her legs and stayed there. He was sitting on the opposite end of the Formica kitchen table, holding a can of Genesee beer and looking like an ad in a magazine—his handsome face, neatly trimmed mustache, and slight smile, as he held up the red and white can that matched their dinette set.

Then Vic was beside her, his voice booming. "Josie! Sleeping beauty. This here's a new friend of mine, Jay."

Vic was always making new friends. He drew people to him like some movie star, she thought, yet he'd never been a star at anything. He just seemed to pull people in. Being near him made you feel good. That was it, she decided, as he hooked an arm around her neck and led her into the brightly lit kitchen: He made you feel as if *you* were the star.

"Now Josie's goin' to college, too, someday," he was saying. "I'm seeing to that. Hell, she's so smart she's gonna get her picture in the *National Geographic* magazine one day." Then he pulled her down onto the red and white chair beside him and said, "Jay here goes to Penn State. He's from Wilkes-Barre but is on his way to Syracuse to visit his girl. Car broke down on 81, got towed to our service station. I've been showing him the town a little."

Briefly glancing at the dark eyes, Josie laughed and said, "I'll bet you've seen the real high parts of Binghamton tonight." She was glad she had left her long, wavy hair loose, covering her breasts on both sides. Without a bra, she felt exposed.

"Yeah," he said with a slight laugh. "It's a nice town though, kind of like my own." Then he shrugged and looked down at his hands. When he looked up again, he tried to smile, but his lips seemed to settle in a frown.

The next day felt like the longest day of her life. Josie was certain that something had happened the night before. She felt it, though she couldn't put her finger on what it might be. She'd slept till ten and woke to find that "The boys're already down-at-the-station," as her mother said in one quick breath, "working on Jay's car." Josie had left them at the table the night before talking baseball, although there'd been tension, some awkward pauses, that Vic seemed to be easing with small talk. But later, she'd heard their voices rising and falling, a continuous ebb and flow that seemed to vibrate up the walls to her room long into the night. She wondered if they'd slept at all.

Her mother left for work early to run a couple of errands, then called at four to say she'd be working a double. That meant she'd be gone until the morning.

"I called Vic at the station," she said. "Told him not to stay out too late." Her mother paused and Josie said, "Mom, you didn't have to do that. I'm okay alone, and anyway . . ." But she couldn't finish. They both knew calling Vic would not be an option soon.

When his Mustang pulled up shortly after nine, Josie met him at the door. "Vic, you don't have to stay. God, it's only nine! Mom is nuts. You can go out. I'm fine." But he just walked past her to the sofa, where he sank down, head back, eyes closed.

"You okay?" she asked, sitting across from him on the edge of the coffee table.

Vic opened his eyes and looked at her a long time. "You're growing up," he said in a soft, strange voice. "Most times I look at you and don't really see you. I just see my little sister. But you are."

Josie hit him on the leg. "Cut it out," she said. But he kept on staring at her with a seriousness that made her uncomfortable.

"That guy, last night, Jay, he didn't look at you like you were some kid," he said with a slight smile. "I could tell."

"Why? What did he say?" Her voice sounded childlike, yet a part of her felt older inside, like she was two people in the same body.

"He didn't say anything. I could just tell . . . just like I knew he wasn't on his way to visit some girlfriend." He studied his hands for a minute. When he looked up, she saw his eyes were wet. He leaned forward.

"He was on his way north," he said slowly. "Goin' to Canada. When we finally got it all out in the open last night, he almost had me talked into goin' with him. He's got a place to stay, a job waiting. It's all been arranged. He flunked outta Penn State. I guess he was on one of those college deferments. And now his lottery number is pretty low, like mine, and . . ." He paused and shook his head. "His dad doesn't believe in the war, so he worked it all out for him."

Josie heard the words and tried to sort it all out in her mind. "Why?" she finally asked. "Why didn't you go?"

Vic shook his head and lowered it into his hands. "I can't. I just can't. It's not right . . . for me. It's not *my* life."

"What do you mean?" she cried. "My god, it's a way out of that war. That's not your life, Vic. Why didn't you go with him?"

"I almost did," he said, pushing up from the sofa and pacing around. "Right up until he drove away. But all I could think about was . . . *him*. Two kids and a wife and just running off with some bitch!"

The mention of their father, so unexpectedly, hit Josie like a blast of heat. Her face felt hot, but her hands felt prickly and cold. She struggled to catch her breath.

"But it's not the same, Vic," she said. "It's not. You've been given a chance, a choice. And . . . and you said he has a place and a job. That's not running away."

"*He*, Josie. Jay has the place and the job. That's his life, not mine, that I'd be chasing."

Josie shook her head. She knew he was wrong, irrationally wrong. She wished there was someone or some way to convince him.

"All right then," she said, standing to face him. "What you're saying is I'm crazy to dream of being anything but a nurse. Staying in this town, at that hospital, as a nurse. That's what you're saying then."

Vic looked at her a moment with a tenderness that made her want even more to send him north. "Oh Josie, that's just it. You have a gift that has to come first. You have to see that through to the end. Not doing it would be your desertion. But me, this is where life's put me. And Jay's been put in a car heading north. That's his life. And he's not so crazy about what he's got ahead either. He's leaving a girl behind, a family, a town. Man, he's scared of all that too. But that's his life. He's gotta face it, and I gotta face mine. That's all there is to it."

What silenced Josie more than the words were the set of his chin and the hard look in his eyes. Vic seemed to age years right before her.

What she regretted most was agreeing *not* to tell their mother. Several months later, after Vic had shipped out to Vietnam, she ached to talk about it, wondered if perhaps together she and her mom could have persuaded him to ride it out in Canada. Then, at least, she wouldn't feel so responsible, especially on those long, empty nights when her imagination, fueled with graphic news footage from Vietnam, created endless visions and versions of his possible death.

One such night, Josie fell asleep on the sofa and awoke in complete darkness just as her mother came in the door. Expecting her to turn on a light, Josie quickly closed her eyes, but instead, her mother carefully made her way in the dark and eased down on the sofa by Josie's feet. She heard the click of a lighter, a deep inhale.

Through squinted eyes, Josie watched the angry glow in the darkness. One drag on the cigarette . . . then two.

Josie shifted slightly, resting her feet on her mother's lap.

"You okay, baby?" her mother asked.

As Josie tried to answer a simple, "Uh huh," instead a croaking sound leapt from her throat, split right through the air with an unexpected force. It startled her at first, pulling her forward, eyes wide open. For a moment, she felt suspended, until the shaking began, convulsive sobs that seemed to come from deep inside her chest. At first, there were no tears, but soon they came, cascading down between gulps and gasps.

Her mother was holding her, rocking her, crooning like she was a baby. "Jo-Jo," she kept saying. "Jo-Jo."

When the shaking eased a bit, her mother softly said, "Oh, I miss him, Josie. I miss him, too."

Josie heard her own voice whimper from somewhere far away. "But it's not fair. It's just not fair. Why did he have to go? Why?"

"I don't know, baby," her mother said while she smoothed Josie's hair back again and again and again.

Suddenly it struck Josie that, perhaps, if she started out small, a chip here, a chip there, it might somehow all make sense.

She looked up into her mother's weary face and asked gently, carefully, "Tell me, Mom. Tell me about Dad. What was he like . . . before things got bad? Tell me any little thing that comes to your mind."

Her mother was startled at first, a quick intake of breath, then slowly, haltingly, she began. Together they talked until dawn.

Lethe Bound

February 2001

VIC

Vic knew they had a plan—Josie and Rodrigo—but plans were for the living. No amount of exercise or healthy food could bring him back from the dead. And since the dead couldn't fight, he would acquiesce. He liked that word—*acquiesce*. It sounded like what it meant: acquire some peace by saying yes. Yes, it took less energy to do what was asked than to refuse, so he had agreed to work out once a day with Rodrigo, in the cluttered garage that Vic and Irma had made into a gym of sorts.

Closing his eyes, Vic pumped away until his arms faltered and Rodrigo grabbed the weight and set it on the frame.

"Take it easy, *hermano*. You'll pull a muscle if you're not careful." Rodrigo's voice was tender, and that pissed Vic off. He was tired of kindness and patience and pity, weary of any emotion at all—even of being pissed off.

Rodrigo leaned against Irma's stationary bike, chewing on his lower lip and playing with the pink streamers that she'd added to the handles. He was uneasy, Vic could tell.

"How 'bout a jog?" Rodrigo asked. "We could do an easy mile or two before I go to work."

"Yeah, let's go, Rodrigo! How about a ten-mile run? Better yet, how 'bout a fuckin' marathon?" Vic stopped to catch his breath. That took more out of him than fifty push-ups.

Rodrigo remained silent, eyes downcast, then quietly said, "Man, I know how you feel, I do. What can I say? I miss them, too."

Vic couldn't go there. If he did, he'd begin to picture Rodrigo wrestling in the grass with Miguel or mixing margaritas with Irma in the kitchen. Looking up at his old friend, he said, "Listen, man, I'm sorry. I'm just not good company today."

"I didn't come here for good company, but I understand." Rodrigo stood to go. "You okay? You need anything?"

"No, I'm fine. Got everything I need," Vic said, motioning about the garage. "Josie should be back any minute."

Rodrigo forced a weak smile, "Okay, adios. Take it easy. Probably see you later."

Vic watched him stride the length of the driveway on his short stocky legs. Black T-shirt, black jeans, black K-Mart athletic shoes. After first meeting Rodrigo, Josie had joked that Ellie would admire his fashion sense—always in black. Vic hadn't yet told Josie all of Rodrigo's story, only that they had met back in Arizona when Rodrigo was fleeing Guatemala. Vic hadn't added the fact that he'd lost his father and brothers in his country's civil war.

Vic lay back on the padded bench, his forearm across his brow. With eyes closed, he could imagine that any minute Miguel or Isabel would pounce on him, with Irma right behind them in her bright pink exercise tights. He couldn't remember exactly when they'd converted the garage into their own private exercise studio, complete with bench press and weights, treadmill, a stationary bicycle, and an exercise mat—all picked up second-hand. Was it after Isabel was born and Irma put on a few pounds? It seemed like it had always been like this, the extra room in their tiny house, gradually acquiring a boom box, an old card table and chairs, and even a mini-refrigerator. Evenings and weekends, they'd all be hanging out there, working out or dancing to Bruce Springsteen, Enrique Iglesias, or Disney songs, depending on who got to the boom box first. He could see it all clearly in his mind, so he opened his eyes to force the image away. Something between a grunt and a roar burst from the depths of his chest.

Vic couldn't cry anymore. Tears came from the soul, Irma once said, and his soul was as dry as the dust gathering in little Miguel's room. His only wish now was to feel nothing. Oblivion. So far, he hadn't succeeded, though he sure as hell had tried. That's when he saw, secured in the beams above, two clear plastic boxes that Josie had packed. Since she'd taken Isabel's bedroom, they had moved some of Isa's things to Miguel's room and packed the rest in plastic boxes. Rodrigo must have put them up there. At some point—when Vic was ready—they were going to go through everything. Irma's, Miguel's, and Isa's belongings. Some would be sent to Irma's relatives in Mexico and some donated to the Vietnam Veterans Association. The rest would be packed and stored. For what purpose, Vic wasn't exactly sure. He could see Isa's books stacked in one of the boxes, and suddenly he was curled around her in her bed, smelling the Strawberry ChapStick that she always smeared on and beyond her little lips, reading story after story to her until Irma would finally drag him away saying, "Enough you two, it's time to sleep."

What Vic would give for oblivion now—not *then*. *Then* he was in a blissful state of ignorance, interviewing some old woman at the law office where he worked as a paralegal. Meanwhile his babies were waiting at the bus stop, glued to their mama's side. The three of them were coming to surprise him with lunch. The girls at the office told him later that they'd been instructed to keep him there until his little family arrived. Even the old man, Harry Smithson, hadn't a clue as he turned his big old Buick onto Ventura Boulevard, oblivious to the blood clot that would render him senseless, causing his car to veer out of control. The Buick slammed Irma into a nearby windshield and dragged Isabel and Miguel across the pavement, where they remained trapped under the car. What Vic couldn't bear, what just drove him out of his mind, was that for a good thirty fucking minutes, the kids were *dead* and Irma *dying,* and he was still talking and laughing with people at work. Oblivious.

The sound of his van turning into the driveway startled Vic awake. It took a moment before he realized that it was Josie, not Irma, walking toward him, her arms full of groceries. He rolled to his side and pushed up.

"I stopped at that Italian market on Sherman Way and got some cannoli and pizzelles." Josie dumped her load on the card table. "I know Rae's on a diet, but you can't have an Italian dinner without dessert." Glancing around the garage, she asked, "Where's Rodrigo?"

"Went home," Vic said with a grunt.

"Went home?"

"Yeah, he left. Abandoned me. Shall we fire him?" Josie looked tired, and he knew he should quit, but he couldn't stop himself.

"I didn't know we had hired him," she said dryly. "Can you fire someone for being a good friend?"

"Well, he's as good as a babysitter, isn't he? The way he shows up whenever you have somewhere to go? Might as well pay him."

"Vic, for God's sake, he's always stopping by. What is it with you today?" Josie's thick dark hair was pulled back tightly off her face, and Vic noticed the gray at her temples and the lines around her eyes.

Something in her face reminded him of his mom. He looked away. He'd always felt such guilt about not settling back home after his discharge from the army. They'd both needed him, especially his mom, yet he'd lied about job opportunities and stayed away.

When Josie touched his arm and asked, "You okay?" Vic didn't have the heart to look her in the eye, so he stood up and headed for the van to get the rest of the groceries. He heard her voice crack as she added, "And no, I don't call Rodrigo every time I go out."

Poor Jo, Vic thought, hadn't she been through enough? Now here she was, putting up with his shit. He shook his head. And here they were again, the two of them, leaning on each other in a small rundown house. The image of Josie's colonial-style brick home outside of Binghamton, at least twice the square footage of Vic's house, made him cringe at the thought of her sleeping in Isa's cramped bedroom. But Josie had insisted this was where she wanted to be, that she was plenty comfortable and glad to be with him. Thank God she'd only leased her house on a temporary basis.

Vic slammed the van door and headed for the kitchen, bags in hand. He knew he had no monopoly on losing loved ones. He remembered Jo's thin tight voice the whole time she visited after Ben died and her frustration over Ellie's pain-in-the-ass attitude. Ellie had been petulant only with her mother. "Christ, Ellie, give your mom a break. She's going through hell. She needs you, man," he'd said, but Ellie had flipped her hair back and snapped, "Well, it's a little late. She sure as hell hasn't needed me before."

God, how he needed Josie now. Vic knew he couldn't make it without her, yet this dependence seemed unfair. The burden laid on him was unbearable, but he couldn't expect her to carry even a small part of it.

It's fucking time I get my shit together, he mumbled to himself.

He'd start right now, helping her with the dinner. The Serafini siblings would make the best damn lasagna west of the Mississippi, Vic decided, as he lumbered into the kitchen, set the groceries down on the counter, and turned to give Josie a hug. His head sagged onto her shoulder as she sobbed into his chest. For a moment, he was so exhausted, he actually felt nothing.

While Vic was glad that Rae had accepted Josie's offer for dinner, he had to admit that he was a little heavy-hearted at the thought of seeing her again. Rae was the head nurse of the Intensive Care Unit that cared for Irma that horrendous week. Vic remembered very little of the days that he'd sat helplessly by Irma's side, praying for a miracle that never came and then letting go. He had a vague memory of Josie and Rae talking with doctors, poring over test results, explaining medical terms to him, and then, finally, sitting on either side of him, holding his hand in those last hours, minutes, seconds, after they had turned off the machine. That's one thing he did remember—the deflating whir of the machine as it shut down. Josie told him later that Rae had often stayed beyond her shift and even came in on days off to lend support and comfort. Since Josie was a nurse herself, whenever Vic started in with his frequent "what if's," she would reassure him that Irma had been in the best of hands and there was no way she could have survived with so much brain damage.

Vic now realized that it was the intensity and intimacy of that week that had led to a firm bond between Josie and Rae. They had stayed in touch, and since Josie moved in, they'd spoken several times. A friendship seemed to be evolving, and he was grateful for that. If Josie was going to stay a while, he wanted her to have a life beyond looking after him. For her sake, he had agreed to this dinner, but he wasn't certain how he'd feel once he saw Rae.

As it turned out, it wasn't so bad. Rae didn't look familiar or trigger any memories. Fact was, Vic didn't remember anyone he met that week—none of the police officers, doctors, nurses, nor the funeral director. He didn't even know which priest said the goddamn Mass.

Since Josie was busy in the kitchen, Vic had answered the door. Rae was dressed in a bright pink blouse, gray pants and jacket, not the surgical scrubs he pictured from the ICU. She had the warmest smile, and, despite the bottle of wine in one hand and bouquet of flowers in the other, she reached out and folded him in her arms. She was large and soft, and, Vic had to admit, her firm embrace was comforting.

"I see you knew Josie's favorite flower," Vic said, stepping back and relieving her of the bottle of wine. They both looked at the flowers, as Vic added, "sunflowers," nodding at the three in the center of the arrangement. "Josie's always loved them. When she was a little girl, she picked out clothes with sunflowers. I remember a dress, a T-shirt, and even something she put in her hair."

"Perfect!" Rae exclaimed, following him into the house. "I had no idea. I chose these because they looked so cheerful."

As they settled into the living room, Vic watched Rae's eyes linger on the two photos displayed on the entertainment center. One was his favorite wedding photo—Vic gazing at his stunning bride while Irma beamed at the camera, her dark eyes full of light and love. The other, their family portrait, which was taken two months before the accident, was supposed to be used on their Christmas cards. All four were wearing red sweaters even though the temperature had been in the eighties that October day. Miguel had been crying, but Vic coaxed him into smiles by promising him a Happy Meal on the way home. They'd all peeled off their sweaters as soon as they got into the car, except Irma, who insisted on staying in the holiday spirit.

"A beautiful family," Rae said softly.

Josie entered, exclaiming about the flowers and setting out appetizers that Rae picked at so she could save herself for the lasagna.

It wasn't until they sat down at the dining table in the small room off the kitchen that Josie and Rae had eased into a more natural conversation, something about a nursing conference they were going to attend together. Vic was lost in reverie, looking at the wall he promised Irma he'd remove one day to open up the kitchen and dining area.

Conversation tapered off as they ate. The wine and heavy food left Vic feeling tired and bloated. He loosened his belt to the previous hole, leaned back, and shrugged. "Sorry."

Rae laughed and reached across the table to tousle his hair like he was a schoolboy. Her long pink nails matched her shirt. "So much for the twenty-five pounds I've lost," she said. "Must have put on at least five tonight. But Lord, it's worth it, seeing you eat and smile a little. Oh Vic, it warms my heart."

"It's the most I've eaten in a while," Vic said, which meant that he actually took a few bites of everything. "Josie cooks like Mama."

"Were your parents from Italy?" Rae asked, looking from Jo to Vic.

"Mom's parents were," Vic answered. "I have vague memories of them. Before Josie was born, when I was maybe three or four, my mom and dad separated for a while, so Mom and I moved in with her parents. I remember Italian music, platters of veal cutlets, and homemade wine in a large jug that I thought was grape juice. I'm not sure how long we were there before Mom and Dad got back together, but shortly after, both Grandma and Grandpa died—within a few months of each other—and we moved into their house for good. And after that, all things Italian seemed to fade—except for mom's cooking."

"In what way?" Rae asked.

"Well, within a decade the neighborhood was no longer an Italian neighborhood as the first generation died out and their kids moved to other parts of town or away completely. Even the local Italian church was eventually torn down and its members directed to another Catholic church."

Rae touched her chest. "Oh my, how sad. And you say your grandparents died within a few months of each other?"

"Yeah, I remember them both being kind of sickly and feeble. I think they married later in life and had Ma when they were pretty old."

"Yeah," Josie said. "Old like us—in their forties!"

"Well, my mom was sixteen when she had me," said Rae. "And I was nineteen when I had my firstborn. I sure as hell feel too old to have one now." Leaning toward Vic, she added, "Don't ask, I ain't tellin'!"

"At least thirty-five, right?" Vic tried to play along. "Like me?"

"Exactly like you!" Rae slapped the table. "Actually, I have two grandbabies—and they are the joy of my life right now. Rashida's three and Renay is two." She reached into her purse and pulled out a small photo album. Flipping it open, she hesitated. Vic knew what she might be thinking. Since his energy was fading, it took some effort to reassure her.

"It's okay, Rae," Vic offered, glancing at the Sears wallet-sized photos, just like the ones he still carried—but his would never be updated. Both he and Josie leaned in to admire the cherubs smiling up at them. Vic was running out of steam.

Sliding the little album back in her purse, Rae asked, "And your dad?"

"My dad?" Startled, Vic snapped upright in his chair.

"Yes, is he from Italy?"

"Oh." His heart skipped a beat, then recovered. "Our dad, uh . . . his parents were born here in the US . . . in Brooklyn. He left home at a young age, ran away, he said, so we never met any of his family. His father's father was from Italy, but his mom's family was from Switzerland or Austria—I can't remember which—so we're not pure Italian, despite the cooking." He nodded toward Josie but didn't meet her eyes.

Josie jumped in like he knew she would. "A runaway, all right. The son of a bitch left my mom with two little kids to support. Completely disappeared, can you imagine? He's never even tried to see us. But even before that, he was gone all the time anyway, playing gigs. He was a drummer." She rolled her eyes. "Ran off with some woman when I was only five. Bastard."

"I know the type," Rae said. "Sounds a lot like my first husband, except he wasn't no drummer. Hell, he wasn't anything. Now my second husband—wouldn't trade him for the world. PE teacher at a high school in South Central. Coaches track. A real gem," she said with a smile. "A genuine diamond in the rough."

Suddenly, Rae looked at Vic in alarm and asked, "Are you okay, hon?"

Vic knew he must look like he'd seen a ghost, which was pretty close to how he felt. The topic of his father being discussed in front of Josie had knocked him off balance. All he wanted was to get the hell out of there. He tried to be nice, to make apologies and convince two RNs that he was just fine, even though he wasn't, so he used his grieving card to make his escape. "Man, I'm sorry, I just get worn out easy . . . ya know?"

Rae nodded. Josie looked at him with a mix of concern and curiosity. "You sure you're okay?" she asked.

Vic pushed himself from the table. "Yeah. Yeah. I'm fine. Just tired. Anyway, you girls probably have nurse stuff to talk about. I'll get out of your way." He stood up. "Go ahead and get out the hard stuff now. The big kid's going to bed." He tried to crack a smile.

Rae stood and hugged him tight. "You're doing great, Vic. Really. You know you'll be riding a roller coaster for a while. Up and down. But the dips will get less and less steep. And the pain, don't let anyone fool you—it never goes away. But it's not as sharp and harsh, more like an ache—an ache deep in your soul."

When Vic stepped back, he saw that Rae's dark eyes had filled with tears, and they were not for him—he could feel it. "You've been here, haven't you?" Vic said softly.

She nodded. "Lost my son when he was five. Fell off a slide in the park. Landed just right—just wrong. Twenty-two years ago, seems like it was yesterday."

A sacred silence floated like a feather in the air.

Lying on his bed a few minutes later, Vic could hear bits and pieces of their conversation, voices rising and falling.

A little about him: ". . . plans on going back to work next month, part time. He's a paralegal at an immigration law firm. God, I hope he's gonna be okay."

Their voices got soft then, clearly whispering about him. He couldn't make out another word until he heard something about their kids.

". . . a pre-school teacher and my son just started as a firefighter in Reseda."

"Mine's a musician, living in Seattle."

Then their voices rose in excitement.

". . . that's when I went back to school—when the kids got older."

"Me too!" Josie's voice, loud and clear. "Just seemed like the right thing to do. Went back to the college where I had majored in geology and picked up all the nursing classes. I loved it. It felt so purposeful. Worked in the Coronary Care Unit and in the Cath Lab for a while, then switched full time to Ben's cardiology office where we started a cardiac rehab program that was super successful." Talking rapidly, Josie sounded just like Ellie, animated and passionate.

Vic sighed and rolled over. He knew he had to tell Josie soon. He'd been wanting to for years, but he never knew quite how to broach the subject. *Oh yeah, by the way, I've been in contact with Dad since 1972.* Perhaps she'd understand the part about a letter right before he shipped out to Vietnam, but how did he explain the rest? Dad questioned whether Josie was his daughter. In fact, he was pretty convinced she wasn't.

Vic had wanted to talk to his mother about it, but how? Where do you begin with something like that? *Who'd you sleep with besides dad?* How do you ask your mother that? And besides, Vic had never seen his mother with another man. She'd never even dated after his father left—just worked her ass off.

When Vic had asked his father to explain, he just kept repeating, "Because she can't be mine. We split for a while back then, off and on. I hardly touched your mother for years before I left. Hell, she wouldn't let me near her, made me sleep on the damn couch most nights."

Off and on? Hardly? Most nights? Sounded like a window of

opportunity existed there. When he pointed this out, his father had gotten angrier. The only thing Vic could figure was his dad associated Josie with his mom, and that fact closed all doors.

But he had to tell Josie before she found out on her own. His dad tended to call out of the blue. No rhyme or reason, no holiday, no one's birthday. Just suddenly called. He lived in Las Vegas, and, once or twice a year, he and his wife drove to Southern California to visit his wife's sister in Anaheim. Occasionally, like last spring, his dad came by Vic's house for a short visit.

It had been a while since they'd spoken. In fact, his father still didn't know about the accident. Vic knew he should contact him before his father called here first. What if Josie answered the phone? Vic shuddered at the thought. He had to tell her as soon as possible.

Turning on his side, Vic gathered Irma's pillow to his chest and buried his face in the center of its softness. He could no longer smell her scent. Her shampoo, her perfume, whatever had been there, was now gone. Attempting to stifle the sobs that came, Vic burrowed in deeper. What he heard made him catch his breath—that same sad sound of his mother's muffled sobs from her bedroom all those years ago. That made him cry even harder.

Foxy Lady
Binghamton 1981

Josie and Vic sat at their childhood Formica kitchen table, its red and white vinyl seats now cracked with wear. They each cradled a cup of coffee that hadn't been touched. Josie watched the steam rise in a swirl through misty eyes.

"I can't believe it," Vic said, his bloodshot eyes brimming with tears. "She's too young for a death sentence. Not even try chemo? I don't understand."

"It's everywhere, Vic," Josie said softly. "I guess there'd be no point. I just can't believe she let it go so long."

Vic had flown in from Arizona on the red-eye and gone directly to the hospital early that morning. Josie, a senior at the local college and part-time nurse's aide, had been at her mother's bedside almost constantly since she'd collapsed three days before. A subsequent MRI had revealed abnormalities in her lungs and intestinal tract. Exploratory surgery that day confirmed their worst fears. Cancer had snaked its way throughout her major organs.

Josie pushed her mug to the side and shook her head in disbelief. "She must have had a ton of symptoms, but she's so stubborn. Just kept working. You'd think she'd know better!" Josie groaned. *Know better?* Who was she to talk about "knowing better"? Two months pregnant, and by a man who would rather spend the night with a stack of books, and whose last words to her were, "I'll write once I get settled," referring to a semester of graduate study in Ireland. But she knew he wouldn't.

Josie pictured her mother shoveling snow the previous week and sank her head into her hands. "Oh Christ, Vic, I should have picked up on this—but I didn't realize—I didn't see. She's had that cough for years—smoker's cough she called it, remember?" Vic nodded. "It woke me up every morning like a harsh alarm," Josie continued. "And the weight loss, I assumed that was the result of the stomach flu that went around just before Christmas. She even called in sick one day, and you know how unusual that is."

Vic sighed. "I don't ever remember her sick. Just that damn cough, like you said, but never sick. Not Foxy Lady." His eyes smiled as he used his affectionate name for her.

Their mother had always admired Eleanor Roosevelt and read several of her biographies. "Dignity personified!" she would say of the First Lady, head held high, cigarette balanced between two fingers. Ever since Vic saw a photograph of Mrs. Roosevelt with two dangling fox furs around her neck, he had dubbed his mother "Foxy Lady."

"And just a few weeks ago," Josie said, suddenly remembering, "I was in the elevator with Dr. O'Neill—the cardiologist that Mom saw last year?"

Puzzled, Vic raised his eyebrows.

"She was having heart palpitations, increased heart rate," she explained, "but it turned out to be nothing, I guess. Anyway, he said something about Mom not looking so great that day—and I, oh Christ, I thought he meant her appearance. You know how some days, especially after a double shift, her hair and her uniform . . ." She shook her head, unable to finish. "In fact, I was rude to him. I gave him a dirty look and made some sarcastic remark." Josie sat up. "Vic, I should have noticed. I should have done something. Instead, I've been all caught up in myself—school and some other stupid-ass stuff that's been going on in my life—and there's Mom, dying of cancer right before my eyes!"

"Josie, stop," Vic said. "You can't blame yourself. Hell, if you want to place blame, put it on me. I should have been here—helping her. I should have come back home and lightened her load a little." He slumped in his chair, tipped his head back, and moaned.

Josie glanced away. So many times, she had wished Vic was here to lean on, but what good would it do to acknowledge that now? Instead, she said, "No Vic, she's so proud of what you're doing—helping those desperate people. She thinks you're a saint."

"Some saint," Vic scoffed, running a hand through his bushy mass of curls that Josie called an Italian-Afro. "If she knew all of what I was doing, she might not approve. I don't know."

"What do you mean?" Josie asked, noticing the sudden shift in his tone.

"I'll tell you some other time. Right now this saint is tired and desperately needs a shower," he answered wearily.

"And a shave," Josie added, wrinkling her nose.

We all have our secrets, she thought. Josie hadn't told anyone hers, and she certainly wasn't ready to share it with Vic. She'd been to the women's clinic in Syracuse and left with a positive pregnancy test, a bottle full of pre-natal vitamins that she kept in her backpack, a pamphlet on abortion (now stashed in one of her textbooks), and enough confusion to last a lifetime.

She'd met Paul at the beginning of her senior year. They'd both sat in the same spot at the library. When she agreed to have coffee with him, she found out he was a teaching assistant and a graduate student specializing in the poet Yeats. He later confessed that she reminded him of the fiery Maud, love of Yeats's life—something about Josie's wild hair and her intensity. She had never encountered such passion. The world of poetry seemed exotic and romantic compared to her geology major. Soon she was so swept up that for the first time, her studies suffered. As the relationship began to lose momentum, she started to panic. When Paul canceled a date just before Christmas, Josie sheepishly sought him out at the university. Her period was late, and she was anxious. But her presence in his corner of a cluttered TA's office was clearly an annoyance. That's when he made his curt statement about writing once he got to Ireland—and Josie made her decision not to talk. Now here she sat, one month later, about to become a mother and lose a mother in the same year.

Looking up at Vic, who had stood, mug in hand, she cried out, "Oh God, Vic, she can't be dying?" Bursting into tears, she laid her head on the cool Formica and sobbed.

Vic came around the table, set down his mug, and placed his hands on her shoulders. "It'll be okay, Jo," he began, but she could feel his arms shaking as his own emotions took over.

Paul left for Ireland without so much as a goodbye. Josie's mother slipped into a godsent coma. Neither ever learned of her pregnancy.

Their mother, Rita Serafini, died three weeks after her surgery, leaving Josie and Vic stunned at the suddenness, yet relieved that she hadn't endured a long, painful death. To Josie, those weeks were a veiled, muted dream as she sat by her mother's bedside, watching her drift in and out of consciousness then into a deep coma, and at the very end, listening to the labored breathing that seemed to go on forever, until finally—and strangely unexpected—that last breath. It wasn't until it was well over that it all began to replay slowly and vividly in Josie's mind, and that hazy state gave way to the agonizing pain of losing her mother.

Somewhere in those weeks, Josie had made the decision to have an abortion as soon as Vic returned to Arizona. She was approaching the end of her first trimester, and she knew it was best to do it soon. No one would ever know of her foolish mistake.

Josie had told Vic that she needed to finish her last semester at college and that Mom had already paid her tuition. She'd be fine on her own in their old house until summer. Then, together, they would talk about the future and what she would do next. Possibly work and save up for graduate school, or maybe move out to Arizona.

What Josie didn't tell Vic—besides that she was pregnant—was that she had *not* finished her last semester and had *not* registered—or paid—for the next one. The whole senior year was gone because of her foolish fling with Paul. She'd never been so distracted before, so swept up that she'd skipped classes, neglected to turn in papers, even declined a great opportunity to do field work in the Catskills with her favorite professor. Josie couldn't tell Vic what a mess she'd made of her life.

Insomnia for Josie meant falling dead asleep, then waking up at 3 a.m. saucer-eyed, her mind racing, tragic dilemmas paralyzing and unsolvable. This 3 a.m. awakening brought her face-to-face with the day's event: abortion. She was scheduled for that morning in Syracuse: nothing by mouth after 7 p.m. Arrive at the clinic at 7 a.m. accompanied by someone who would drive her home.

Josie had had nothing to eat or drink since the evening before, but the escort—that part she would fake. Tell them "someone" was having breakfast and would be there in time to take her home. She'd either drive herself back or stay at a motel. She figured this would be like a heavy period. No big deal. At least that's what she kept telling herself without much conviction. But what else could she do? Who could she tell?

Her friendships at college had been scattered and momentary, linked to a class or a project. Most students lived on campus and formed friendships with those in their dorms. While Josie sometimes took part in weekend hikes and occasionally attended an event on campus, she always felt like the odd woman out. Working the evening shift most weekends at the hospital and living off campus kept Josie fairly isolated from the college-coed life.

Her two close childhood friends had both left Binghamton. One had moved to Florida with her family, and the other had married a guy in the military. Josie had no idea where she lived now.

At the hospital, everyone knew her mother. It was like a small town in itself. If she confided in anyone there, it would travel quicker than the mouse that lived behind the bathroom sink. A flash of gray in the corner of your eye. Then everyone would be looking at Josie with sideways glances—and raised eyebrows.

As for Vic, she'd come close to telling him, but each time Josie had swallowed her secret, choked it back down, and kept her lips firmly sealed on that option. And why? Certainly, she didn't want to burden him during that difficult time—the weeks at the hospital and then the funeral. He had enough on his mind. Not to mention that he'd abruptly left his responsibilities in Arizona to come to their mother's bedside. He'd been on the phone almost daily to Tucson, sometimes speaking in Spanish. When he finally told her about the Sanctuary movement and how he was helping refugees from wartorn Central American countries find homes and jobs in a country that did not legally welcome them, that had humbled her. And when he added that what he was doing was illegal and he could be arrested, well, that had worsened her insomnia.

But those were not the real reasons Josie didn't tell Vic she was pregnant. The truth was that she feared his response. If he acknowledged the life within her for even one moment, if his eyes softened and warmed at the news, even for an instant, she'd have no choice. She wouldn't be able to go through with the abortion. No, he could never know. In fact, as long as no one knew, then it would be like it never happened.

At 5 a.m. Josie decided to head out for Syracuse. What normally took an hour might take two on snow-covered, sleet-slick roads. She'd get ready, get going, and get it over with.

She packed a peanut butter and jelly sandwich, a bag of chips, and a can of Coke into her backpack. Sliding into the old Datsun that she and her mother had shared, she inhaled the faint smell of cigarettes that still lingered. Vic had insisted on installing new snow tires before he left; that was after the oil change and tune-up. She had to admit it gave her more confidence as she set out.

The drive proved to be smooth and strangely comforting. The white-blanketed countryside glowed faintly in the dark, a mesmerizing journey along the mostly deserted highway. Josie got there half an hour before the clinic opened. Pulling into the empty parking lot, she stopped at a spot close to a streetlight. For a few minutes, she kept the motor running, heat full blast. Then realizing that she'd be wasting gas, she turned it off. Silence. *Thunderous silence*, Paul had once said, quoting Shakespeare. It had sounded strange to her at the time, but it described this moment perfectly. The abrupt quiet was startling.

Hungry and thirsty, but unable to eat or drink before the

procedure, Josie shivered and burrowed into her jacket. Finding a diner for warmth would be pointless. The smell of the food would either make her nauseous or drive her crazy with hunger. *Should have brought a textbook* was her next thought, then she remembered, no books to read, no papers to write—and no one waiting for her at home.

Just Vic's frequent calls from Arizona.

"You sure you're okay, Jo-Jo? God, it drives me crazy picturing you all alone in the house with Mom's things everywhere." That was last night—the fourth night she was on her own.

Yes, it was unbearably lonely, and yet, since Josie started college, she and her mom had spent little time together. When Josie wasn't in class, or at the library—or with Paul those few short months—she was working at the hospital herself. More often than not, when Josie was home, her mother was working or sleeping. Yet how she missed her mom's presence—her coffee cup left in the sink, the cigarettes stubbed out in the red pedestal candy dish that she used as an ashtray, her blue robe hanging on the back of the bathroom door, and all her magazines and paperbacks stacked on the coffee table. Josie had spent the last few days flipping through her mother's weathered celebrity biographies—Doris Day's was her latest—and looking through her closet, smelling her clothes, putting on old costume jewelry, like her large clip-on earrings and fake pearls. The last two nights, Josie had cried herself to sleep in her mother's bed, wrapped in the faded blue robe that reeked of cigarettes.

"Foxy lady," Josie whispered through chattering teeth. She had started talking to herself as well. *Time for bed . . . Should get a few groceries . . . You sure fucked things up royally.* Little comments like that, to no one in particular—just the silence that enveloped her life since Vic had left.

"Foxy lady," Josie repeated softly. Then, as she reached to start the engine to warm up the car again, she felt a fluttering in her abdomen. She froze. *No,* she thought, *it's too soon, isn't it?* She had avoided reading anything about what to expect at this stage of pregnancy, such as when you might first feel movement. She decided it must be gas. The angry moans of an empty digestive system. Josie held her breath and waited.

But it isn't empty down there, is it? She sat with her gloved hands tightly gripping the steering wheel, contemplating this thought: *There is a baby inside me. A baby. Maybe a boy. Maybe a girl.*

Josie took a deep breath, let it out, and watched the warm air rise, like cigarette smoke, then disappear. *A boy or a girl.*

Then out loud, to the now frosted windshield, she said, "There is a baby inside me. Maybe a boy—or a girl." Josie pictured tufts of dark hair, then a white dress with little red hearts embroidered on a tiny collar. *Maybe a daughter?*

"Foxy lady," she whispered, then laughed a quick, short chortle.

The tears that started to come weren't from a depth of sadness, but from somewhere lighter, with hints of hope.

Then, spiced with the zip that Vic always added when their mom entered a room, she said, "Foxy lady!"

With that, she reached up again, this time starting the engine and cranking up the heat. She sat quietly, watching the ice begin to melt. Opening the backpack beside her, Josie dug deep to the bottom and pulled out the pre-natal vitamins and sat reading the label. Her cold cheeks felt the warmth of her tears as they ran down to the corners of her mouth. Licking the salty droplets, she said, "What do you say, little Foxy Baby? Shall we have a peanut butter and jelly sandwich before we drive home?"

This time Josie wasn't talking to the silence.

That week Josie felt a quiet joy, cleaning up the house and putting small things in order. She planned to return to work at the hospital the next weekend and request more hours. School was clearly in the past, at least for now. One month at a time. That was her plan.

She still hadn't told Vic. First, she wanted answers to the questions he would surely ask and without which he might come flying back. She was almost twenty-two years old and could handle this herself.

In some ways, Josie was glad Vic hadn't returned home after his military discharge six years before. She might have fallen back into her earlier dependence on him. He'd been a father and, at times, a mother to her for so many years, that when he left for basic training, she'd felt a void much worse than after her father's abrupt disappearance. But Josie had learned then to take care of herself. She'd made her own meals, washed clothes, done her homework, noticed when things needed fixing around the house—and she'd taken great pride in that newfound confidence and maturity.

That was why, even now, Josie wanted all bases covered when she told Vic about the baby. The old house was paid for, left to her mom when her own parents died and now left to Josie and Vic. The life insurance had covered the funeral expenses. Since her mom had added Josie to her bank account when she started college, Josie was already comfortable using that to pay bills. Before Vic left, the hospital had spoken to them about their mother's last paycheck and her retirement fund, which would be forthcoming once processed. Vic and Josie were going to discuss all of those financial details come summer. For now, Josie's main concern was adding more hours at work, hopefully full time. But what had occurred to her the night before was medical insurance. She wasn't sure if she was covered—for the baby. When she had all these answers, especially more hours at work, then she'd tell Vic.

Now, instead of talking to herself, Josie was talking to the baby. She'd read that a fetus could hear its mother's voice and feel its vibrations, so Josie talked or read aloud often. That Sunday afternoon, stretched out on the sofa, Josie was telling the baby about "The '80s Look" and Brooke Shields, who was on the cover of the *Time* magazine that was opened and resting on her slightly rounded stomach.

"Now in this photo, Brooke's hair looks a lot like mine, all bushy and wavy, but those eyebrows! Wow, hers are thick, not like mine at all. Mine are so thin. Almost as thin as the ones Mom used to pencil in after shaving hers off. I guess that was the style when she was young. My mom said movie stars like Jean Harlow, Marlene Dietrich, even Lucille Ball, used to do that. I wonder what will be stylish when you're my age?" She patted her belly.

As she flipped the pages, Josie heard a car pull up out front. Its motor stopped, a car door slammed, and then, to her surprise, there were footsteps on the front porch. She jumped up as the doorbell rang. Through the curtained door window, she could make out a man in a dark suit and tie. She was thinking "funeral attire" as she opened the door with a frown. Just like at the funeral, the familiar face that greeted her smiled slightly, but immediately reverted to that pained grimace that accompanies mourning.

"Hi, Josie. How are you doing?" It was Dr. O'Neill, the cardiologist that she had insulted in the elevator after his misunderstood comment about her mom's appearance. "May I come in for a moment? There's something I'd like to discuss with you, something I have for you." He was a handsome man, close to forty perhaps, with receding blond hair and blue eyes—thin, but fit.

As Josie opened the door and said, "Of course, of course. Please come in," she remembered her awkward apology at the wake, her convoluted explanation, and his kind insistence that it had never been an insult, rather his miscommunication.

As his eyes swept the room, Josie wondered what he saw. A faded green sofa with a crocheted afghan neatly folded on its arm; a coffee table stacked with *National Geographic* magazines and two paperbacks, one about Lauren Bacall and the other Grace Kelly; a green swivel rocker, its cushion sewn in two places; and the TV tray beside it with the remains of Josie's morning tea. All neat and clean, thought Josie with a sigh.

"Won't you have a seat?" She motioned to the sofa, instead of the swivel rocker, which tended to lean to the right. "Can I get you some tea or coffee?" She felt poised, almost graceful, but then she *had* been reading about Grace Kelly.

Dr. O'Neill sat on the edge of the sofa and reached for a paperback. A slow smile crept up his face, finally lighting up his blue eyes. They seemed to twinkle until Josie realized they were wet with tears. "God, she loved these books, didn't she?" he said. "It seemed every week she had a new one." He turned to the back cover and flipped through to the photographs on the inside. Then he looked up, cleared his throat and said, "Yes, you know, some hot tea would be nice. If it's no trouble, of course."

"No, no, not at all," Josie said, turning toward the kitchen. There was a depth to his emotion that was puzzling. He seemed to *know* her mother. There was clearly affection in his voice and eyes.

"Can I help?" He began to rise.

"No, no, please. Sit down. Take your coat off and . . . Here, let me take it." She fumbled and stumbled, leaving all traces of Grace Kelly in the weathered pages of the book.

When she returned with two mugs, Lipton labels dangling, Josie felt a bit more composed and began again. "Here you go, Doctor," she said, handing him the tea. "My mom saw you last year for palpitations, didn't she?" She sat gingerly on the swivel rocker, being sure to lean to the left and even things out.

He smiled. "Ben . . . please . . . call me Ben. And yes, she did. I ended up sending her to Dr. Waskin, OB/GYN. It was hot flashes, beginnings of menopause." He raised his eyebrows and grinned.

Hearing Dr. Waskin's name—her gynecologist, whom she planned on seeing the next week—made Josie wince. Ben noticed and immediately said, "I'm sorry, Josie. It must be so difficult for you. Your brother's in Arizona? Any other family close by?"

"No, I'm fine, just fine. Yes, Vic's in Tucson now. And no, no family. Mom's brother died a few years ago of Hodgkin's disease." She paused, noting he didn't ask about her father, then asked softly, "You knew my mother well?"

He sighed deeply and sat well back into the sofa, stretching his arm along the top and crossing his legs. He looked at Josie with a sad tenderness in his eyes. "Yes, Rita was a good friend at a time I desperately needed someone . . . someone who could understand." The sound of her mother's name left Josie fighting back tears.

Ben hesitated. "My wife . . . ex-wife . . . was hospitalized a number of times . . . with liver disease." He paused, then added, "She was an alcoholic, also addicted to Percodan, and your mother and I . . . ."

"Please, you don't need to explain." Josie wasn't sure she wanted to hear just how intimate their relationship was, although she couldn't imagine this handsome man and her mother.

But he continued. "Rita took care of her; that's how she learned the intimate details of my life. Over time she told me about your dad—his alcoholism and what she went through. She was always supportive and understanding, so strong and solid, like the big sister I never had. She was a treasured friend, Josie."

Suddenly Josie could see her mother, sitting in the hospital coffee shop, puffing away on a cigarette, listening, nodding her head. And it gave her insight into some of the thoughts that might have drifted through her mother's mind late at night in this living room. A tear dripped slowly down her cheek. She wiped it away with the back of her hand.

Ben leaned forward. "The reason I'm here, Josie, is because I took the liberty of taking up a collection at the hospital. Nurses, technicians, aides, orderlies, and of course, a number of physicians. I know how proud your mom was of you and your hopes of going to grad school. Geography, or is it geology?" He nodded to the stack of magazines. Josie's eyes blurred through the tears. He reached into his pocket and unfolded a check. Handing it to her, he said softly, "It's ten thousand dollars. I hope it helps a little. I know how expensive education is today, but it's a start."

Josie's hands shook as she took the check and stared at the numbers.

"Your mother was loved by many at the hospital," Ben added gently.

"I can't," Josie began, her voice trembling. "I can't accept this."

"Why? Josie, what's wrong?" He had reached his hand out and placed it lightly on her arm.

"I'm not going to school, not finishing this year." She looked him square in the face and straightened her shoulders. "I'm pregnant," she said firmly. "I'm expecting a baby in August. And the father . . . the father is gone. He doesn't even know. He's not a part of this . . . I can do this on my own."

Josie waited, not for *his* response, but for her own, for this was the first time she had said the words out loud to anyone. What she felt with this release was a calm certainty, a sense of purpose, and, to her great surprise, pride.

Smiling through her tears, Josie held out the check and said, "So school will have to wait, for now. In fact, I plan to add more hours at the hospital, hopefully full-time nurse's aide status, if I can." Then as an afterthought, she added, "Maybe I could use you as a reference?"

Ben had moved his hand to the arm of her chair, but he remained there beside her, silent, yet close. The check, still in her hand, was extended in the air. He reached out and gently squeezed her forearm, pushing it and the check back onto her lap. "Well then," he said softly, "looks like you need this even more."

Josie looked up into his eyes, just inches from hers. His hand still rested lightly on her arm, his clear blue eyes, so different from Paul's that bordered on gray. Neither moved nor spoke.

Clearing his throat, Ben sat back, paused, then reached for his tea and took a sip.

Josie sat nervously staring at the check in her hands, wondering if it was polite to keep it. Ten thousand dollars was a lot of money.

Ben kept sipping his tea, deep in thought. She was just about to thank him again, when he said with a nod, "Josie, what do you think of this idea? I could use some help in the back office, assisting with EKGs and treadmills. That'd be a hell of a lot less strenuous than hospital work—in your condition. Let me look over the books, talk to my office manager, and then I can give you a good idea of salary and benefits. What do you think?"

Josie's mouth hung open, her heart racing. "Wow," she heard herself say. "Seriously? That would be amazing!" Then catching her breath, she asked, "Are you sure? I mean, maybe you need to give it some thought first." But before he could respond, she added, "I'm a really hard worker. Responsible. I learn fast."

Ben laughed, his face boyish and soft. "Josie, I'm sure you are. Knowing your mother, and just seeing the young woman you are right now—how you're handling all of this—I have no doubt you'll be a great asset to the office." Then standing, he said, "Well, I still have to make rounds. I'll give you a call tomorrow. Sometime in the late afternoon? How's that?"

"Great, that's great," Josie answered, struggling to keep her voice as calm as she could. "I can't thank you enough." As she handed him his coat and walked him to the door, all she could think about was calling Vic.

Re: My Sincere Apology
March 2001

JOSIE

To: cayugaequine@aol.com
From: jserafini@aol.com
Subject: My sincere apology

Doc Lucas,

Or should I say Doc Peterson? I am so sorry. I don't know why I thought that Lucas was your last name. That's the name Jennie used when she first referred me to you—Doc Lucas—and since I made the checks out to Cayuga Equine, I never got your full name. Lucas Peterson! Sorry!

AND I'm also very embarrassed about the confusion with your mother. Somewhere along the way, I assumed she was your wife. My previous vet's wife always answered the phone and relayed messages. I thought the woman who answered for you was also a wife because she often referred to home. "He'll be home shortly, so I'll have him give you a call." Anyway, your *mother* was very nice about my mix-up. I'm sure she told you. She was quiet for the longest time when I asked when I might be able to speak with "her husband." Then when I called her Mrs. Lucas, well, she began to understand my confusion and kindly explained that she is your mom and that your *first* name is Lucas! Once we set things straight, we had a good laugh and a lovely conversation.

She was so thoughtful, inquiring about Vic and asking how we were doing. Clearly, she—and you—have known what it is to lose a loved one. She told me about losing your dad in '93. And she also told me about your tragedy, losing your wife at such a young age. I lost a good friend to ovarian cancer, so I know how cruel and quick it can be. But what wonderful news about your son, Jacob. Congratulations! You must be very proud of him following in your footsteps. Cornell is the best veterinarian school in the country.

I'm glad my sweet old Fire is in your hands. I hated leaving him most of all. He will officially turn thirty this month, though I've been referring to him as a thirty-year-old for months already. Let me know if his appetite picks up. He can be finicky. I hope it's nothing else. How is Jack? And Luke? I actually call him Lucas sometimes—Lucas Andronicus—just because I like the way it sounds. Is he picking fights with his stall mates? He always snaps at Jack to keep him in line. I hope he's not bothering your horses.

Yes, Vic is back to work two days a week, which is clearly the best thing for him right now. They are easing him in slowly and giving him lots of leeway since he is still not able to sleep much at night. He's utterly exhausted, yet once he lies down, he says his heart starts racing, panic attacks, I guess. I've asked him if we should find another place to stay for a while, but he says no, they are still here.

Their spirits. Their memories. He feels close to them here, and yet . . . Thanks for asking about him.

Despite your comment that it's not necessary to end all of my emails with a profound thank you, I cannot tell you how much I appreciate that you are taking care of my boys.

Embarrassed, humbled, and ever-so thankful,

Josie Serafini

To: jserafini@aol.com
From: cayugaequine@aol.com
Subject: Re: My sincere apology

Josie,

I hope my mother didn't talk your ear off. Once she gets started, she'll tell you her whole life story and probably mine, too. No problem about the name. It's an honest mistake.

As for your Lucas, I must tell you that I have been thinking of adding Andronicus to my business cards, but now that I know it's taken, guess I'll have to nix that idea.

I have to admit, I can't stop thinking of Vic. Jacob was only five at the time that my wife died, and as difficult as it was, Jacob was what actually kept me going. For your brother to lose them all, I don't know how he copes. You must be his lifeline right now. My mother was mine, and my dad. I ended up leaving the vet group I was working with near Cornell, moved back home, and eventually started my own practice here. My mom manned the phones. Once my dad retired, he used to come on calls with me, as my assistant. If it wasn't for them and Jacob, heck, I don't know what I would have done. So, I'm happy to help with your horses, especially knowing how important it is for you to be there.

Fire slowly polished off a bran mash this evening. Sir Lucas Andronicus has met his match in our donkey Spartacus—and I'm not joking—he was named by my dad twenty years ago. A Kirk Douglas fan. As for Jack, he has taken to our ranch hand, Charlotte, a neighbor's daughter who helps with chores. Mom says he nickers when he sees her. Your boys are doing fine.

Yes, I'm very proud of my son.

Storm expected this week, possibly two feet or more of snow. Enjoy sunny California.

No further thanks needed,

Doc Lucas (Andronicus)

To: cayugaequine@aol.com
From: jserafini@aol.com
Subject: Re: My sincere apology

Doc Lucas,

Spartacus? What a great name for a donkey! My mom loved Kirk Douglas, too. She read celebrity biographies voraciously, so I'm sure she read his. She could probably list every movie he made, and every wife or lover.

I'm so relieved to hear that Fire ate the bran mash. As for the snow, tell Charlotte that Jack loves the snow. He will roll and roll, making horse versions of snow angels. Can't say that I'm missing the weather at all.

My daughter was supposed to come down from Seattle for a visit, but the storm you are expecting there already swept through the Pacific Northwest, and her ride canceled. I offered to pay for a flight, or even a train or bus, but she hasn't responded yet.

I'm not sure how well Vic is coping. I'm really worried about him. He eats very little and is getting quite thin. He promised me he'd see his primary doc and get some lab work done, but I'm not sure he's followed through on that.

It's so comforting knowing the horses are in your hands. I miss them so much, but I know they are doing fine, and that helps.

A simple thank you, but I promise it's my last, maybe,

Josie

To: jserafini@aol.com
From: cayugaequine@aol.com
Subject: Re: My sincere apology

Josie,

Our internet has been out for a few days. We ended up getting close to three feet of snow. Hope your daughter made it down. Does she attend college in Seattle? A friend of mine teaches at UW. How's Vic? Horses fine. Sorry this is short, been busy digging out.

A simple you're welcome,

Lucas

To: cayugaequine@aol.com
From: jserafini@aol.com
Subject: Re: My sincere apology

Lucas,

I don't miss the snow at all; in fact, I could get used to this weather year-round. Right now, it's cloudy and what they call "cool" here in Southern California—in the low 60s! Perfect hiking weather. I've hit a few of the local trails, although I don't like to be away from Vic too long. On days he goes to work, I explore a few that aren't too far away, but if he's home, I stay close.

Lately, Vic's been calling himself "The Hollow Man," which pierces my heart because he is. I'm so worried. After Ben died, I remember feeling listless and numb, but I wonder if that's how I looked to my friends and to my daughter, kind of empty? I sense you know what I mean, having been through it yourself.

As for my daughter, still no word from her. So frustrating! Attending college? How I wish she were. No, she's a musician. Singer-songwriter, plays guitar, has an alluring voice, I have to admit, with a rich, smoky tone. Whenever she sings, people stop what they're doing and listen—and keep listening. A part of me is hopeful and supportive, sort of. I wish she was doing this while going to college though.

Sorry! I keep going on and I know you're busy. Don't mean to take up your time.

Tell Fire I said "Happy Birthday." This may sound silly, but maybe you could call me when you're not busy and you're in the barn, so I can talk to Fire myself? It's such a special birthday—thirty years young! If not, if you're too busy, I certainly understand.

And please say hello to your mom for me, and tell Charlotte thank you for spending time with my horses.

Not thanking you this time,

Josie

To: cayugaequine@aol.com
From: jserafini@aol.com
Subject: New thread!

Lucas,

I'm tired of seeing the "Re: My sincere apology" subject, so I'm starting a new thread. I almost wrote "Thank You" as the topic, but I knew you'd object. Instead, I am simply thanking you in the email itself.

You were kind to call so I could sing "Happy Birthday" to Fire, and even kinder including Charlotte so I didn't have to sing alone. She sounds like a sweet girl. Kind of reminds me of Ellie at that age, still little girlish, not quite ready to push mom away yet.

Just hearing the horses snort in the background made my heart ache. I miss them so much! There's a neighborhood not far from here that has horses. I'm going to have to pay a visit and get a whiff of horse.

Goodnight, although you've probably been in bed for hours with the time difference.

Josie

P.S. I swear, if don't hear from Ellie this week, I'm going to hire a private detective!

Ways of Loving

Binghamton 1997

Josie ferociously raked the brilliant crimson, orange, and golden leaves into a pile, while Ellie scooped them up in armfuls and tossed them into a black trash bag.

"I still don't understand why we have to do this!" Ellie groaned, struggling with Ben's work gloves, which wouldn't stay on her hands. "We could pay someone, or even ask one of our neighbors. They'd help us. And anyway, more leaves'll fall this week. Why not just wait?"

"Ellie, I'm not going over this again. The yard is a mess, and I just want it done. Now. Today." Josie glanced toward the house anxiously. She should check on Ben; she'd been out here for over an hour. "God, I wish you were ten again. You used to love to help us rake and garden. Now you make me feel guilty if I ask for just a little help."

"I can't believe you made me get up at 9 o'clock on a Saturday. Can't I sleep in one morning?" Ellie stood, hands on her hips and two long braids hanging down, looking like a little girl throwing a tantrum.

Only, as a little girl she hadn't, Josie thought. She'd always been sweet, loving, and agreeable. But since she'd hit her mid-teens, she'd developed a rather disagreeable disposition. Josie assumed it was hormones, as well as identity issues, especially since Ellie had become obsessed with finding her biological father. While Josie had been patient, understanding, and tolerant of some uncalled-for outbursts, lately, not only was her patience wearing thin, but Ellie's contentious nature was escalating. Now Josie wished she had been difficult at six, not sixteen.

"Listen," Josie said, thumping the rake handle on the ground, "you said the band was practicing this afternoon. That's why we started early. I didn't say you had to help with barn chores or stay home the entire day; I compromised with you. Now stop being so difficult."

"You're the one who's difficult," she heard Ellie say under her breath, but she let it slide. If Josie challenged her, Ellie might fly into a rage and leave, and Josie couldn't bear to do this alone. Not that the work itself was overwhelming; Josie loved working outside. But yesterday she had tried—starting on the front yard—only to find herself in tears, unable to go on.

Josie and Ben had spent a good part of every weekend doing yard work together. Mowing, clipping, trimming, planting, weeding. They had every garden tool known to man, and then some. What Josie hadn't realized, until yesterday, was just how much she loved that simple weekly act. What she had thought was routine, she now knew was a very special part of their life together, a part that might very well be over.

Four months before, Ben had experienced a ruptured cerebral aneurysm and subsequent stroke. Ben—who played tennis, hiked frequently with Josie, and looked as trim and fit at fifty-eight as he had at forty-two. Despite his attention to diet and exercise, he had fallen victim to a congenital weakening in the arteries of his brain. Complaining of a severe headache after a vigorous afternoon on the tennis court, he'd been rushed to the hospital one fateful Sunday afternoon. Within the hour, the emergency room was teeming with doctors—a few even dressed in their weekend summer attire of polo or Hawaiian shirts and shorts. Josie remembered, in the midst of her own confusion, the bizarre contrast of their casual dress and serious demeanor, as they pooled their expertise to help their friend and colleague. Despite immediate intervention and subsequent surgery performed by two top neurosurgeons, Ben had been left with some neurological deficit: slurred speech, significant weakness in his right arm and leg, and occasional short-term memory loss. But he had survived the worst and was home now, recovering and rehabilitating with a determined and upbeat attitude.

"So I retire a little early," Ben had slurred a few days after his aneurysm had been surgically clipped. "Means the sooner we travel." His blue eyes twinkled devilishly, so vivid against his pale skin and bandage-wrapped head. "We could take Ellie to London and Liverpool. She could rock and roll."

Their dream had been to travel once Ellie was settled into college. But seeing Ellie settled *anywhere* was unimaginable, so the reality of their plan never took focus in her mind. It just remained a hazy dream.

Now it was Ben's motivation. He'd become computer literate almost overnight in his quest to research countries, cultures, and travel information online—that, and following the stock market. In fact, that's where she'd left him over an hour ago, seated in front of the computer.

"I should check on Ben," Josie said aloud. Though he rarely complained, she was certain that his headaches were persisting. She'd seen him rubbing the back of his neck and his eyes, but when she asked, he insisted he was fine. Setting aside the rake, Josie began removing her gloves.

"I'm not doing this alone! I'll check on him," Ellie insisted, pulling off her gloves and tossing them on the ground. She stomped toward the house, leaving Josie staring at Ben's weathered gloves on the pile of leaves.

Picking them up, she touched the bends and creases that had molded to the shape of his hand. Thank God she hadn't lost him. Racing to the hospital that frightening day, all she could think about was how much she cherished this man. All he had done for her and Ellie. How much he loved them both. Had she loved him enough in return? That's what had plagued her as she rushed to the hospital, and that's what drove her now.

When she agreed to marry Ben, Josie had been working at his office for over a year and Ellie was seven months old. Their lives had become so intensely intertwined, it seemed the right thing to do. In their first months working together, Josie had assumed that the source of Ben's concern and attention was related to his generous nature and his respect for her mother. While this was certainly true, something more had developed, something that at first took her completely by surprise—and which tapped into a side of Josie she didn't know she had.

Ben had been eager to make Josie comfortable and give her whatever she needed at work, but she attributed this to the fact that she was pregnant, and therefore, in his eyes, somehow delicate. Then she began to notice the way his hand would linger on her back or the way he'd be looking at her when he should have been focused on someone or something else. This utterly confused her, partly because she was twenty-two and he forty-two, but mostly because he was a successful doctor, well-traveled, highly respected in the community, experienced and worldly—what could he possibly see in her? Sex was the obvious answer, but when she looked at herself in the mirror, she saw swollen breasts, a large belly, even a puffy face. Unable to understand the source of his attentions, she had chosen to ignore them.

The night they first made love, Ben had taken her to dinner, as he had a few times before on the spur of the moment right after work. Afterwards he'd insist on following her home, where he would walk her to the door and say goodnight. But this time, he lingered, gazing into her eyes, then softly asking if he could kiss her. Speechless, she had stood there until he took her face into his hands and kissed her on the lips. Her own response surprised her more than his kiss. She returned it with a deep, hungry passion that had them clinging and kissing, until she drew back, confused and questioning. "I don't understand," she had said, referring to her own feelings as well as his, but of course, Ben assumed she meant him.

He immediately composed himself and apologized, asking if he could come in and explain. "Please, I don't want you to get the wrong idea, and I . . . I think it's time we did talk," he said hesitantly, "about us."

Her mind raced with all sorts of thoughts as they settled themselves a foot apart on the sofa. What did this mean for her job? Was he going to ask her to be his mistress like a few of the nurses and doctors she knew at the hospital? Why was she sitting there, wanting to feel his touch again? Her mouth was dry and her hands felt ice cold—until he took them both in his and began speaking of his admiration for her: her independent spirit, her determination to take care of herself and the coming baby, her lack of self-pity. "I've never known a woman like you," Ben said. "You're amazing." He reached up and stroked her cheek. "God, I can't stop thinking about you. I've come close to calling you several nights. I even thought of driving over. Actually," he said, looking down, "I did. Once. I drove over and sat out front a few houses down and saw a light on upstairs, but I didn't know what to say. Or what you'd say. I guess I was most afraid of that—what you'd say."

Josie didn't say anything, nor did she remember who moved first. Ben later said it was her, but she only remembered the feeling of wonder—that he cared for her so deeply. That he saw her as a woman. And what followed only pulled her in deeper. His passionate love-making was gentle, and tender, and focused thoroughly on giving her pleasure in a way that she'd never experienced before. Whether due to hormones or some deeper unfulfilled need, from that night on, she hungered for him daily. Despite her pregnancy, they managed to enjoy each other right up to Ellie's birth. And to her delight, the tenderness that she thought had been because of her pregnancy was just Ben's way of loving.

Ben's way of loving. That was what tore at her before the wedding and on that frantic drive to the hospital fifteen years later. Had she married him because she loved him, or because of the way he loved her? From the day that their relationship first took that decided turn, he had lavished her with gifts, large and small, like the diamond necklace that she'd insisted they exchange for a simple one—a sunflower pendant encircled with tiny diamonds. He'd been present at Ellie's birth and, together with Vic, had made her first weeks as a mother almost as stress-free as if her own mother had been there. What a hilarious pair Ben and Vic had made, fretting over both mother and child, as if they were royalty.

When Josie finally said yes to his frequent suggestion that they marry, Ben was clearly overjoyed at his good fortune to have her and Ellie in his life. He had no problem at all when she said she wanted to keep Serafini as her name, and Ellie's. They bought an old-style colonial brick house just outside of Binghamton, on an expanse of land near trails that Josie could hike daily. When Josie decided to go back to college and pursue a degree in nursing, Ben often rearranged his busy schedule to accommodate both Ellie's and Josie's needs. When Ellie first expressed an interest in playing guitar, Ben purchased the finest acoustic and a year's worth of lessons. And when Josie fell in love with a neighbor's horse—a neighbor dying of cancer—he suggested building a barn on their property and bringing sweet Fire home. It seemed Ben could not do enough. While Josie had tried to love him the same in return, she was often left questioning the source and strength of that love.

Yet on that critical Sunday afternoon, Josie found her answer as she flew through those intersections on the way to the hospital, desperate to kiss his warm hands, his face, his lips. Whatever she'd felt at twenty-two, she now knew she loved him deeply. Her hunger for him continued, but it encompassed so much more than their physical relationship or his devotion. She wanted every part of him, every day, forever. It was that simple.

Josie finished two more bags of leaves, then headed toward the house where she found both Ellie and Ben in the family room. Ellie was curled up on the sofa, bent over some papers.

"Ellie!" Josie began, but Ben, still at the computer, held up his good hand to silence her before she could scold her daughter.

"It's my fault, Jo," Ben said with an apologetic grin. "I found something online for her, something important."

"What?" Josie asked, peering over Ellie's shoulder. She was thinking it had something to do with music, but what she saw at the top of the page made her heart palpitate: "Making Contact After the Search." Speechless, she turned to Ben, who motioned her to come sit beside him. As Josie sank onto the soft ottoman, Ellie clutched the papers and ran tearfully to her room.

"Oh God, Ben, this scares me to death. He hasn't a clue that he has a sixteen-year old daughter. There's no telling how he might respond. I mean, how would you feel?"

"Well, this is a good article. Covers all different ways of making contact and the advantages and disadvantages of each. Phone, letter, third party." He rubbed Josie's back with his strong left hand. "She needs to think about all of this, imagine different scenarios in her mind, before she's ready."

"I wish she'd just leave it all alone."

"Could you? If you were Ellie?"

"But she has a wonderful father. Why does she need anything more?"

But Josie did understand. A part of her wished her own father would suddenly seek her out. But the resultant pain at the thought of him only left Josie wanting to protect Ellie all the more.

There was also the undeniable fear that she might somehow lose her daughter. What if after meeting Paul, Ellie wanted to live with him? What if he wanted to make up for lost time? This question she kept to herself. To speak it out loud made it too close to a possibility.

Ben reached for the small therapeutic ball beside the computer and began exercising his right hand. "She's growing up, Jo. We have to give her some room to breathe. This is one decision she has to make on her own. And I think she's right; it should be *her* making the contact, not you."

"I know. But I think it should be a letter, not a phone call. Give him time to adjust before he responds." She buried her face in her hands. "I can't believe she called him."

"Not exactly called him. . ." They were referring to the fact that shortly after getting the computer, Ellie had searched for her father online, checking English Department faculty at numerous universities. She had finally tracked him down at a small state college in Illinois. Apparently, she had placed several calls, only to hang up when he answered or acknowledged his name. She knew where he was, so now what?

"Maybe I should check on her?" Josie said, glancing helplessly toward the hallway.

"No, let her read in peace. We'll talk to her later, when she's had some time to digest it." Ben swiveled in his chair. "How about a hike?"

"Cool," Josie said, wrapping her arms around his neck and laying on a big kiss. His speech and memory were improving rapidly, but his arm and leg required hard work.

"Hmmm. I don't know, maybe I should conserve my strength for some other physical activity?" he said, stroking her thigh.

"I don't think those are the muscles you're supposed to be working on."

"True. Then let's hike all the way down the road and maybe later we can work on those other muscles, when Ellie's rockin' and rollin'."

"Do our own rockin'?"

"Maybe even some rollin'."

Despite the side effects of the various medications that Ben was on, they had eased into a playful intimacy. While nothing had been spoken, Josie knew how much of his manhood was tied up in his need to give her sexual pleasure. Rather than deal with the frustration of his own limitations, he focused intensely on her. With her desperate need to shower him with love now—to let out all this newfound certainty—it had actually been difficult to let herself lie back and enjoy his touch. Some days, when she was particularly pre-occupied with worry, she just couldn't let go, but she'd learned to fake it, rather than

face his disappointment. Afterwards, she'd tap into his ensuing con-
tentment and find calm wrapped in his embrace.

Josie pushed the ottoman aside and reached for Ben's four-prong
cane.

"Been sitting too long," he grunted as Josie helped him up. "Stiff.
God, I hate this."

That was the extent of his complaining—*God, I hate this.* She
knew he was holding it all inside. Maybe verbalizing to Jack Mills,
his psychiatrist—at least she hoped so. But for her benefit, he kept it
hidden, and she silently thanked him for that.

Their new definition of a hike entailed a walk from their front
door to the road, then left to the end of their property, usually with
all three horses playfully trotting along their fence line. At that point,
they'd stop to rest, chat with the horses, and then, at a much slower
pace, they would all head back home.

At the door, Josie grabbed Ben's Yankee cap and put it on him
backwards, catcher style. He was wearing a Nirvana sweatshirt that
Ellie had given him last Christmas. It was faded from being worn and
washed so often. Josie's heart gushed just looking at him, and her face
must have shown it, for Ben hesitated.

"What's so funny? What are you grinning at?" he asked.

"You. I just love you more than you can possibly know."

"Oh, I know, Josie. Don't ever forget that. I know." And with that,
he kissed her lightly on the forehead, then said, "Beat you to the road."

A few days later, Ellie sat down for breakfast, her usual somber self,
only this time she actually spoke to them. Reaching into her French
book, she pulled out some folded papers and gingerly pushed them
across the table. "I wrote him a letter. I'd rather mail it than send an

email. It seems more personal. I wondered if you'd read it and tell me what you think," she said.

Josie could feel the blood draining from her face. She sank down onto the kitchen chair, coffee pot in hand.

"Did you want us both to read it, or just Mom?" Ben gently asked.

"No, you too. I mean, Mom's got other feelings mixed up in this. So, I'd like you to read it, too."

"Wise answer," Ben said.

Josie thought she noticed a slight smile begin and then fade on Ellie's face. Her copper-colored hair was swept up in a high bun, accentuating her cheekbones and displaying her stunning blue eyes. Even without make-up, she was beautiful. Josie always marveled at this child she'd produced. Nothing in Ellie's features or coloring reminded her of Paul, the biological father, yet neither did she strongly resemble Josie. Apparently, she was a blend of genes that created her own unique physiognomy.

"And, I want to send a couple of pictures. One of me when I was little and one of me now."

Josie nodded. "Of course," she said, her words barely audible.

Ellie took a deep breath and pushed back her chair. Stuffing her book into her backpack, she stood and slung it over her shoulder. She paused for a moment, then turned to Ben. "How are you feeling today?" she asked meekly.

Ben smoothly masked his surprise and answered, "Not bad, El, thanks for asking."

She glided out the door, leaving the two of them wide-eyed, looking first at each other and then at the letter folded between them.

Josie felt her stomach churn. "You read it. I'll listen."

Setting the newspaper aside, Ben reached for the letter and slowly unfolded the pages. It was neatly handwritten on lined school paper.

Adjusting his reading glasses, he took a deep breath and said, "You ready?"

Josie bit her thumbnail and nodded.

Ben began: "*Dear Professor Paul Reid, I am not sure where to begin this letter. I am really nervous about writing to you, but what I have to tell you is very important. I hope you will not be too upset. And I hope you will understand why I needed to write.*

"*Here goes. I guess I should just come out and say it. So please sit down and get ready.*

"*My name is Eleanor Serafini. Everyone calls me Ellie. My mother named me after Eleanor Roosevelt, who I'm sure you know about. I am sixteen years old. This is the part that is hard to say. I am your daughter. My mom is Josephine Serafini. She was your girlfriend for a while at SUNY Binghamton. I guess when she found out she was pregnant, you were not dating anymore. Her mom was dying of cancer at the time, and she was very confused. I know I would be if I were her.*"

Ben paused and looked up at Josie. "You okay?" he asked.

Josie reached for a napkin and wiped her eyes. "Yes, go on," she said.

"*At first, she was thinking of having an abortion, but then she changed her mind. You were in Ireland. My mom decided it was best not to tell you and to take care of me on her own. I think she was very brave to do that.*"

"Oh my God," Josie gasped. "I can't believe she said that."

Ben looked over his glasses and smiled, his eyes wet as well.

"Go on, go on."

"*Anyway, I am not writing to ask you for anything. I just want to meet you. I want to know if I have any half-brothers or sisters. I'd like to know about your mother and father because I guess they'd be my grandparents.*

"I know this must be a big shock for you. I keep wondering how I would feel if I were you. I'm sorry if I have upset you. I just really want to meet you.

"I'd like to tell you a little about myself. (And I'd like to know stuff about you too.) I love music. I play the guitar and sing in a band called Bliss. We're all girls, except for the drummer. We're just beginning, but we've written a couple of our own songs. Basically, we're into alternative rock. I love Nirvana, Hole, Sleater-Kinney, and No Doubt. I do okay in school, but I'm not an A student or anything. I played some sports when I was little, like soccer and softball, but it's not my thing now. Music is. Actually, if you're interested, I could send you some of my song lyrics. They're like poetry, I guess. Let me know when you write back if you'd like me to send them.

"So that's probably enough, I mean, probably more than you want, right? You must be in shock. I'll stop now and just say PLEASE WRITE and let me know what you think. I'm going to include my address and phone number and my email address, so you can answer me in any way you want. Also, I'll send some pictures so you can see what I look like.

"I hope you understand why I wrote.

"Sincerely,

"Your Daughter, Ellie."

Ben took a deep breath, refolded the letter, and set it down. "Wow. Quite a letter. I think she did a good job."

Josie reached for the letter and scanned it again. Ellie probably re-wrote it a million times, she thought, starting over each time she made even the slightest error. It was neatly written in dark purple ink, not one cross-out or correction. Her stomach burned just wondering what Paul Reid would think and how he might respond to Ellie.

"Well," she sighed, "I guess it's time to let it go. It's out of my hands and up to him now. I just hope she can handle the outcome."

And me too, she thought, biting her lip. She'd always assumed that this knowledge would come as a burden to him, that he'd be grateful that Josie had kept him ignorant and, therefore, not responsible. But what if she was wrong? What if he would have embraced this daughter, despite their relationship? Would he be angry that Josie hadn't informed him all these years?

"Don't worry, Jo," Ben was saying. "Ellie isn't facing this alone. We'll be there to help her through." He reached across the table and, with his finger, traced the vein down the middle of her forehead. "Relax, sweetheart. It's going to be okay."

"You think so?" Josie asked meekly. She couldn't imagine this ending well, but it was comforting to hear just the same.

Four weeks later, Josie called home at the end of her work day. She had returned to the office three days a week, and she and the staff were putting things in order for Ben's part-time return the next week. He was going to try to see a few patients, and then they'd determine if he should officially retire.

Ellie answered on the fifth ring, her voice sullen. "H'lo."

"Hi honey, how was school?"

"Sucked."

"What's wrong? What happened?"

"Nothing. Just sucked."

Josie knew that whatever did or didn't happen at school had just as much to do with Ellie's lack of correspondence from Illinois. Her letter had been mailed over three weeks before. So far, no response. When Josie suggested that perhaps he was out of town, Ellie's immediate comment, "No he isn't," confirmed the fact that Ellie must have called the college. Josie decided it was time to intervene. Tonight, she'd talk to Ben about what she might say to Paul Reid when she contacted him.

"What's Dad doing?"

"I dunno. Haven't seen him. Been in my room."

She could picture Ellie storming into the house and then her room. No "Hello." No "How was your day?" Just that door-slamming "Stay out and leave me alone!" attitude that made Josie want to pull her own hair out.

Exhausted, Josie sighed. "Well, what do you guys want for dinner? I thought I'd stop for pizza or whatever. Ask Dad, or put him on the line."

"Ben!" Josie could hear her calling out. "Ben!"

On occasion, Ellie didn't call him Dad. They had told her the truth when she was five. She had asked then if she could still call him Daddy, to which Ben had replied "of course," because he was in every way. When at fourteen, Ellie had first called him "Ben," he had been deeply hurt. That was the only time he'd ever raised his voice to Ellie, explaining that no matter what she called him, he would always be her father. He'd adopted her as an infant, loved her as his own, and would always be there for her.

Josie had noticed that her use of "Ben" was usually done to irritate her mother, like now. Only this time, what followed several shouts of "Ben!" as Josie shuffled files and set them aside, was a sharp, desperate, "Daddy!"—then a blood-chilling, "Mom, Mom, Mom!" that got louder as Ellie raced back for the phone.

By the time Josie got home, the paramedics were huddled over Ben on the floor of the family room. Desperate to see his face, Josie made her way around the feet of a kneeling EMT only to meet her daughter head on. A sobbing Ellie flung herself into her arms, crying, "I'm sorry. I'm sorry. I'm sorry."

Josie managed a quick hug as she strained to see over her daughter's shoulder, then made her way to Ben.

Kneeling above him, Josie cradled his head and bent her forehead to his.

"Ben, sweetheart. Ben," she whispered in his ear. Then, sitting back on her heels, she took him in. His pale face was placid, his eyes closed, his mouth slack and open. He was breathing but unresponsive.

Bending forward again, she said, "Please stay with me, Ben. Please!" As her tears fell onto his face, she felt her daughter wrap herself around her from behind. The two sobbed in unison as the stretcher was bumped into the room and the paramedic said, "Ma'am, I'm sorry, but we need you to step aside, please."

Ben had suffered a subarachnoid hemorrhage in an area close to the brain stem. Despite severe damage to the brain revealed on the CT scan, aggressive measures were still exhausted. Comatose, Ben barely clung to life for two weeks.

Josie remembered little of those weeks. Night and day were indistinguishable, as she slept when she could on a cot beside his bed. Phone calls to Ellie, who was staying at a friend's house, were short, with silent pauses that Josie was much too weary to fill. Phone calls from Vic, who was busy with work, little Isabel, and newborn Miguel, were one source of comfort and support. That, and simply resting her head on Ben's chest, hearing his heart beat, feeling the warmth of his skin—savoring it as long as she could.

Once, Josie woke to find Ellie sitting on the side of the bed, holding Ben's hand, tears flowing down her cheeks. When Josie rose to hug her, Ellie had said, "He looks so old. Why does he look so old?" Then, in a whisper, "If I had just found him sooner, he might be okay now." And Josie had rocked her, saying, "No, no, no. I should have been there. I shouldn't have left him alone for so long."

In early December, Josie buried Ben beside her mother. On the tombstone, she had inscribed: "Devoted Husband, Loving Father." She would long for every part of him, every day, forever. It was just that simple.

On New Year's Eve, Josie spent close to an hour on the phone talking with Vic and Irma. The week of Ben's funeral, baby Miguel had been rushed to the hospital after an intestinal virus left him dangerously dehydrated. Unable to fly home for Ben's funeral, Vic had felt terrible and still couldn't let it go despite Josie's reassurances. She decided the best approach was to focus their conversation on her trip to LA that upcoming summer.

"It will be good for Ellie, too," Josie said. "In fact, I wish we could come sooner. But I want to stay more than one week, which is all she gets for spring break, and she sure can't afford to miss any more school." Ellie's grades had plummeted, and once classes resumed, Josie was planning on speaking with each of her teachers.

"I just wish we weren't so far apart and airfare so damn expensive." Vic said. He sounded tired. Josie knew that both he and Irma had had a stomach flu as well.

"I know. I miss you so much. Can't wait till this summer," Josie said.

"You sure you're okay? I could come out for a few days—no problem."

"No, Vic, I'm okay, really. Don't worry. Summer will be here before we know it."

The truth was, Josie just wanted to be alone, for that's when she felt closest to Ben. No one distracting her or trying to pull her back into real life.

After hanging up the phone, she decided to check on the horses. A kind neighbor had been helping with their care, but it had snowed earlier and there was talk of more to come. Josie wanted to be sure they were set for the night. The horses were such a comfort since Ben's death. They asked little of her and gave so much. Whenever she found the strength, she made her way to the barn.

Slipping on her boots and jacket, Josie stepped out the side door. An almost full moon lit up her yard, now covered in white. Something about the blanket of snow was so soothing that, for a brief moment, Josie was tempted to lie down. Instead, she stood still and took in the untouched beauty.

Slowly, she crossed the yard, the crunch of her boots disrupting the silence. As she approached the side of the barn, she peeked through the bars of the first window. A beam of moonlight softly illuminated the interior of the three-stall barn. Josie was pleased to see that in anticipation of the snow, her neighbor had added fresh shavings.

Her oldest horse, Fire Mountain, was lying down, legs curled up beside him, head upright but eyes closed. He was aptly named, for in sunlight, Fire looked ablaze, as his sorrel coat was more orange than red. Even now, bathed in moonlight, he cast a gentle glow. Jack, her quarter horse, all black except for a white diamond on his forehead and a white snip on his nose, stood with head bowed, most likely asleep. Of course, it was her buckskin miniature horse, Luke, standing guard, eyes alert, ears upright, for despite being gelded a few years back, he still thought himself a stallion and very much in charge.

Luke turned slightly, but when Fire opened his eyes and glanced up questioningly in the direction of the window, Josie stepped back. If they made eye contact, Fire would push himself up and come to her.

And while the thought of opening the window's grill so she could press her forehead to his was inviting, Josie didn't want to disturb him. She knew his arthritis acted up when it rained or snowed, and he looked so peaceful. They all did. Instead, she gingerly made her way back to the house.

All Josie wanted to do was curl up on the sofa and sleep. Friends and neighbors were still bringing endless offerings of food and doing grocery runs for her, so most of the time, Josie flopped on the family room sofa, slept, wept, watched old movies on TV, and slept and wept some more. Ellie came and went quietly with friends. Josie was grateful for that. In fact, that was why she gave Ellie permission to attend a friend's New Year's Eve party despite the coming snow.

Unable to hear one more person shout "Happy New Year!" Josie switched off the TV, pulled up the granny-square afghan that Ellie had made her years before, and buried her face in the soft blue sofa pillow. Nothing could be happy about this new year.

When Ellie stumbled in the door at 2 a.m., Josie woke with a start.

"Where have you been? I told you 12:30. Welcome in the New Year, but then home—12:30!" The smell of beer hit her just as Ellie heaved and ran for the bathroom.

Holding Ellie's hair back over the toilet, Josie felt a mixture of anger and deep sadness. "Oh, Ellie. That's it! No guitar. No band practice. You're grounded. One week."

After rinsing her mouth, Ellie spun around. "Why? Since when do you care?"

"What the hell does that mean?"

"Or do you just want me to be as miserable and pathetic as you are?" Her thick tongue could barely articulate the words.

Josie held back an urge to slap her daughter's face; instead, trembling, she said, "Get to your room right now."

"Exactly. Send me to my room, so you can be alone, in that stupid Nirvana sweatshirt or that old flannel shirt he always wore. Just sit around and cry all day."

"Ellie, what a mean thing to say!" Josie sobbed. "I have every right to cry my heart out. And so do you."

"Yeah, so do I. At least he cared about me, not like you."

Josie followed her into her bedroom, where Ellie had flung herself face first on the bed. She sat down beside her and tried to collect her thoughts. What was all this about? She reached out and began rubbing her daughter's back, but Ellie yanked away and said, "Don't touch me. Leave me alone."

"Why do you make it so difficult to love you?"

"I don't make it difficult. I just don't want to be second all the time. Sometimes *I* want to be first."

The words hit Josie like a blast of cold air.

"Oh God, Ellie, don't you know you were always first—always." Josie struggled to find the energy to continue. "And Ben was second, in a way. But this year, well, he needed me. And even that didn't mean you were second. You know how much I love you. And your father . . . how he loved you."

She rolled onto her side. "My father?" An edge of sharpness sliced the air.

"Yes, your father. The man who helped you with algebra, taught you to skate, and set up a fund for your college education. That father," Josie said firmly.

Ellie remained silent.

Josie hadn't thought about the letter and Paul Reid in weeks. All of that had gotten lost in the nightmare that followed. At least for me, she thought, certainly not for Ellie.

"Honey," Josie began tenderly, "I'm sorry if Paul didn't answer you. God knows what he thought—if he did in fact get your letter. For all you know, he never received it. But . . ." She sighed heavily at the thought, then forced the words out anyway. "I'll try to reach him. Give me some time to . . . get it all together . . . and then I'll contact him. Okay?"

Ellie rolled onto her back and put her arm across her eyes. She was silent for a few minutes, then quietly said, "Don't bother."

"Oh honey, it's no bother," Josie began, but Ellie interrupted.

"I already heard from him."

"What? When?" Josie leaned forward, her eyes wide.

"When you were at the hospital, staying with Ben. He . . . emailed me."

"Emailed?"

"Yes. He said . . ." Ellie hesitated, then snorted through her nose, a harsh sarcastic sound. "He said the timing was bad. I think that's how he put it. He just got married and the timing was . . . *unfortunate* . . . that was the word . . . *unfortunate*."

"Oh Ellie." Josie wanted to touch her again, but feared she'd pull away, so she waited.

"He said he appreciated my letter, and that one day, when the time was right, he'd contact me. But *to please respect his privacy at this crucial time in his life.*" These last words were spoken in a mocking tone. "Oh, and I sounded like a very nice young lady—and no, there were no brothers or sisters."

"That's it?" Josie asked, gently.

Ellie paused uncomfortably. "He did say one more thing. He said to keep in mind the possibility that perhaps he wasn't my father after all. It was a complicated time back then, he said. *Complicated* then, *unfortunate* now." Ellie grunted and rolled back onto her stomach, her long hair covering her face.

Josie closed her eyes and imagined that she was leaning back against Ben, his arms around her, holding her tight. She held on to this moment, gaining calm, and finding strength.

"Ellie, I know this must be painful, maddening, frustrating, but you have to look at what you have, not what you lack. Think about it. You have . . ."

Abruptly, Josie was interrupted by the wild eyes of her half-drunken sixteen-year-old daughter, who flung her pillow across the room and exclaimed, "I'll tell you what I have and what I lack. I have *half* of a mother, and I'm *minus* two fathers!"

Blue Eyes

April 2001

VIC

Vic closed the file and leaned back in his rickety chair with a heavy sigh. So many heartbreaking stories. Still, it felt good to be back to work, outside of himself, and immersed in other people's problems. But when he came out of that tunnel of concentration into the bright daylight of "Vic Serafini's Life Today," he was hit with a startling thunderclap that took his breath away. This happened mostly at work, not when first waking from sleep, like for most people—because he didn't sleep. Not deeply and not for more than two hours at a time. He woke in fits and starts and was always well aware of the brutal absence of Irma and the kids—immediately. Work was the only place that he could forget, for a while, that his life was an empty vacuum.

Weeks ago, Vic had made Josie toss out all antidepressants and sleeping pills. The temptation of their presence, even under lock and key, was too real, while the way they made him feel was not. What a dishonor to their memory to blunt his pain—unless he blunted it for good. And he knew now, just as he had known that desperate dawn after swallowing all those pills, that that was not the answer. There was something more he could do—must do—in this world. He'd felt that way after Vietnam. So many young men gone, especially his buddy Castillo. At the time, he wondered if he'd been spared for a reason. He used to think Irma and the kids were the answer, but not anymore. Why he was still left on this godforsaken earth was beyond him.

Vic had been working at Santiago's law office since following his friend to Los Angeles fifteen years before. They had met in Tucson where they were both involved in the Sanctuary movement, helping Central American refugees find homes and jobs. Santiago was an attorney, devoted to helping his Latino community in Los Angeles where he had resettled a number of refugees. From the start, Santiago had been impressed with Vic, his disarming way with people, how he put them at ease and gained their trust—even though he was a *gringo*. Santiago joked that Vic's Spanish was as good as anyone walking the streets of San Fernando, despite, or maybe because of, his atrocious grammar. He didn't sound like a schoolboy, but a man of the streets. Most reassuring was his sense of commitment. Whatever task he tackled got every bit of his heart and soul, and that was saying a lot.

Seeing Vic's potential, Santiago had suggested he become a paralegal. Then he gave Vic the best motivation possible: guaranteed employment. At first, Vic simply assisted Santiago with interviews and paperwork while pursuing his paralegal certificate, but then, as his skills and knowledge increased, he took on more complex responsibilities, working directly with clients and courts. By the time he finished the certification process, he and Santiago were an established team. Their focus was deportation defense, asylum, work visas, and family/spouse petitions—all legal channels in a community teeming with undocumented immigrants, or, as the public called them, "illegal aliens."

Vic glanced up at the weathered poster of the Statue of Liberty on his office wall, which read in bold red letters, "No human being is illegal." Try telling that to the men standing on the corner one block down, nervously eyeing every van that passed by and wondering which was a potential employer, looking for day laborers, and which was *la migra,* making sweeps every now and then. It astounded Vic that anyone could call trying to survive a crime.

Working at the law office had given Vic a deep sense of satisfaction, unlike working on cars or helicopters, which left him with grease-stained hands and too many bad memories best left in the past. But whether this was where he could continue to find purpose, he wasn't so sure.

With a sigh, Vic reached for the phone to call home. It was comforting having Josie there. The thought of her going back east anytime in the near future was disturbing, to say the least. Each time he brought it up, she shook her head and said she was definitely staying through summer, most likely longer. The lease on her house was open-ended. Her work was flexible, since she'd been working part time at the cardiac rehab center after turning Ben's practice over to new hands a few years before. Vic knew Ben had left her pretty well set financially, so thank God that wasn't an issue. But the horses were another matter—probably the most important part of Josie's life, now that Ellie was gone. To be away from them for so long clearly bothered her, but it sounded like they were doing okay with her horse veterinarian. Still, this couldn't be easy for her.

What was most reassuring to Vic was the fact that Josie had found ways to enjoy herself in LA. Some mornings she hiked, exploring various trails that she'd read about in a book called *Walking Los Angeles.* She carried a cell phone and sometimes, if she found decent reception, she'd call Vic to tell him about a bird she saw or an encounter with a coyote. She'd met Rae for lunch a couple of times, and once they had attended a nursing workshop at UCLA Medical

Center. Josie wasn't big on shopping or sight-seeing, but she managed to keep busy, and this week she was excited about finally seeing Ellie.

The phone rang once. "Hello," Josie answered, her voice tight and nervous, and Vic knew why. She was waiting for Ellie to call.

"It's just me again, Jo, not the Princess of Punk, the Queen of the Quagmire, the Blue-eyed Baby in Black."

"Quagmire? Queen of the Quagmire?" Josie groaned, and he could picture her rolling her eyes.

"You know . . . mired . . . in a swamp. That's a word, isn't it? Like stuck in a swamp of . . . I don't know . . . the blues?"

"Sounds about right," she said.

"So, I take it El hasn't called yet."

"Nope, any minute I expect. I still don't know why she wouldn't fly. That's a long drive—and with someone she hardly knows?" Josie paused, then added, "She always has to do things the most difficult way possible."

"Well, she says she has a good reason," Vic said. "We'll soon see. The suspense is killing me." Vic knew the exact look on Josie's face, knitted brow that made a defined line down the center of her forehead, top teeth biting her lower lip. "Relax, Jo, everything's gonna be fine."

"God, I can't wait to see her," she said. Then, as an afterthought, "I should keep the line open."

"Relax, *pobrecita*. Listen, the reason I called—one of the girls here says her teenage daughters love that Hawaiian pizza with pineapples and, I guess, ham. Maybe Ellie would prefer that? Or should we stick with Plan A?"

"Ham? I doubt she'd eat a pig. Just get the veggie one. Plan A."

"Okay. Good luck. See ya later."

"Thanks. I'll let you know when we're on our way home."

An hour later, Santiago walked into Vic's office, keys in hand. "You mind taking off now?" he asked. "Ana called and she's running late. I have to pick up the girls from soccer practice in thirty minutes." Santiago looked more like a musician than an attorney, with his long, dark hair pulled back in a ponytail and his almost daily wardrobe of T-shirt and jeans. When he went to court, though, it was suit and tie.

"We can pick them up first if you want, drop me off after," Vic offered, though he dreaded the thought of stopping by the park—and seeing the girls.

"No, no problem. Anyway, I'll have a carful." His eyes were warm with unspoken sympathy. He most likely knew where Vic's thoughts were.

Relieved, Vic grabbed his jacket and followed him out the door. It was still difficult for Vic to socialize with Santiago outside of work. His daughters were close to Isabel's age, and his son was one year older than Miguel. Even looking at their pictures on Santiago's desk or their artwork on his wall was painfully disturbing.

As they approached the small parking lot, the *thwop, thwop, thwop* of a helicopter vibrated down his spine and made him shiver. Vic glanced up at the low-flying police helicopter scanning a street beyond. He was relieved that it wasn't the LA Fire Department's red-and-white aircraft. That one always reminded him of the 'Nam-era Huey Cobra, its nose painted with the bloodstained teeth of a shark. The *chop-chop* sound was enough to make him wince, but the sight of the red-and-white copter always brought back images of the fierce-looking gunship. The first time he'd seen that sharp-toothed beast in 'Nam, he'd been paralyzed with regret. While other guys had cheered at its sight, Vic had felt remorse for maintaining a machine that brought terror and death to innocent villagers.

"You okay?" Santiago asked, well aware of Vic's Vietnam triggers.

Vic nodded, then did what he'd been told by another Vietnam vet: he focused on the present moment. "Appreciate the ride," Vic said. "Josie's on pins and needles waiting for Ellie, thought she'd arrive earlier, which is why she has the van. This morning Ellie called from Santa Cruz—said they'd spent the night there and were heading on down. The guy driving lives in the Sunland-Tujunga area. That's where Josie will pick her up."

"Isn't she nervous about driving there?" Santiago asked as he unlocked the door of his Dodge Ram van. "Ana would be afraid to drive to a new place alone."

Vic glanced at the car seat in the back and felt that ache in his chest again. How many times would Irma doublecheck Miguel's seatbelt? She'd fuss and pull, tighten and recheck. Vic wondered when these memories would cease. Turning his mind back to Santiago, he said, "Josie, afraid? She's never been afraid of anything like that. She's had an adventurer's spirit since the day she was born. She and Ben had been planning to visit every continent in the world once he retired. She wanted to start with Africa, and her intention was to travel to small villages, not resorts or tourist sights. She still talks about doing that someday."

Vic suddenly realized that his life was such that he could actually join Josie. His restless soul could wander the world. Maybe he'd find *theirs* somewhere—Irma's, Isa's, and Miguel's.

"So how long is Ellie staying?"

"I guess about a week, maybe ten days. She's getting a ride from someone who's on spring break. Says she can't fly—she'll explain when she gets here. Some big mystery. Josie is exhausted trying to figure her out but beside herself with excitement. She hasn't seen her since last summer."

Vic tried not to look at any bus stops, but this one was unavoidable. They were taking a right, hugging the curb, when he caught the eye of a little boy, his arms wrapped around his mother's leg. Vic closed his eyes.

"Maybe she's afraid of flying, read about some plane crash or something," Santiago offered.

"I don't know. But it should be an interesting week."

"Sure you don't want to take tomorrow off?"

"No, no. Thursday and Friday are fine. Thought I'd give them a day alone first. They need it." Vic opened his eyes and decided to keep them firmly on the road ahead.

They had just turned into Vic's cul de sac. Some neighborhood boys were skateboarding in the street. At first, they rolled by, glancing casually at the car. When they saw it was Vic, they skidded to a stop, picked up their boards, and stood solemnly beside the curb. Vic glanced in the side mirror after the car passed them. They stood there still, side by side, at attention, eyes right, skateboards vertical at their sides, as if paying tribute to a fallen soldier.

Two hours later, as Josie and Ellie pulled into the driveway, Vic bounded out the front door with a burst of energy that surprised him.

When Josie had called on her cell to let Vic know they were on their way and to order the pizzas, he had been stumped by her tone. Usually he could read her pretty well.

"There's more than one surprise," Josie had said, and he honestly couldn't tell if her voice conveyed awe or anger. "One big one, so to speak, and one, uh, well . . ."

"No, no, no," he could hear in the background. "Don't tell him. Let him see for himself." Then Ellie came on the line. "Hi Uncle Vic. I love you!" Her voice wrapped around him like a warm Mexican blanket.

And now, here she was. Ellie's big smile lit up the interior as the van came to a stop and she burst out the side. Tall and thin, she was still dressed in black: long black skirt, black top exposing her midriff, long black sweater jacket, and big black clunky boots that added another two inches at least—but in startling contrast, she wore a multicolored scarf, that covered her head, wrapped around her neck, and draped over one shoulder.

Vic swept Ellie up in a bear hug, and she immediately began to sob. "Oh God, I'm so sorry I didn't come down for the funeral . . . I couldn't. I just couldn't."

"I know, I know," he said. "It's okay, sweetheart."

As he set her down, her scarf fell back, exposing her hair—or lack of it. Her long copper-colored hair was gone, and in its place, short golden spikes. "Whoa!" Vic said, standing back, taking in this new look. "Stunning," he said. "You're something else, Ellie."

"We shaved our heads about six weeks ago. Wild, huh?"

Vic turned his attention to Josie who was leaning into the back of the van. "Some big surprise, huh Mom?" Vic said, straining to see her face and wondering how she'd responded.

Josie lifted her head and said over her shoulder. "That's not the big one. This is—and she's plumb tuckered out, El."

Josie stepped back as Vic approached the van to peer in. Curled up on the seat was a large black and white Siberian husky with stunning facial markings. White face, black forehead with a blaze of white up its center, and ice-blue eyes accentuated by a mask of black.

"God, she's beautiful," Vic said. "What magnificent markings, and those eyes!"

"I can't believe you said that!" Ellie exclaimed. "That's her name. Maggie the Magnificent. That's what her owner called her. He was an old guy down the street from our apartment house. He used to walk her every day, and we'd pet her and talk to him. And then . . ." Ellie climbed in again and sat beside the dog, who immediately put her chin on Ellie's leg. "Then one day, well, we see a coroner's van outside his house and then animal control comes and takes Maggie. So, we go to the shelter, and there she is. It took a while, but we brought her home." Maggie's eyes moved upward as Ellie leaned down to kiss her forehead.

"We?" Josie said. "Don't you mean you? Who's taking responsibility for her?"

"Well, Kelly and I both brought her home, but she's always with me. Sleeps with me, follows me everywhere."

"Even to LA," Vic said with a wink to Josie. "That's why you couldn't fly."

Ellie nodded. "That, and I was afraid to leave her." She looked nervously at her mother. "Our apartment doesn't allow dogs. I was afraid she wouldn't be there when I got back. The manager was pretty mean about it. Said if she wasn't out immediately, he'd have us evicted. We told the whole story, about the old guy down the street—thought maybe he might know him—but it didn't make any difference. He wanted her out right away. Kelly said she'd keep her quiet until I got back, but . . ."

"Pretty hard to hide a husky." Vic stroked Maggie's ears; only the blue eyes moved in his direction.

"Yeah, not like hiding a cat. Anyway, I'm gonna try to find a new place when I get back—one that will let me keep her." She looked apprehensively at Josie. "I hope it's not too much of a pain. She's really good, doesn't bark much, just an occasional howl, and I'll pay for her food." She glanced down.

"Oh, Ellie, of course it's okay." In Josie's face was all the pain and tenderness that Vic knew weighed down her heart. "She's a wonderful surprise! Which is more than I can say for this," she added, rubbing what there was of Ellie's hair. "All' that beautiful hair, oh honey."

Ellie turned to her mother and opened her mouth to speak. There was a sadness in Ellie's eyes that spoke to Vic's sorrow. He leaned forward to catch her words, but Ellie stopped short—even flinched—when Josie added, "You just don't know a good thing when you have it. What most women would give for hair like yours! And you just cast it away."

Attempting to intercept Ellie's expected retort, Vic reached for the Guatemalan duffel bag in the back and said, "Let's get in the house. I'm starving. Been smelling that pizza forever. You girls are damn lucky I didn't devour the whole thing."

But Ellie hadn't responded. Instead of her usual rapid-fire defense, she had sat back, quiet and sad, and then, like certain flowers at twilight, closed up tight and firm.

Sitting on the tiny plot of grass in the backyard, Vic and Maggie watched Josie plant a small lilac bush. "I can smell them already," Vic said, attempting a joke, but his voice fell flat.

Josie sat back on her heels and rubbed her nose with the back of her hand. "Amir said they were in full bloom in my yard, and his wife had placed lilacs in every room. 'The house is pungent with their fragrance!' he said." Josie accentuated "pungent" with a nod of her head.

Vic scratched behind Maggie's ears, and she looked up adoringly at him. "She's a great dog, isn't she?" he said. "So gentle and serene. Almost queenly."

Josie smiled and said—more to the dog than to Vic—"She's a very special lady. Yes, she is."

"Seems to have a quieting effect on Ellie, too. Don't you think? Or maybe it's just being here, in the house, with the kids gone." Vic said the last words slowly, gently. He paused, then let the thought go with a sigh. "But the dog, I do think she has calmed Ellie. I do."

Josie frowned. "Ellie does seem subdued. At first, I thought she was exhausted from the long drive, but she still seems kind of serious and quiet. Of course, being here, she's forced to confront the loss."

Vic nodded. "When you went hiking yesterday, what did she talk about? Anything seem to be on her mind?"

"No. Just Maggie and finding a place. A little about her music . . . and of course, you." Josie paused and gave him a slight smile. "But nothing that went very deep into *her* life. Again, she seemed tired, so I didn't push it. I just enjoyed the fact that she was there with me, along the trail."

Vic stretched out his right leg. His calf muscle had been sore since he and Rodrigo had raced up a hill on their last run. Maggie rolled over, a complete 360, then gazed up with her blue eyes. "Maggie could be Ellie's daughter—they've got the same eyes." He laughed.

"Good God, don't say that to Ellie. The topic of eye color always sets her off!"

"Why?"

Josie patted the earth around the plant, then came and sat beside Maggie, stroking her side. "People used to tell Ellie that she had her father's eyes—meaning Ben. Once, she asked me, tentatively, if it was possible that Ben was really her dad. God, she was so pained and hopeful. And you know, Vic, I wanted to say yes . . . maybe I should have . . . maybe I should have lied and avoided all this anguish. But they did have the same eyes—a clear light blue—not grayish like her biological father's. I always loved that—as if she did belong to Ben."

Josie picked at the grass at her feet. "Who's to say what constitutes being a father," she said softly. "Ben loved her like she was his own." She threw a handful of grass in the air. "Not like our father," she said, with an air of disgust.

Vic took a deep breath. Perfect segue. He couldn't have planned it better. His intention was to tell her tonight, after some wine. He'd come close several times, but just couldn't rouse the necessary energy. Now he had no choice. Their father was stopping by that weekend. He cleared his throat.

"Josie, I've wanted to tell you something for a very long time. Hearing what you just said, maybe you can understand why I chose to . . . well . . . lie . . . in a way." He looked at her with as much tenderness as he could muster. "Before I left for 'Nam, Dad wrote to me. Then when I came back, I . . . I visited him in Vegas."

Josie eyes widened. "What? You've seen him? But why didn't you tell me, and why didn't he . . . ?" She stopped.

Vic placed his hand on her arm. "Wait. Let me explain."

"Is he still living?" she immediately asked. "Have you seen him since? Where is he now? Does he know about the accident?"

Vic pressed his lips together, wishing he didn't have to let out the next words. "Yes, to all of the above. In fact, he's coming to LA— this weekend. He just found out about the accident recently when he called. We don't communicate that often. But I want, I hope, that you two will talk. Except Josie, there's something I have to tell you first." He knew she hadn't digested all that he'd said yet, but he figured it was best to get it all out quickly.

"The reason he hasn't gotten in touch with *you* is because . . ." She was ghostly white, and he worried how she'd take the rest. "This is insane, but . . ." He stopped again. Then, gently, almost in a whisper, he said, "He doesn't think you're his daughter. Isn't that the weirdest thing? I mean, you know Mom. But he thinks . . ." He couldn't finish the sentence, let it hang in the air like the worst of summer smog, dark and dense. But it was out, after all these years, his burden was lifted—and dumped on Josie, which didn't make him feel any better.

She sat quietly, her chin quivering. "Not his daughter? Then whose?" She sat for a moment, her brow furrowed. "How weird is right. But how can I not be his?" She straightened up. "That's a cop-out if I ever heard one! Of course I'm his daughter! He just doesn't want to face what a pathetic deadbeat dad he is."

Suddenly Josie drew back and looked at Vic in disbelief. "Don't tell me you believe him?"

"No, of course I don't." He paused, then added. "I've gone over it a million times, and I think he's trying to convince himself for whatever reasons. But then again, we have to be honest. We don't really know. We can never really know."

She frowned. "Is it possible Mom was with someone else?"

Vic pictured his mother sitting alone at night, cigarette in hand. "I have vague memories of him coming in the door, probably drunk, saying 'Daddy's home!' and both of us running to him. I never questioned it before. And Mom always referred to him as our father."

Josie sat deep in thought. "I suppose I could do a DNA test or something." Then tossing her head back, she moaned. "But Christ, why even bother? He's not worth the effort. Some father either way." She stopped and looked at Vic. "Or has he been—to *you*?"

Vic rubbed his forehead. "No, Josie, not a father by our terms. But he *is* my father—*our* father." They sat in silence. Maggie's ears perked up as a car door slammed out front.

Josie laughed. "What an ironic story for Ellie to hear. Incredible!"

"Helloooo!" Ellie called from inside the house. Maggie jumped up and ran for the door.

"We're out back," Josie said weakly, then to Vic, "Why didn't you tell me? Since Vietnam?" Her eyes had filled with tears.

Vic reached out and took Josie's hands. "Josie, I'm sorry. It was all so awkward. His communication with me has always been sporadic. I just put it out of my mind. For what it's worth, he's an old man now, even older than his years. He lived hard, drank hard. Just talk to him when he comes. Just see what happens."

"Oh Maggie, Maggie, Maggie, Maggie." They could hear Ellie prattling on in the kitchen. "Such a good girl. Look at what Mama got you, yes. You're such a good girl."

"Absolutely not," Josie said firmly.

"At least give it some thought."

Josie shook her head. "Not necessary. I do *not* want to see the man." With head held high, she rose and walked into the house.

Josie and Vic both struggled to keep awake. Ellie had begged them to stay up with her to watch *Saturday Night Live*. Dave Matthews was the musical guest and she wanted them to hear his music. That Ellie wanted to share this with Josie had lightened the mood that evening. Dinner conversation had briefly touched on their father's upcoming visit since Ellie would still be there when he arrived. After hearing a few of the details of Vic's reconnection with him, Ellie had started asking questions, but Josie, her voice breaking, had quietly asked if they could change the subject. There'd been an awkward silence, with Vic anticipating Ellie's response. To his surprise, Ellie had glanced at her mother's downcast eyes, then without missing a beat, she'd started talking about Dave Matthews's music and the show later that night. When she asked her mother if she'd stay up and watch it with her, Josie's eyes had brightened and her mood had lifted for the rest of the evening. Vic was beyond grateful for this perfect antidote to the day's painful revelations, even if it meant staying awake past nine. He tended to conk out early, then wake sporadically throughout the night. Maybe staying up late would help.

Vic was just nodding off when Josie slapped his thigh. "Wake up. Wake up. We can do this. We still have it in us." Ellie was still on the phone in the bedroom.

"Alright. Alright," he murmured.

Josie was sitting up on the sofa, legs crossed yoga-style, wearing her new oversized Washington Huskies T-shirt. "You know what I just realized?" She glanced toward the hallway. "I can't believe it didn't occur to me before. Ellie didn't bring her guitar. She never goes anywhere without that guitar. Do you suppose she sold it?"

"I can't imagine that. She said she's been playing in coffee houses." Vic reached for a handful of popcorn and thought of the contests he and Isa used to have, seeing who could toss it the highest and still catch it in their mouths. Irma used to freak for fear Isabel would choke. He played with the kernels in his hand.

Ellie emerged from the bedroom, a somber look on her face. Vic tossed the popcorn back into the bowl.

"Ellie, how come you didn't bring your guitar?" Josie immediately asked. "I just realized that something was missing."

Ellie had the same defined crease down the center of her forehead as Josie. Flopping on the chair, Ellie propped her bare feet on the coffee table. Her toenails were painted a dark blue with silver glitter. Irma and Isa usually had pink, although Vic suddenly remembered that Ellie painted Isa's when she was here in the fall. He wondered what color.

Ellie shrugged and said, "It was either Maggie or the guitar. Wasn't room for both." All three looked at the sleeping ball of fur curled at Josie's feet. Her nose was buried in her tail, so she looked like one round circle.

"Well, I admire your choice. I know it must not have been easy." Josie paused, then finally acknowledged the long face. "What's wrong? Something happen in Seattle?"

"Yeah." Ellie bit her lip. "I have a problem, Mom, and maybe you can help."

Vic watched Josie's eyes brighten. "What is it, honey?" Josie asked.

"Well, like I told you, our landlord said he'd kick us out if we didn't get rid of Maggie. Kelly says he's stopped by a couple of times to check. And Kelly claims that she looked around for new places, but couldn't find one that allows dogs. Thing is, I doubt she really did. So, I don't know what to do." She hugged her knees to her chest and rocked slightly. "I guess I'll just hide her the best I can and start looking for a place as soon as I get back. Unless . . ." she paused and looked at Josie and then Vic. "Could you maybe keep her here for a while—just until I find a place? Maybe till summer when I can get a ride down again and take her back?"

Josie didn't answer right away and Vic wondered why, knowing how attached she'd gotten to Maggie in just a few days. Then he got his answer as Josie said, "Ellie, why don't *you* just stay here? We could drive to Seattle together and get your stuff, and you could pursue your music here—and maybe take some classes at the community college."

Vic frowned. Josie thought she had it all figured out. Wrong!

Ellie jumped up and began pacing, her long limbs taking the length of the small living room in three strides. "Mom! I don't want to stay here. I like Seattle. I have a life there."

"What life? You've barely settled in. You don't have a steady job. You don't know any dependable people—for heaven's sake, they talk you into shaving your hair! I don't understand. This isn't Binghamton; it's Los Angeles. A bigger music scene. You could make a life here."

Maggie woke and lifted her head.

"Sorry I asked!" Ellie thundered. "I'll just take her back and manage on my own!"

"I didn't say I wouldn't take her, did I? I just offered to have you stay here, too."

Vic's head started pounding. He clenched his fists.

"Offered? I didn't hear an offer. I heard a command. I'm a grown woman. I can take care of myself. I don't need your money—I'll find a way on my own. And no one talked me into shaving my head. I did it entirely on my own. For a good reason."

"Ellie, settle down!" Josie shouted, standing up and startling Maggie who jumped to her feet.

"You settle down!" Ellie stepped forward, squaring off with her mother.

"That's enough, both of you!" Vic leaned forward, knocking the bowl of popcorn and spilling it onto the rug. "Do either of you have any idea how fucking lucky you are to have each other? To be able to sit here and talk and make plans for any fucking future!"

Both of them stood silent as Vic continued. "This is ridiculous. You have two days left and you waste it with this shit." Tears filled his eyes, surprising him. He hadn't been able to cry in weeks. "Just like tomorrow, Josie. What's the big deal. Just talk to him."

Josie sank back down onto the sofa. "Vic, you're right, about *this*," she said motioning to Ellie, "but not *that*. That's different. *He* did the wasting, not me."

As Ellie bent down, scooping up the popcorn into the bowl,

Maggie ran up to her and began eating the scattered kernels. Throwing her arms around the dog, Ellie buried her face in her fur. Little tufts of golden hair stood out in contrast to the gray-black fur.

Josie knelt beside them, hugging both and rubbing Ellie's back. "Oh honey, I'm sorry. I just worry about you. But don't worry about Maggie. We'll keep her here." She glanced up at Vic. "Is that okay with you?"

"Of course," he answered.

"And come summer, or whenever you want, you can come get her. Or I'll bring her to you."

Ellie sat up, pulling herself away from Josie's arms. "Thanks," she said. "I'll find a place as soon as I can."

"And, of course, I'll help you with money. You'll need a security deposit, maybe first and last month's rent. Don't you need some furniture?"

"Mom, I'll work it all out. I'll let you know," Ellie said, exasperated.

"Alright, alright," she paused, then added, "Ellie, you're only nineteen. That's not exactly a grown woman."

"Almost twenty! I am a grown woman in a lot of ways. Just like you're not in some."

Vic lowered his head to hide his grin.

"What is that supposed to mean?"

"Well, do you always do the grown-up thing? I mean, Uncle Vic has a point. Shouldn't you at least talk to your father tomorrow? Wouldn't that be the grown-up thing to do? I mean, as much as I hate the man who is my biological father, if he ever contacted me, I'd at least give him a chance to speak."

Vic waited for Josie to retaliate with something about Ellie and Ben, but to his relief she didn't.

"Ellie, he abandoned us. I was only five. I waited for him night after night, for years, although I'm not sure why. I have no memories of him being affectionate or attentive. He was gone most of the time, or home arguing with my mother and making her cry. I have nothing decent to say to the man. In my opinion, it's wisest to leave it as it is. If Vic sees him, that's his business. But I certainly don't want to." Josie didn't mention the part about him questioning his paternity. Too delicate, Vic thought.

Ellie seemed to consider her mother's words, then said softly, "I'm kind of curious. I'd like to meet him. He is my grandfather."

Josie sat back on the floor, leaning against the sofa. She looked at Ellie. "I hadn't even thought of that. That you might want to meet him. What do you think, Vic? You said he doesn't expect me—just you. How might he react to Ellie?"

Suddenly weary, Vic sighed. "I don't know. I really have no idea, but I think he should see both of you. Let what happens, happen."

"No, I do not want to see him—under any condition. But Ellie, if she wants to, that's up to her."

They both turned to Ellie, but she was watching the TV screen. "Oh, that's him, Dave Matthews. Turn it up," she said excitedly.

Vic reached for the remote. They all focused on the screen. Ellie began singing along, something about getting out of your head and being somebody else.

Vic watched Ellie, lost in the music, nodding her head to the beat, playing air guitar, singing. He ached, wondering what Isa and Miguel would have been like when they grew up. What would have been their passions? Music, sports, art? He'd never know. In his mind, Isa would always be a six-year-old version of her mother, wide-eyed, affectionate, always wanting to please. And Miguel would be a three-year-old tyke, kicking around a soccer ball bigger than his head and following his sister everywhere.

Vic closed his eyes and leaned back. Oh yes, he thought, it certainly would be better, much better, to be somebody else.

Sundays were the hardest for Vic. Park day. Irma would pack an elaborate lunch, or they'd plan a barbecue, and everyone would meet there. Her cousins, Santiago and family, sometimes Rodrigo would join them. They'd spend the whole day, eating, drinking beer, and playing soccer. It was always someone's kid's birthday, so there'd be a piñata strung up in one of the big oak trees. Today was Alba's birthday, Irma's cousin's daughter, and they had called to invite Vic and Josie. But he couldn't go, not yet, maybe not ever. He was relieved to say that his father was going to be in town. "We mees you, Veek," Irma's cousin had said, sounding so much like Irma that Vic couldn't speak for the lump in his throat.

Vic glanced at the clock: 12:50. His father would be here soon.

Vic had stretched out on the sofa as soon as Josie and Ellie left in the van. The house had suddenly gone quiet without them. The heaviness was settling in again. Having Ellie here all week had been great, her vibrant energy filling the vacuum a little, but she was leaving the next day and taking the lightness with her. Josie would be heavy-hearted, too.

Vic closed his eyes and sighed. "Irma," he said out loud, just to hear her name, the way she pronounced it: "Earrrma," with the trilled r. How he missed her, her laugh, her perfume, her sweet smile, her girlish ways that could so swiftly turn into a sultry woman's. They'd met at a party at Santiago's sister's house. Irma was the sister's best friend, and she had offered to help serve food and drinks. She kept coming back to Vic with a flirtatious smile, and he would polish off whatever she brought so she'd return again and again. He hadn't been in a relationship since Tucson, but from the minute he got Irma's number that evening, they'd been inseparable. He had offered to help her study for her upcoming citizenship test, only to find that she knew more about American Civics than he did. They had married less than a year later. Happiest day of his life, until the kids were born.

Tears dripped from the corners of his eyes and trickled down his ears. Hearing a car pull up out front, he sat up and wiped his face with the sleeve of his T-shirt.

Vic hadn't seen his father, Tony, since a visit the previous summer. His father's wife, Sally, visited her sister in Anaheim once a year. Since it was only fifty miles from Vic's, Sally would drop Tony off on a Sunday afternoon, then the sisters would go shopping and pick up Tony afterwards. It made for a long day: Anaheim to LA, shopping, LA to Anaheim, but when Vic offered, instead, to put his dad and Sally up for a night, they always said no. And Vic knew why.

Sally had set foot in the house only once, and that had been awkward enough. Vic had noticed the fake eyelashes and crooked blond wig, while Irma had caught the source of the underlying tension.

"I'm Mexican, Vic," she had said. "You married one of *those*. You know, she had the nerve to ask me how I got into this country? I couldn't help but have some fun, so I told her I was strapped to the bottom of a car. I even showed her my scar." He remembered her strained grin, how she had tried to mask the hurt.

"What scar?" he had asked.

"I don't know, but when I pointed to the side of my face, she seemed to see it."

"Your trip across the border was dangerous enough," Vic had said, referring to her trek on foot to San Diego at the age of sixteen with an uncle and two cousins. They'd been robbed at knifepoint.

While she'd lived in the shadows as an undocumented immigrant for six years, she'd achieved legal status with the amnesty of 1986 and became a US citizen the year before they married.

"She even asked me why I didn't stay in my own country," Irma had continued, hands on her hips. "When I told her how poor our village was and that it gave me great pride to send money home from here, well, she just looked at me and said, 'I went to Mexico City once and there seemed to be lots of jobs there.' Can you believe it?"

And Vic could believe it. He'd seen it in Vietnam, the way some soldiers treated the Vietnamese. He'd seen it in Tucson with the desperate Guatemalan refugees who were at everyone's mercy. And of course, he saw it still with the immigrants in his community. People judging others because of the color of their skin, or their religion, or their ethnic background. In this sad, brief world, that he now knew could be altered forever in a matter of moments, how could anyone, *anyone*, not love and accept someone like sweet, kind Irma, just because of the color of her skin?

Vic heard his father's slow, heavy steps on the stairs, then the doorbell. Taking a deep breath, he headed toward the door.

The plan was for Ellie to drop off Josie and Maggie for a hike and come back alone around 2 p.m.—to meet her grandfather. That'd give Vic an hour to prepare him. She'd stay for a half hour or so, then head back out for the trail. She and Josie would return later, long after his dad was gone. Vic braced himself for a trying afternoon.

As soon as the screen door swung open, his father had him in a bear hug, tight and hard. Vic could smell a strange mixture of beer and Old Spice aftershave. His father stepped back, pulled a wrinkled white handkerchief from his trouser pocket, and blew his nose.

Tony's thinning gray hair revealed white patches on his scalp. The bags under his bloodshot eyes and the spider veins on his cheeks were more pronounced. He seemed to have shrunk since the last visit. His shoulders slumped forward under a loose-fitting green plaid shirt, and his tan pants sagged so low beneath his protruding belly, they gathered at his feet, covering his shoes.

"Oh son, what can I say? What can anyone say?" He swiped the hankie several times across his nose. Looking around the small room, no Irma and kids to greet him, then back at Vic, he said, "Just God bless ya. God bless ya. So, how *are* ya doin'?"

"I'm okay, Dad. I'm doing . . . well . . . the best I can, I guess. Come on in, have a seat. I'll get us a couple of beers."

Vic led him into the living room, noticing how slowly Tony walked. He'd be seventy-two next month, and with the drinking he'd done—still did—he looked more like eighty-two.

"Doing okay, huh?" Tony mumbled absently.

"Yeah, Dad, I'm okay. I don't know . . . what can I say? One day at a time . . . I'm hanging in there. Back to work. And Josie, she's been great. I couldn't make it without her."

His father nodded and looked down at the floor.

"Let me get those beers."

When he returned, his father was sitting forward on the sofa, flexing his fingers and rubbing his hands together. "Damn arthritis. Got it in my knees and especially my fingers and wrists. Can barely hold a drumstick anymore."

"Do you still play at all?" Vic asked, handing him his beer and noting a slight tremor in his hand as he reached for it.

"Oh, I mess around a bit—at home and sometimes at the Blue Star. Jam now and then with other old cronies like me, and sometimes with the young ones, too. But I can't play very well. Sound like the old bag-a-bones that I am." He laughed. "Hell, the only way I'll sit behind the drums is if I'm loaded. Can't bear to hear myself sober."

Vic nodded, then asked, "Hungry? Would you like something to eat?" He remembered how Irma would wait on the two of them, scurrying in and out with drinks and food.

"No, no. Just had a big breakfast—big Mexican Sunday brunch, all-you-can-eat at some place in Anaheim. No, I'm fine." He paused. "Actually, you look a bit thin, looks like ya could use an all-you-can-eat brunch. Ya eating okay?"

"Yeah, I'm eating. Josie tries to fatten me up. So, how's Sally?" Vic asked, not really caring to know.

His father shrugged. "Pain in the ass, what can I say? Her sister's just as bad. You have no idea how good it is to be here."

Vic laughed nervously, not sure how to respond.

"Hell, if it wasn't for her social security, I'd rather be on my own," Tony continued. "But when you're my age, what can you do?"

"Are you serious?" Vic asked.

"Hell yes. We're like a couple of cats and dogs at each other. But neither one of us can manage on what comes in every month. Need both checks to get by."

They'd never talked like this before, but then Irma and the kids were always there. No chance to really talk beyond the surface.

"How can you live with her if you feel that way?"

"I leave, or she does—go into town, play the slots." Tony laughed. "One time I ran into her at Caesar's. We just looked at each other and kept walking." He laughed so hard, that he started coughing. "The only time we really talk at all is when we watch TV. 'Course she usually watches in the bedroom and I sit in the living room—but sometimes we watch together—like the game shows or Jerry Springer."

Vic couldn't resist. "Where do you sleep?"

"In my goddamn bed. Woman's not gonna kick me out of my own

damn bed. We keep to our own sides. And at my age, that's where it stays."

Vic knew his father had lived with several different women over the years, but when he'd met Sally twelve years ago, she'd been intent on marriage. He remembered his father making some comment back then about being too tired to hold out—that and being in Vegas where any drunken fool could get married and not know it until they sobered up the next day.

His father was not a man to admire, but he was his father. Many times throughout the years, Vic had found himself being thankful, for his mom's sake, that his father had left. He couldn't have been easy to live with. Vic had vague memories of his parents' fights when he was quite young, but in the years just before Tony left, when Vic was nine or ten, it was mostly silence. Silence and long spells of his absence.

"Hell, you don't want to hear about that," his father was saying. "I should be cheering you up, not bitching about my wife." He took a long draw on his beer. "So, what the hell happened to the old coot that killed your family? Will he be tried or anything?"

Vic closed his eyes and lowered his head. "For chrissakes, Dad, the guy that hit them had a fucking stroke. He passed out, lost control of his car—it was an accident." Turning his head away in disgust, he finally said, "I'd rather not talk about this. In fact, there's something else . . ." Vic sat up and looked directly into his father's eyes. He no longer felt any apprehension about Ellie's imminent appearance.

"Dad, Josie's daughter Ellie has been here all week. And frankly, she wants to meet you. You're her grandfather—whether you want to acknowledge it or not—the closest she's got to a grandfather. She should be here shortly. Just her, alone. She wants to meet you, just talk for a few minutes, then she'll head back out."

His father kept his eyes down, his lips pressed firmly together. "I don't know," he finally said, looking up. "Why does she wanna talk to me? About what?"

"I don't know. It doesn't matter really. She just wants to meet you. She's a pretty interesting kid. Spunky. Took off on her own. Gives her mother a run for her money. You'll like her. She's a musician."

His father's eyes widened. "A musician?"

"Yeah. She plays guitar and sings."

"I don't know. I just don't see the point. I mean—what must she think of me? I'm sure she's heard plenty."

"She's nineteen. Has a mind of her own. Maybe she wants to decide for herself what she thinks of you."

Thirty minutes later, Ellie screeched the van to a halt and took the five stairs in two thuds. She didn't pause for even a second, but strode right into the room, arm outstretched. Vic grinned with pride.

"Hi, I'm Ellie," she said.

She was dressed in jeans and a black Dave Matthews Band T-shirt. Wrapped around her head and tied in back was a short, colorful scarf that gave her an exotic look.

At first, his father didn't move, but sat speechless, his usually flushed face now pale. Clearly flustered, he reached out his hand, first upward as if to touch her cheek, but quickly lowered it toward Ellie's, and they shook—like two men meeting at a business conference.

"I don't know what to say," Tony stammered, his eyes suddenly wet, surprising Vic with this show of emotion. "Uh . . . the name's Tony . . . nice to meet ya."

Ellie sat cross-legged on the floor. "So, you played the drums, in Vegas?"

"Yes, yes. All sorts of places." He seemed to be struggling, fidgeting in his seat and licking his lips nervously.

"You okay, Dad?" Vic asked. Maybe this wasn't such a good idea.

His father placed both hands on his knees and straightened his back. "I'm fine, just fine. Though I could use another beer."

"Me too, Uncle Vic. Just one."

"Hell no. You're not even twenty yet, let alone twenty-one. And you're driving. I'll get you a Coke." He left the room, wondering what he'd miss while he was gone. He could hear Ellie talking, then his father's brief answers, but he couldn't make out the words. When he returned, they were talking about Tito Puentes and Gene Krupa.

"I can't believe this girl knows about Gene Krupa!"

Ellie grinned. "Actually, my boyfriend was a drummer, and he used to talk about Gene Krupa and Baby Dodds."

"My god, yes, Baby Dodds. Christ, I haven't heard that name in ages!" The color was returning to his animated face.

"Boyfriend? You told me you didn't have a boyfriend," Vic said, holding back her Coke.

"*Was*, the lady said. He *was* her boyfriend. Didn't you catch that?" His father grinned and winked at Ellie.

The conversation continued, rapid fire, covering Krupa's drug arrest, his use of press rolls, the big band sound, Cuban music, and Ellie's recent fascination with congas and the drum circle movement.

"I want to learn about all types of music, incorporate all kinds of sounds, you know?" Ellie said, her eyes bright.

The planned thirty minutes turned into an hour, until Ellie jumped up and proclaimed that she had to split; her mom was waiting on some trail in the mountains.

Vic watched his dad rise slowly to his feet and then struggle to stay up as Ellie crushed him in a fierce embrace.

"Well, sweetheart, it was sure nice talking with ya," his father said.

"Well," Ellie said, "I'll see you again sometime. Maybe this summer? I'll be back again in August—to celebrate our birthdays—mine and Vic's. Maybe you'll come?"

His father half-shook and half-nodded his head, ending with raised eyebrows and a "Sure, maybe." Then in a flash, Ellie was gone, and they stood for a moment, readjusting to the atmosphere now clearly devoid of her vibrant energy.

"That's Ellie," Vic said simply.

"Yep. She's quite a spark, all right." His father sat down and rubbed his face with both his hands.

"You okay?" Vic asked. Something seemed to be bothering his father.

"Yeah, just a bit tired. Been a long weekend. The drive from Vegas, listening to Sally whine for five damn hours, then hearing it in stereo once we got to her sister's."

"Maybe you'd be better off renting a room somewhere, alone. Why live like that? It must be exhausting."

His father paused and looked at Vic. "Son, it's nothing compared to what you have to live with."

What I have to live with, Vic thought, is nothing.

The next hour went slowly, for both were emotionally drained and pre-occupied. Small talk was exhausted, and anything more was beyond either's capability. When Sally and her sister finally arrived, Vic was relieved. He managed to be polite, accepting their condolences and agreeing that, yes, this had to be the worst thing that could happen to any human being. It wasn't until after Vic had thanked them for their prayers and they were heading for the car, that his father stopped on the front stoop. He told the women to go on ahead, he'd be right along, then he turned to Vic.

"Have I ever told you about my sister, Angie?"

"The one who died of TB when she was a kid?"

"Yes, she was almost seventeen when she died. And she . . ." Tony's eyes welled up again, and he pulled out his hankie to wipe them. "She used to wear these kerchiefs on her head, kind of like what Ellie had on, only they tied 'em under their chin." He stopped and swallowed hard. "Son, Angie had the most beautiful blue eyes, like my mother—your grandmother."

"I don't remember ever meeting my . . ." Vic began, but stopped when Tony grabbed Vic's forearm and looked him square in the face.

"Ellie is her spittin' image. I swear it was Angie walked in that door. Spittin' image." One lone tear dripped down the deep crevice that lined his cheek.

Vic's face softened. "I'm not surprised, Dad," he said.

His father's voice cracked. "All these years . . . is it possible? Your sister?" He glanced at the car, then back at Vic.

Vic sighed. "Maybe it's time you and Josie had a talk."

Once again, his father's face blanched. "Oh, hell!" Vic heard Tony say as he turned and lumbered down the stairs, raising his arm in farewell.

Fight or Flight

Ellie's Songbook: May 2000

Fight or Flight
Words and Music by Eleanor Serafini
*Acoustic guitar only.

Verse 1
Seems like we're never on the same page
No matter what I do, you end up in a rage
You see red when I see blue. I just can't stay
Don't know what else to do. Need to find my own way
My own way

Chorus
Fight or flight
Don't know what's right or wrong
I'm so confused
Don't know where I belong

Fight or flight
You light my fuse
My head explodes
So confused
Guess it's time for me to go

Verse 2

I know you're going through your own hell, too

I just don't know what else to do

We're both so broken, just limping along

If only one of us was really strong

Really strong

Chorus

Fight or flight

Don't know what's right or wrong

I'm so confused

Don't know where I belong

Fight or flight

You light my fuse

My head explodes

So confused

Guess it's time for me to go

Bridge:

Seems to me since the men in our lives leave

There's no reason why the next one can't be me

Perhaps, they feared their souls would slowly die

So they had to leave to survive and thrive

Like me

Chorus

Fight or flight

Don't know what's right or wrong

I'm so confused

Don't know where I belong

Fight or flight
You light my fuse,
my head explodes
So confused
Guess it's time for me to go

Some Birthday

May 2001

JOSIE

Smoothing out the striped Mexican blanket that covered the van's rear seat, Josie signaled Maggie to jump up. Maggie obeyed, settled on the blanket, then hung her head, her eyes glancing up sheepishly. Josie's heart sank. "Oh, Maggie, I didn't mean to yell at you." She reached in, found the sweet spot behind her ears, and gave it a good scratch. Once again, Maggie had dug up new plants in the garden, even though Josie had barely stepped away to get a cup of coffee. In the past four weeks, Maggie had taken down two lilac bushes, four tomato plants, numerous flats of snapdragons and petunias, and every sunflower seedling that Josie had lovingly planted. Vic said he didn't know whom to admire more, the determined gardener or the persistent excavator.

"I know you're just following your instincts." Josie sighed. No more attempts at gardening until Maggie was gone, although the thought of her leaving put a lump in Josie's throat. So far, Ellie hadn't found a place, so they still had time.

As Josie stepped back to close the door, her cell phone rang. Who would be calling at six in the morning? Her heart raced as she glanced at the number, fearing something happened to Ellie. It was Lucas, which wasn't good either.

"Lucas?" she said, trying not to sound too alarmed.

"Yeah, hi Josie. Listen, sorry to call so early, although I assumed you'd be getting ready to hike. But it's Fire, early signs of colic. I'm treating him. Banamine. Tubed him with mineral oil and some fluids. Drew some labs as well. He's not rolling or kicking at himself. Just not eating. Minimal bowel sounds. Lying down more than usual. I wanted you to know right away. I'm keeping a close eye on him." He paused. "You okay there?"

Josie sat on the seat beside Maggie. "What do you think? Is it serious? How serious? Should I come home?" Josie knew that colic could go in either direction. A quick recovery if any blockage was passed or a rapid emergency if the bowel twisted on itself. Sometimes surgery could correct an extreme case—if caught in time. Josie knew friends who'd lost their horses prematurely to colic.

"Time will tell if it clears or not. Rushing home wouldn't accomplish anything. Just sit tight. I'll let you know how he's doing throughout the day." His voice softened. "I promise. Okay?"

"Oh, Fire, I wish I was there," Josie said in a whisper.

"Hang on a minute," he said. She could hear movement, then Lucas's voice from a distance. "Talk to him. Fire's listening." So he was calling from the barn. She pictured Lucas holding the phone to Fire's ear.

Josie sat up, then in a high-pitched voice that made Maggie snap her head up, she said, "Sweetheart. How's my guy doing? I love you, Mr. Mountain. You're gonna be fine. Just relax and rest. My heart is with you. I love you." She could picture his ears cocked in the direction of her voice—alert, listening.

Lucas's voice confirmed it. "He hears you. And so do your other boys, I think. They both picked up their heads just now. Neither has gone far since I turned them out. They keep wandering back. Jack

keeps a close eye on Fire, as always, but even little Luke keeps mosey-
ing back and sniffing at Fire's gate. That's where they are right now."

She could picture it somewhat, though she'd never seen his property. Fire wouldn't be allowed to graze, so he'd be kept in his stall, but
the boys would be turned out to wander at their leisure. She ached
to see them all, but especially to sit with her devoted Fire Mountain.

Josie had first fallen in love with Fire over the months that her
neighbor, Sally—his original owner—was dying of cancer. Visiting
both of them daily had eventually led to talk of Josie possibly taking
Fire, even though she had never ridden a horse before. Since Josie
brought Fire carrots regularly, he would nicker whenever he saw her.
A gentle horse, with soft, soulful eyes, he was irresistible. One day,
when she asked Fire if he'd like to come live with her, he had lifted
his head, rested his chin on her shoulder, and nestled into Josie's
neck. That sealed the deal. Sally was immensely grateful when Josie
promised to love and care for Fire for the rest of his days. Though
Josie worked with a trainer the first year Fire came to live with her,
it was Fire himself who taught her about the horse and rider bond.
Once Josie learned to relax and feel his movements beneath her, she
came to trust his every move. Her most peaceful moments were with
Fire, either riding the trails beyond their home or sitting with him
in the pasture.

"Listen, I'll call you in a few hours," Lucas said, "let you know
how he's doing. Okay?" He paused, then in a softer tone, he added,
"Try not to worry. I don't have any calls too far from home today, so
I'll be close by. Plus, Mom's keeping an eye on him too."

Biting her lower lip, Josie wanted to linger but knew she had to
let him get on with his day. "Okay," she said, hanging up the phone
after his final goodbye.

Josie sat for a minute debating if she should hike or just stick around where cell phone coverage was better. Instead, she decided on the dog park where Maggie could run and dig to her heart's content.

One hour later, Josie and Maggie were home again. Vic was still asleep. He'd been struggling at work, unable to concentrate on occasion, and although Santiago suggested he take some time off, Vic kept plugging away. Like a robot, Vic would go to the office, shuffle through paperwork, then make a few phone calls, until he was either asleep at his desk or staring blankly into space, according to Santiago. Finally, Josie contacted Vic's psychiatrist, who convinced Vic to go back on his meds with Josie's close supervision. They were told to be patient. It would take a while to find just the right balance. He was also seeing a therapist, who had encouraged him to join a grief group, but Vic had adamantly refused. In the meantime, Vic resisted being placed on disability, preferring to work part time and do the best he could.

Josie was grateful for Santiago, who gave Vic as much leeway as he needed. "He's like a brother to me," Santiago had told Josie. "He got me out of jams because of my short fuse and helped me stop drinking. Saved my life, my marriage, my career. Nothing I wouldn't do for him. Whatever it takes. He didn't deserve this fate." As a result, Vic's schedule for the month was flexible. If he was up for it, he could put some time in at work, even take paperwork home. Once the meds kicked in, they would take it from there.

Not wanting to wake Vic, Josie ushered Maggie back into their bedroom and closed the door behind them. Flopping onto Isa's twin bed, she stared at her phone. She couldn't resist and dialed Lucas's office number, which Josie knew his mother would answer. To Josie's relief, she picked up on the first ring.

"I'm sorry to bother you, Mrs. Peterson. I'm just checking in on Fire. Any change?" Josie asked, though she knew it was too soon, at least for any good news.

"Oh, Josie, it's no bother at all. No change, sweetheart, but it's a bit too early to see improvement yet. These things tend to take a while." His mother's voice was soothing and calm. "But don't worry, dear. We're on top of this. I've been checking him every thirty minutes, and Charlotte will be here early. It's her short day at school, so she'll be out there the whole afternoon. If there's any problem, Lucas is close by and will hurry home. Right now, Fire doesn't appear to be in any acute distress. We're just waiting. It takes time. I'm sure you know that."

"Yes, I know, I just . . ." Maggie jumped onto the bed and sprawled across Josie's legs.

"Oh honey, I understand," his mother said. "You're so far away. Listen, you feel free to check in as often as you want."

"Will you call me if there's any change at all?"

"I certainly will, dear."

Then, as Josie thanked her for a tenth time, she'd added, "And sweetheart, please, call me Alice."

After hanging up the phone, Josie exhaled so deeply that Maggie opened her eyes and lifted her head questioningly.

"Go back to sleep," Josie said, "but give me a little room. This is supposed to be my bed." Then maneuvering her legs around Maggie, Josie turned onto her side, curled up, and closed her eyes. Maybe the worry dolls on Irma's embroidered wall hanging above the bed would ease her anxiety a bit.

The sound of an angry voice startled Josie awake. Groggy, she sat up, realizing the voice was Vic's and that it was coming from the backyard. Sliding to the window beside the bed, she glanced out and listened.

"Why not? It's her birthday for chrissakes!" Vic was pacing on the patio, his phone to his ear.

Josie's heart sank. Was he talking to Ellie? Had Ellie forgotten her birthday? She'd been expecting a call from her later in the afternoon, before Ellie left for work. Why was Vic talking to her now?

"You said you wanted to set things right, so now's your chance. Just a brief call to wish your daughter a fucking happy birthday!"

Her father! He was talking to her lame excuse for a father. And a fucking happy birthday it was. Why was Vic wasting his energy? She didn't want to speak to *him* any more than he wanted to call her.

"Asshole!" she said, alarming Maggie, who responded with three loud barks.

Vic whirled around toward her window. Their eyes locked. Turning away, Vic spoke briefly into the phone, then hung up.

They met in the kitchen.

"What are you doing home? I thought you were hiking?"

Glancing at the clock above the sink, she saw it was almost 10 a.m. "We didn't go," Josie said. "Fire colicked. I needed to stay near the phone."

Vic's face changed from angry-weary to worried-weary. "Oh Jo, I'm sorry. Is it serious?"

Josie grimaced. "Hard to know yet. Lucas treated him with mineral oil and some meds, but only time will tell if it worked or if it's more serious." She held up her cell phone. "I'm waiting for an update."

Vic stepped forward. "Jo, go home. Book a flight. You don't need to stay here."

Josie paused for just a moment, thinking of Vic and his meds and his fragile state.

"The truth is," she said, "if it's serious, I wouldn't make it in time. If it's mild, he'll recover shortly." She pulled out a stool and sat, leaning forward, her arms resting on the cool white tiles of the small kitchen island. "I could sure use a cup of coffee."

After dumping his cold coffee into the sink, Vic reached for a second mug and filled both. Setting them on the counter, he pulled a stool around and sat across from Josie. With a shrug, he motioned to the backyard and said, "Sorry about that."

"What were you thinking?" Josie asked. "You know I want nothing to do with that—"

Interrupting her, Vic reached across and touched her arm. "Happy Birthday, Jo."

"Thanks," she said. Then, for the umpteenth time, she asked, "Are you sure you don't mind that I'm going to dinner with Rae? That is, if Fire's okay. I won't be late. She has to work early tomorrow."

"Of course not. In fact, Rodrigo's coming over. Soccer match on TV. He's bringing In-N-Out burgers. That should put you at ease. I want you to enjoy your dinner and celebrate. I'm no help in that department."

Josie looked down at her coffee. "I'm not in a celebratory mood myself. It's just another day." She thought of the fuss Ben and Ellie used to make with decorations, a cake, and even sunflowers, when Ben could find them.

"Another year!" Vic said, lifting his mug to toast. "Forty-three years *old*," he added, wrinkling his nose and accentuating "old."

"Sometimes I feel much older than that—except when I'm hiking. Then I feel nineteen again." Josie raised her mug and met his. With a tilt of her head, she said, "But, really, Vic, please give up on playing Oprah. I don't want to reconnect with that man." Josie couldn't even say the word "father."

"I was thinking more like Jerry Springer," Vic said with a wink.

"Exactly!" Josie said.

Vic set down his mug, folded his hands, and looked at Josie.

"What? What?" Josie could tell there was something more.

"He wants to come in August. Ellie mentioned coming down to celebrate for her birthday and mine. *She* invited him—not me."

"What? You've got to be kidding! Do you think he will?"

Vic shrugged. "I don't know. He just said he's thinking of taking a bus to visit us in August. Who knows if he really will? I'm just letting you know. And you can blame Ellie, not me."

"Oh, I will. You better believe I'll give her an earful!"

Later that evening, Josie stretched out on her bed, her back against propped pillows. The twin felt roomy now without Maggie pushing up against her legs. Vic and Rodrigo were watching soccer in the living room and Maggie was sitting eagerly at their feet, waiting for a few French fries to fall. Josie had canceled dinner with Rae. Her stomach was in knots about Fire, and she knew she wouldn't be good company. They would reschedule another night, if all went well.

For now, Josie just wanted to be alone—near her phone. She told Vic she might join them after she heard from Lucas.

"Sorry about your birthday," Vic had said, the dark circles under his eyes deeper than usual.

Some birthday, she'd thought, grabbing the half-bottle of wine on the counter and heading for her room. Ellie had called earlier to wish Josie a happy birthday, but she'd been moody since her search for a dog-friendly place wasn't going well. When Josie offered to help with rent to increase the possibilities, Ellie had gotten annoyed and cut the call short. At least she called, Josie kept reminding herself. Then thoughtful Rodrigo had picked up a small birthday cake decorated with cherries, but Josie hated cherries. And Vic had surprised her with new gardening tools—and a flat of herbs. Great, Josie thought, Maggie will enjoy those!

Scooting up on the bed, Josie reached for the bottle of Chianti and poured herself a glass, then glanced at her watch. 7 p.m. here. 10 p.m. back east. Why hadn't Lucas called yet? Had something happened? Last update on Fire had been a brief call from Alice late in the afternoon, saying there was no change for better or worse and that Lucas would call once he had some news this evening. Apparently, he'd had a busy day.

Taking a sip of wine, Josie closed her eyes. As good as it tasted, she felt the wine burn as it eased down into her already aching stomach.

The shrill ringtone sent the wine halfway back up.

Though he sounded out of breath, Lucas's voice was upbeat. "Happy Birthday! We have shiny poop!" His laugh was deep and warm. Josie had never heard him laugh quite like that before.

She let out a long sigh. "You have no idea! This is the best birthday gift possible! Thank you!"

"Don't thank me. It's all Fire. He didn't want your birthday to pass without something special . . . to pass. Hey, I didn't even plan that!" His laugh again. "No, really, Josie, I was hoping I could give you good news tonight. I hated the thought of you being sad or worried on your birthday. I have to say the sight of that oily manure made my day, too." He paused and cleared his throat.

"How did you know it was my birthday?" Josie suddenly wondered.

"You mentioned it the other night, when I asked if you'd heard from Ellie. You said she'd be calling on your birthday, Thursday. It was too late to send a card or anything, and it slipped my mind this morning when I called about Fire, preoccupied of course, but . . . Happy Birthday! That one was from me, not Fire, and my mom said Happy Birthday as well."

"Your mom was so kind this morning on the phone. She helped

calm me down. Oh, and she told me to call her Alice. I've always loved that name. So, please tell her thank you for me." As an after-thought, she added, "I really like her."

"She likes you, too." The warmth was still there. It was soothing. Nice. A silence followed, then he asked, "So, what did you do today? Anything special?"

Josie sat up straight, her legs crossed yoga-style. "You really want to know?" She felt her own spirits rise as she described her misera-ble day, a day that now actually sounded funny. Garden destroyed. Moping, guilty dog. Sick horse. Argument with brother about dead-beat dad. Canceled dinner. Vic's well-intentioned gardening gift. Moody daughter. And finally, the difficulty of sharing a twin-sized bed with a husky, even after making a cushy dog bed on the floor using a crib mattress and old blankets.

"You and Maggie, sleeping in a twin? I'm trying to picture that one."

Josie smiled. Lately, Lucas had called a few evenings a week, not just to talk about the horses, but to ask about Vic and Ellie and whatever else she had done that day. She looked forward to those calls.

"Thoughtful gift," he said, "gardening tools and herbs."

"Do you mean for me or for Maggie?"

"Both?"

"Exactly!"

Leaning back and stretching out her legs, she looked up at the collage of photos on Isa's wall. Josie hadn't packed those away because she liked looking at them, especially the largest photo in the frame—Vic holding up baby Isa at eye level, the two grinning at each other with utter delight.

"And get this," Josie continued, "apparently my *father*"—that word said with as much sarcasm as she could muster—"wants to come here in August for Vic and Ellie's joint birthday party."

"Uh oh, doesn't sound like a very good plan. I take it you're doing it for Vic?"

She paused. For Vic? She hadn't thought of that. "Well, it was Ellie's idea, not Vic's. But . . ."

"How's he doing? Vic, I mean. Are the meds helping at all?"

"Good question. He still has trouble falling asleep, then he's sluggish in the mornings. But he is watching soccer with Rodrigo right now, which is encouraging. I heard him shout and cheer a couple times." She closed her eyes.

"What hell he must be going through," Lucas said, echoing her thoughts. "How do you keep going after losing so much—wife, and kids, too?"

"I know," she whispered.

"He has to find some purpose, something that makes him feel of value in this world. But, Josie, he's so lucky to have you there."

She pictured Vic playing monster with the kids, chasing them around the house Frankenstein-style. "You know, you're right," she said softly.

"Usually," Lucas chuckled, "but what am I right about now?"

"About the party in August. If it would make Vic happy, or at least make him feel good about something, then maybe I should stop being so difficult."

"You're a good sister, Jo," he said.

It was the first time he had called her Jo. Only Vic, and her mom, and Ben did that.

"Well, thank you." Josie felt her face flushing. "And thank you for giving me the best birthday present of the day."

"The poop?"

"Yep, the shiny poop." Josie laughed. Fire's improvement was certainly the best news of the day, but she was grateful to Lucas for so much more.

After they said their goodbyes, Josie slid down under the covers and smiled. Not such a bad day after all.

Her Letter
June 2001

VIC

Dear Sweet Irma,

My therapist says I should write to you. First, she told me I should try keeping a journal, like a diary, but about my feelings or important memories. Can you picture that? Me sitting down with a little notebook and pen and writing my *feelings*? I can hear you laughing, that little girl giggle.

Christ, I miss you.

She told me to buy a notebook and just sit and write whatever came to my mind. Let it just pour out, she said. It's healing, she said.

Remember that notebook that Ellie carried with her to write song lyrics? You commented on the cover, said how it definitely fit her. Had a colorful design like the Guatemalan fabrics you love. In the center was a young woman floating through the air, her wavy hair flowing behind her like a long veil. Her tears, all the colors of the rainbow, were dropping to the ground beneath her and blossoming into colorful flowers. Yeah, that certainly fit Ellie.

What would *my* notebook look like?

Black. Black cover with empty pages.

No, I can't write about my feelings. I try not to feel, not to remember.

So, when I told her that I couldn't do the journal thing, she suggested I write you a letter. She said to imagine that I'm talking to you and to write what I would want to say.

Be honest, she said. Don't say what you think she wants to hear, say the truth.

The truth. What's the truth? What do you want to hear?

How much I love you? You already know that. You've always known that.

How will I go on without you? I don't even know that. It's been almost six months and I haven't gone on. I've been stalled in a fog. Barely existing. Day after day.

I feel like a ghost, haunting these rooms.

In fact, I feel like I did after 'Nam. Utterly lost. Uncertain where I belonged. Home didn't feel like home. I lied to my mom and said the army helped me find jobs working on helicopters in different states. It was partly true. Alabama, Texas, Kansas, until I ended up in Arizona.

You already know about 'Nam. My few months there that felt like years. The two gruesome deaths I witnessed—saps, trying to infiltrate our base, that got hammered instead. Or the guys I heard about but didn't see, only imagined, guys I knew. And how fucking lucky I was to be part of the early withdrawal of troops in '72.

But I didn't tell you about Castillo. Those times when I was quiet and you'd ask and I wouldn't answer. Maybe that's a truth I should tell you. Maybe that's what you would want to hear.

Carlos Castillo was a mechanic buddy of mine. We'd done our advanced training together in the states and ended up at the same base in Vietnam, repairing and maintaining Hueys mostly. We were going to meet up in Arizona once we both finished our service in '75. I always wanted to see the Grand Canyon, and he was from Tucson.

Plus, he and his dad ran Castillo Auto Repair, so if I was interested, I had a job. That was the plan.

There'd been talk of major troop withdrawals for months, so when I got news that I was shipping out of 'Nam to Germany, I thought for sure Castillo would be going, too. We'd been a team since the first days of aviation mechanics training. We were like brothers, or at least what I felt it must be like to have a brother. But he didn't make that list. He'd have to put in a couple more months. Word was they'd be pulling out thousands before year's end, so we were hopeful.

Then, just two weeks after I left, I heard the base was hit. Mortar attack. One helicopter badly damaged and one mechanic killed instantly. Castillo.

It took me five years to make it to Arizona. It was his father who went with me to the Grand Canyon. We drove like five, six hours, got out of the car, and just looked at the immense, jagged scar carved into the earth by the Colorado River. Neither of us said a word, just looked, got in the car, and headed back.

He offered me a job at his garage, which I accepted. When he offered me a room in his house as well, I knew I couldn't go that far. I rented a trailer nearby. That's when I started to learn Spanish since most of his customers were from Mexico. I took a Spanish class at night. Dated the teacher for a while. That didn't go anywhere. I told you about her. Anyway, it was through Castillo's church that I got involved in the Sanctuary movement as refugees from El Salvador, and then Guatemala, started coming across the border. That's when I met Santiago and Rodrigo, and you know the story from there. A few years after I had moved to LA, I learned that Castillo's dad passed from cancer. It happened quickly, like in a matter of weeks. By the time I heard, he had been buried already, next to his son.

So why didn't I tell you about Castillo? Partly because I just couldn't bring myself to talk about him and partly because I never felt like I was living *my* life then. It was his life I was living. Even his dad called me Carlos a few times. Like I said, I felt more like a ghost. Castillo's ghost.

It wasn't until you, my Irma Camila Limon Estrada, my own Irma Serafini, that my life started. For a few, bright, glorious years, I was alive. With you. With Isabel and Miguel. Finally, I was living Vic Serafini's life.

But now, once again, I don't know who I am or where I belong. I'm just floating.

I'm sorry. I know this isn't much of a letter. Not what I think you'd want to hear. But it's the truth. My truth.

I'm supposed to write letters to the kids, but that, I cannot do.

Oh Irma, my heart's been ripped out of my body. I just want to be with you. With them.

No more. I can't write anymore.

Keeping Cool
Mid-Summer 2001

JOSIE

Only 9 a.m. and already the heat was intense. Though not as humid as summers in Upstate New York, they were just as debilitating in Southern California. By noon there was still that oppressive blast that hit like a shock wave when she stepped out from the air-conditioned house. No matter how early Josie got started on the hiking trail, it wasn't early enough. The heat lay in wait, catching her on some long, unprotected stretch, and leaving both her and Maggie panting hard and draining whatever water they'd brought along.

Josie looked down at her constant companion and choked up again at the thought of their parting. Ellie was flying down the next week, and when she returned to Seattle by rental car, Maggie would be with her. She'd found a house to rent with a fenced-in yard. Ellie and Kelly had just moved in, and come September two college students would join them, bringing down the monthly expenses. Until then, Josie was helping out financially.

Squatting down, Josie hugged Maggie, then reached into her bag for their third, and last, water bottle. They'd just hiked the old Stagecoach Trail in the Santa Susana Pass called Devil's Slide, a steep, perilous road on the route from Los Angeles to San Francisco. After saluting the historical marker left in the rock by the Native Daughters of the Golden West, they'd headed back down the dry, dusty trail. Josie could not imagine anything on wheels making it up this terrain, let alone an old rickety wagon. To think people had traveled on horseback—even on foot—in this glaring sun was enough to make anyone thankful they lived in an age of air conditioning.

Filling the tin cup for Maggie, she watched the dog eagerly lap up the lukewarm water. "Let's get home girl, before we get fried." Reaching for the backpack that she'd set down beside the trail, she froze. Coiled just inches from her bag, tail raised, was a rattler at least four feet long. Josie wasn't worried about herself so much as Maggie.

Glancing at the husky, Josie was relieved to see her still focused on the water, nudging the empty tin in the opposite direction. Slowly she reached out and grasped the dog's collar and moved them both away from the bag and the snake. Should have kept her on that leash, she thought, scolding herself for what could have happened. Stopping a few yards away, she waited. The snake eased around the bag and across the trail, then disappeared into the brush. Keeping a tight hold on Maggie's collar, Josie cautiously approached her pack and inspected its contents before reaching in and securing the leash.

Once they reached the shaded trees of Chatsworth Park, they stopped to rest. Josie hopped up onto a picnic bench, and Maggie flopped on her side in the cool dirt. A woman on a stunning appaloosa slowly ambled up the path and nodded toward Josie. She watched as horse and rider passed, mesmerized by the woman's long yellow-gray braid swinging in the same rhythm as the horse's tail. If it hadn't been so hot, Josie would have struck up a conversation. "Maybe once you're gone, I'll make myself a new friend," she said to Maggie, wondering what it would be like to ride a horse along this type of trail.

She was beginning to feel at home in Los Angeles, at least in its northwest corner. Occasionally, she'd imagine herself buying a small house or condo, perhaps in Chatsworth, and living beneath these hills that she was coming to love. She could be close to Vic and closer to Ellie than if she stayed in New York. Why not settle permanently here? She could easily find a job. But the thought of selling the house, her home with Ben all those years—that's what held her back. The roses they'd planted, the line of sunflowers facing south, the two maples that they named Ben and Jo, and of course, the horses. Moving them was out of the question. Fire was too old to transport cross-country. No, that wasn't an option.

Ultimately, her life was still in Upstate New York. Yet she had to be honest with herself, the house was really much too big for just her. It didn't sound like Vic would ever consider moving in, and Ellie, well, it was becoming clearer every day that she was following her own path. Josie knew she should consider a smaller house with horse property. Of course, there was also Lucas. Their frequent evening phone conversations were the high point of Josie's day. She sensed they were for him as well. Gradually, they had shared their pasts, and they always filled each other in on the day's events.

At the same time, the thought of going back east and leaving Vic and Ellie and Maggie all out west left Josie heavy-hearted and confused. At some point, before year's end, she would have to make a decision.

Sliding down from the table, Josie took up the leash. "Let's go home," she said to Maggie, who had leapt to her feet, eager to move on. "At least where home is today. Gonna change for you soon—and who the hell knows where home's gonna be for me."

Later that evening, sitting on the patio sipping margaritas, Josie and Vic laughed at Rodrigo's imitation of the singer Ricky Martin. "Living La Vida Loca," he crooned, his hips gyrating and his head bobbing back and forth. Rodrigo's solid, stocky frame tried in vain to mimic the lanky performer's seductive movements. Vic laughed so hard, he choked on his drink.

The sprinklers whirled, cooling the air, and finally, Josie sat back and relaxed.

"Stick to your woodcarving," Vic said between coughs, "and don't quit your day job either."

It was comforting to see Vic laugh. Lately he'd been moody, either quiet and somber or downright irritable. She'd heard him up at night, pacing or just watching TV. The few times she came out, saying she couldn't sleep either, he didn't buy it and sent her back to bed, telling her he just wanted to be alone. Being a nurse and having been through the grieving process herself, she knew the stages of anger and depression that often recycled on the path to acceptance— not that acceptance was ever really attained. More like a resignation. A survivor's surrender.

But Josie was worried about Vic. He told her one night that he felt like he was perpetually falling, never landing, just flipping and tumbling through the air, with no ground in sight. And while this was understandable and even expected to some extent, Josie couldn't help but wonder if he'd ever pull out of this—or worse, plunge even deeper.

Rodrigo had picked up on it as well and tried to get Vic out with others, playing soccer or basketball. But even after these outings, he'd been concerned.

"There's a hard edge to him," Rodrigo had said to her just last night, "a meanness on the field that I never saw before. He almost got in a fight last weekend. Vic! Can you imagine?"

So tonight, they decided to barbecue and drink margaritas—just take it easy in this blistering heat.

"Almost finished with the flute?" Vic asked Rodrigo, referring to the wooden double flute he was carving for Ellie's birthday—a gift from Vic. Josie had already claimed as her gift his ornately carved huehuetl drum, which Josie knew Ellie would love. Rodrigo, a construction worker by day, was a talented woodcarver and instrument maker who fashioned works of art out of wood, clay, gourds, and deerskin. He lived in a converted garage two doors down, where he worked on his craft late into the night. Occasionally, Vic would wander in that direction when he couldn't sleep.

"You're so talented," Josie repeated, as she so often did. "You should be paid a lot of money to do this full time."

"Well, I do okay. It's a nice extra income on the side." Josie knew he sold his creations to Native American markets around the country, as well as for use at local powwows and other cultural festivals. It had become his life's passion.

"I wish I had some talent, some artistic or musical gift," Josie said, draining her glass.

"You do," Vic said. "You have a talent for appreciating nature."

Smiling, Josie glanced at him, expecting to see some silly look on his face, but he was serious.

"No, you do. The physical world holds a spiritual experience for you. Like Rodrigo and his instruments, or Ellie and her music. It's a gift, really. I sure don't find that when I hike with you. To me it's either some kind of physical challenge or it's just plain hot and tiring." He leaned back on the flimsy patio chair, his arms behind his head.

"You see everything out there. Every bird or bug or critter. I just keep walking to the top or bottom. You take it all in. That's your talent, Jo."

"Wow," Josie said, pondering his words. She'd never thought of it that way, but he was right. Nature was her church. Whether hiking, or gardening, or grooming her horses, she came away feeling calm and centered, at times even healed. She wished Vic could find that somewhere, too.

Rodrigo had retrieved the blender flask and was filling each of their glasses with its remains. "So, what's your talent, *hermano*?" he asked Vic. "Where is your spiritual experience?"

"Being a pain in the ass. I'm getting better at it every day." Vic grinned, raising his drink. "*Salud!*"

Josie ran her lime wedge along the rim of her glass, then patted large crystals of salt along the outer edge. Rodrigo paused before sitting and asked, "Want me to prep a fresh glass?"

"Hell, no," Josie replied, tracing her finger along the edge and then licking the salt before taking another sip. "I prefer to keep adding more salt as I go. That's why I keep a small scoop of my own nearby." She motioned to the white mound in a green bowl beside her. Then turning to Vic, she said, "*You* are the most talented of all. And Vic, you can't lose that, you can't let that get away from you."

"What? Being a pain in the ass?"

"No, being you. Listening to people—really listening. And then helping them get on the right track or making them believe in themselves. I've always admired that about you."

Rodrigo stretched out on the chaise lounge. "You got that right, Josie. God knows where I'd be if you hadn't helped me, Vic. Deported to my country. Executed, like my brothers and father."

Vic shook his head. "Someone else would have been there. I wasn't there alone."

"Yeah, well, you were the only one that I saw. No one else took such a determined interest in me." Rodrigo lifted his chin and closed his eyes.

"Vic, how can you trivialize what you did?" Josie said. "Someone else wouldn't have been there. Most people are too busy worrying about themselves. You're out there helping others."

Vic set his drink down and leaned toward Josie. "Jo, you always make me out to be some saint. I went to 'Nam 'cause I had to. Fixed old helicopters so we could pull out and leave those people to pick up the pieces of a mess they didn't ask for." Vic stopped for a moment, then continued. "Then I ended up in Arizona, met Santiago and the first couple fleeing El Salvador with a little baby. And while I may have helped them . . . helped you, Rodrigo . . . I got a hell of a lot more in return. I felt like there was a reason to exist in this world. I felt needed . . . Just like I felt with Irma, and Isa, and Miguel." He said their names slowly.

The three of them were silent, listening to the sound of the sprinklers. Then burying his face in his hands, Vic began to sob. With each jerk of his shoulders, Josie felt her heart would break in two. Kneeling beside him, she squeezed his forearm, but he sat up and shook it off. "I'm okay. I'm okay. Sit down. I'm fine," Vic said. "It's the tequila."

"You sure? Do you need anything? What can I do?"

Vic leaned back. "What can you do? Well, for starters . . ." He cleared his throat. "You could give Dad a chance." He spoke these words firmly, his eyes still wet with tears.

Josie slowly sat back in her chair, picked up her drink, and took a sip. "I agreed to the party, didn't I?" she said. She knew what Vic meant, but the truth was she had no idea how she'd feel when she finally saw Tony. Would she explode with anger or feel utter indifference?

Both her father and Ellie would be here in a few days to celebrate Vic and Ellie's birthdays. Ellie would fly in on Friday, and their
father would arrive by bus on Saturday evening. Since his wife wasn't
planning to visit her sister for another year, their father was making
the trip on his own, something he'd never done before. In fact, he
would spend three nights at Vic's, before heading back to Las Vegas
on Tuesday. Three whole nights.

It was no consolation to Josie that her father had acknowledged
he was, most likely, her father. In fact, it angered her all the more. But
it was Vic's birthday. If Ellie wasn't coming as well, Josie might have
considered staying at a motel. As much as she despised the thought
of her father's presence in the house, the fact that Ellie and Maggie
would be there made it an ordeal she would have to endure. As far
as Josie was concerned, the only time she had to actually sit down
with Tony was Sunday, the day of the dinner. Other than that, she
could come and go, enjoy Ellie and Maggie, and make it to Tuesday
unscathed. On Sunday, the four of them would celebrate. Father, son,
daughter, and granddaughter. That much she could do for Vic. But
beyond that, Josie wasn't sure.

"Vic, I can't help how I feel. I'll be decent to him, but any more
than that? What can I say?" As Josie slid down in her chair, the sprinklers turned off and the cool moist air became uncomfortably warm
and sticky—just like summer nights in Binghamton.

Ellie's hair had grown into a sleek, short style that added a touch
of sophistication to her otherwise funky look. To Josie's relief, the
bleached spikes were gone and Ellie's natural copper color reigned.
Once again, she looked like her daughter, although the jaunty air of
confidence that rode on the clunky shoes gave Josie pause. Her little

girl *was* turning twenty this week, and next year—dare she think it? —she'd be twenty-one!

When she first caught sight of Ellie at the airport, Josie had struggled to hold back tears. She knew a weepy mom would embarrass her and get things off to a tense start, so she'd hugged her tightly, whispered "I missed you" in her ear, and stopped there.

After a quick embrace, Ellie had immediately looked around and asked for Maggie.

"She's waiting for you in the van with Vic. We couldn't bring her in here, of course, but it's awfully hot out, so we'd better hurry."

"Let's go then. Let's go," Ellie had said impatiently, flinging her bag over her shoulder. "I don't need to stop at baggage claim—got everything here." And she'd started off with long even strides that Josie struggled to match, trying to get beyond the distance that Ellie set between them.

Once in the van, all of Ellie's attention went to Maggie, with a little for Vic on the side. Swallowing the lump in her throat, Josie concentrated on navigating the freeways back to the Valley.

Now settled at home, they sat together on the sofa, drinking iced tea and stroking Maggie who lay between them. Both of them had recovered from that initial reunion awkwardness, and they were now laughing together after Josie described Maggie's passionate interest in gardening.

"I hate taking her away from you, Mom." Ellie frowned.

"Oh, don't worry about me. I'm happy knowing you two are together—looking after each other." Josie squeezed Ellie's arm, then went back to patting Maggie. "She loves the trails. You'll have to explore them with her in Seattle. But be sure to use a leash. I learned my lesson this week when we met up with a rattlesnake."

"What?"

"Fortunately, Maggie never saw it," Josie continued, "and I was able to get her back on leash. Still it gave me quite a scare." They sat listening to the whirl of the bicycle in the garage where Vic was working out.

"I can't believe he's in that suffocating garage," Ellie said. "The fan only blows hot air around."

"It's good for him, despite the heat, I think," Josie said unconvincingly.

Ellie leaned in. "How is he, Mom? He seems kind of . . . I don't know . . . empty, hollow."

Josie wondered how Ellie had picked up on this so soon, for that's how she'd seen him for a while now. A hollow man on the verge of caving in. She looked at her daughter, who sat with her right leg crossed over the left, foot moving up and down, and her arm draped along the sofa almost touching Josie. Ellie's look of deep concern seemed to reach out across the distance as an invitation that Josie was eager to accept.

"I'm worried about him, Ellie. I'm so worried."

"Is he seeing a psychologist?"

"Yes, he has a psychiatrist, and he sees a therapist every other week now."

"Does he take any meds at all?" Ellie asked.

"Yes, but beyond keeping him a bit more on track, he's still not Vic. He's either edgy or empty."

"How about, like, a group, you know support group? Share his feelings with someone who's been through this too? Or close to it, at least. I mean, how many people lose their whole frickin' family?"

"He refuses to join a group," Josie said, feeling a sense of release as she opened up to Ellie. It was like talking with Rae or Rodrigo, only more intimate and, Josie realized, much more comforting. Gingerly, she took another step.

"I feel like he needs a change, El. I don't know how he can go on here and at work. I've suggested that the two of us move back to Binghamton or take an extended trip somewhere, but he says no to everything. I don't know how he'll get through this."

Maggie rolled over, spread eagle, her head hanging over the edge of the couch. They both laughed.

"You guys should come up to Seattle for a while. It's such a cool city—except for the rain. That part reminds me of Binghamton." She made a sour face.

"So, tell me about your house and your music," Josie asked, letting the Binghamton slight pass. After all, at twenty, Josie would have loved to leave, too.

Ellie's frown lifted into a wide grin. "Oh, I love Capitol Hill. It's so rad there, and having our own house is gonna be wild. I mean, no neighbors above or below like in an apartment. Truly our own space to make music."

"What are your neighbors like?"

"We've only met the people next door so far. They're a young married couple, artists that work with glass and make these unusual designs. Seem really nice. They're cool about our music and stuff. We're on a corner, so there's only that house next to us. And then behind us is our backyard and then another yard, separating us from those neighbors. We're almost as good as sound-proof."

"Sounds ideal," Josie said, taking in Ellie's energy. "And your music, what's happening with the band?"

"Well, I told you about those guys Kelly and I met when we started working at Pagliacci's Pizza. Eddie plays drums and congas, and Ian, keyboard and guitar. So, we've been putting some songs together. Original stuff. Some alternative, some folksy, and a touch of Afro-Cuban beat. I'm starting to learn flamenco techniques on the guitar, and Eddie's teaching me the art of congas. I love it, Mom, all of it. And I'm getting better and better on the guitar." Ellie spoke so fast the words rose and fell like the melodic sounds of Italian or Spanish. And she glowed: her eyes sparkling like blue topaz and her cheeks flushing crimson.

Josie thought of the day over a year ago when Ellie first told her she was leaving. The band was piling into two vans and heading west with only vague destinations. Someone's relative in Chicago, an old friend in Austin, and another one's aunt in Seattle. Josie had gotten hysterical. It was enough that Ellie had fought tooth and nail the entire year about going to college. She'd refused to go away to any of the colleges in New York that had accepted her; instead she'd grudgingly attended a few classes at the local community college. The band had been her focus. Well-known in the area, they played clubs in a one-hundred-mile radius. Josie knew they had talked about moving to New York City, and she had been ready to take on that fight. But this aimless wandering had come out of the blue. Consequently, their parting had been ugly. Josie insisted Ellie's money in trust was for education only, and Ellie exclaimed that her mother would never hear from her again. But within a week, both had recanted: Ellie finally calling from Chicago and Josie helping financially. Still, that week had been a nightmare for Josie, wondering, waiting, and feeling, once again, abandoned.

Sitting beside her now, Josie still believed a college education was a necessary foundation that Ellie should build on, but she had to admit there was something to admire in Ellie's determination. Looking at her daughter, so self-assured, so passionate about her music, Josie smiled and relaxed. "I'm glad you're here."

The smile on her daughter's lips looked a bit forced as Ellie ran her fingers through her copper hair and said, "Yeah, Mom it's nice to be here." Josie knew those fingers would rather be strumming a guitar in an old house in Seattle.

The kitchen door leading to the garage opened and closed, and Vic appeared drenched in sweat. "Ellie, come here. I need you to turn the hose on me out back. Spray me down." He grinned. "Come on, Maggie, let's go girl."

The three of them, Maggie eagerly in the lead, headed out the patio door laughing. Josie felt a surge of joy. Ellie lifted Vic's spirits. Then she remembered—her father would soon be intruding on anything close to joy.

Josie woke to the sound of mourning doves cooing their low, plaintive song. She wondered—did doves that lost their mates remain alone or find a new companion?

Almost four years had passed since she'd lost Ben, and she still missed him terribly. They'd had fifteen years of a love that quietly stretched thick, deep roots far into the heart of the earth. Despite her longing for Ben, Josie felt fairly grounded and secure, but still—was she destined to spend the next decades alone?

Lucas was the first man she'd felt a connection to, but was it a friendship that was evolving or something more? Josie wasn't sure what she was feeling, beyond looking forward to their talks. In fact, she barely remembered what he looked like. Whenever Doc Lucas would come by on a vet call, Josie's focus was always on the horses or the list of questions she had stuffed in her pocket. He'd deal with the horses, then go. There'd never been any small talk, just business. But this Lucas was different. This Lucas asked questions, and listened,

and laughed. She wondered where it would all lead when she went
back—whenever that would be.

But today had little to do with the future and everything to do
with the past. There was no way around it. Josie had managed to avoid
Tony—as she'd decided to call her father—since he'd arrived the day
before. She had taken Ellie to Hollywood, where they played tourist, then checked out a place called Musician's Institute, and finally
ended the evening with dinner and music at The House of Blues.

With a smile, Josie nestled into her pillow. They had actually had
fun, the two of them, and Josie had even heard herself say several
times, "Cool!" like she was nineteen all over again. Yet she had to
admit, all the noise and people had overwhelmed her. She longed for
the quiet of the mountains, for a long walk in a shaded grove, but
she wouldn't trade a moment of grace and peace for the special bond
she'd felt with Ellie last night. By the time they had gotten home after
midnight, the house was dark and quiet. Vic got up long enough to
report that he had picked up their tired, aching, and stiff father at
the bus station at six in the evening; exhausted, he'd turned in about
nine.

Vic had looked dull-eyed the night before, so Josie made a mental
note to make this weekend as pleasant as possible for him. It was,
after all, his first birthday without Irma and the kids.

The day's plan included a manicotti dinner mid-afternoon—just
the four of them. They'd discussed inviting Irma's relatives, Santiago
and family, and Rodrigo, but Vic had quickly nixed that idea. He
began with the words, "Last year . . ." that needed no explanation,
and Josie had reassured him, saying "Just us, then."

Within an hour, she had coffee brewed, sauce and meat sim-
mering, and the ricotta mixture settling in the refrigerator. She
heard voices in the hallway as Vic gave instructions about the tub

and shower, then Vic was beside her, lifting lids, sniffing and tasting, dripping sauce along the way.

"Happy birthday, Vittorio," Josie said, giving him a big hug. He wore the Pagliacci's Pizza T-shirt that Ellie had given him.

Josie was just about to comment jokingly on how next year he'd be turning fifty, but as she stepped back, she saw that the circles under his eyes were even more pronounced and the lines in his face as defined as glacially striated rock. With his unruly mass of graying curls, he had the look of a weathered rock star.

Setting the wooden spoon down, Vic said, "Remember how Mom used to make that Italian sweet bread with raisins—and we both hated it? But there it would be, first thing in the morning, on our birthdays."

"God, yes. I used to pick out all the raisins and make a mountain on my plate."

"Now I love that stuff," Vic said. "Isn't that weird? I thought of it first thing this morning." He sat down at the kitchen table, staring out the window.

Josie poured him a cup of coffee. "It's so hot again today. Supposed to hit 105 degrees. We should start the air before I put the oven on, try to keep it cool." She handed him a steaming mug, but he was lost in thought. Setting it down, she waited, respecting his silence.

Finally he spoke. "I hope somewhere, somehow, they're all together. Mom, the kids, Irma. She would have loved them."

Josie nodded, then quietly asked, "Do you think, perhaps they are? Do you really believe that . . . ?" She left the rest unsaid, but waited, hoping for an answer that felt true.

His eyes softened as he wearily shook his head. "I wish I did. I just kind of hope, you know?"

"Oh, I know," she said, closing her eyes and listening to the bubbling sauce, the running tub water, and the mourning dove still singing its song.

By the time Tony made it to the kitchen, Josie was taking her turn in the shower. And once he was settled in the living room, she was back at work in the kitchen. Ellie was holding court, jabbering away about Maggie, Seattle, her music. Occasionally Ellie stopped long enough for Vic or Tony to make a comment, then she jumped back in and took the lead.

The temperature hit 102 degrees by noon, and despite the air conditioner in the living room window, the kitchen was quite warm. Josie decided she was about as ready as she could be, so she straightened her shoulders and entered the living room, carrying tall glasses of Hawaiian iced tea.

Tony stood immediately as she entered the room; *something Ben would have done* was her first thought, yet it was an incongruous image. Ben would have stood to help with the tray. Her father's movement was more like a startled snap-to-attention in preparation to flee.

Josie held forth her offering to Tony first, and as his swollen hand reached for a glass, her eyes traveled up to take in his appearance. He looked nothing like she remembered him, though most of her memories consisted of black and white photographs. She did not recall spending any significant time in his presence; he seemed to come and go. Only one vivid memory stayed with her.

A festival in the church basement. A man dressed as a saint chasing a man dressed as the devil. That's what her brother Vic had told her: it wasn't real—just men dressed up, like for Halloween. Only this knowledge hadn't calmed her, and Vic had taken off with friends. Josie remembered crying for her mother, but instead this man—her father—had picked her up and set her on his lap. First, a sharp scent, possibly cologne or alcohol. Then the solid feel of strong arms around her waist as he bounced her on his knee and sang a song in her ear, dissipating her fears. For a while, Josie felt safe.

That man, of course, had been young, with slick dark hair and a long straight nose. Movie-star handsome in photographs, always striking a pose, brimmed hat cocked, cigarette dangling from his lips, and a seductive gleam in his eye. Somehow, Josie always pictured him this way, maturing into an older form of the same smooth character. No father-figure image, that's for sure. It had never occurred to her to compare her mother's early photos with how she'd actually aged. She too had been attractive: lush dark hair, permed and styled, a coat delicately draped over her shoulders, her head turned slightly to the side, and a sweet yet alluring look in her eyes. She must have been nineteen in that photo, with her own 1940's movie star look about her. Yet her mother, Rita, had aged hard; she'd lost weight, carried ever-present bags under her eyes, and neglected her lovely hair, letting it go dull and limp. And of course, she hadn't lived beyond her fifties.

Josie had never considered how her father might look now, despite Vic's comments, but Vic had described him well. Tony was a shrunken, sagging old man with a purple, bulbous nose, spider-veined cheeks, and a haunted look in his dark eyes. His thinning gray hair exposed a pink, scaly scalp. Josie was relieved to find that there was nothing lovable about him. It made it so much easier to turn away toward Vic and Ellie.

Ellie's vibrancy carried them through most of dinner, but after her third piece of manicotti and second glass of wine, she suddenly faded.

Conversation had centered on superficial topics, with neither Josie nor her father speaking directly to each other. Josie wondered if he would make any effort to approach her, alone, before Tuesday. Would he ask for her forgiveness or try to reclaim her as his daughter? If this afternoon was any indication, he would simply avoid any conflict. So far, they were both doing a great job of avoiding even eye contact alone.

With Ellie's sudden silence at the table came a strained tension that Vic tried to fill by thanking Josie for the great meal. As she turned to Vic to respond, she heard Tony blurt out, "Christ, tastes just like your mother's." Josie froze.

How dare he mention her mother? She glared at him, her face flushed scarlet with anger. He was wiping his lips with a napkin, oblivious to the fury building within her, ignorant to his own insensitivity.

"Pathetic," Josie said, in a hiss. "Disgusting and pathetic." The napkin stopped mid-air. She squeezed the sides of her chair, straining to hold in the tirade of words that struggled to escape. She could feel Vic's eyes on her, pleading and weary.

Josie pushed her chair back and stood, meeting Vic's gaze. His eyes were blank, and his face slack; only his eyebrows moved upward slightly, as if the effort to care came from some small dwindling reserve within. He looked utterly defeated. Josie's anger subsided, replaced now with an aching concern.

"I'll make coffee," she said meekly. Vic nodded, but as he leaned back into his chair, the sound of the ringing phone startled him. In an instant, the dull glaze cleared as if a mask had been lifted, and Josie saw, in Vic's widened dark eyes, utter despair.

Forlorn

August 2001

VIC

Vic welcomed the Chianti's dulling of his senses. Despite the passage of time, it seemed the waves of grief were becoming more potent, more compelling, so when at dinner Josie started to erupt—that initial hiss of steam before the mountain blows its top—Vic let the waves tug him under, just slightly. And it felt good. No need to rescue or be rescued. Just let it all go.

Then the phone's shrill ring resonated beneath the surface like the harsh ping-ping of radar tracking an incoming torpedo. Reluctantly, Vic broke through the surface and gasped for air, forced abruptly back to the here and now. Josie, standing to his left; Ellie, slumped in the chair across the table; and his father, head sagging, to his right.

"You want me to get it?" Josie asked, a pained look in her eyes.

"No, no, I will," Vic answered, feeling the need to move, to put one foot in front of the other. "Probably another fan calling to wish me a happy birthday." He forced his lips to curl upward, but it was no smile.

Minutes later, Vic hung up the phone and returned to the kitchen where Josie and Ellie were cleaning up. His heart was pumping with a desperate urgency. Adrenaline had purged all traces of Chianti in seconds.

"I have to go," Vic said matter-of-factly, "east of San Diego . . . Imperial County."

They turned at the same time and looked at him, bewilderment creasing both brows. Each had been lost in thought, immersed in her own troubles, Vic realized, each struggling with her own undertow. He had no right to sap any of their strength.

"What's wrong? What's happened?" his father asked from the hallway.

Vic ran his hand through his hair. "It was an official from the Border Patrol. They found a young man staggering along Interstate 8. He collapsed and is in a coma at a hospital. No ID on him, but they found a piece of paper with my phone number." Vic felt his knees buckle slightly, so he eased onto the kitchen chair and continued. "Before he collapsed, he was frantically mumbling something about his wife. The official said they searched the area, and ten miles away, they found a young woman, dead, in the desert. Probably the heat—dehydration." Vic licked his own dry lips. "I think it might be Ernesto, Irma's youngest brother. He's crossed before to work on farms. Although the part about his wife, I'm not sure. They have a little baby, I think. So, I don't know if she'd be crossing, too. She might. But I have to see if it's Ernesto."

Vic thought first of the skinny kid, nine years ago at least, chasing his cousins with a lizard; then he recalled the serious young man in an ill-fitting suit, pledging eternal love at his wedding about two years ago.

"Oh, Vic." Josie sat beside him and laid her hand on his forearm.

"I need to get down there, see if it *is* him. Christ . . . it must be him."

"I'll go with you. Ellie can take care of everything here," Josie said.

"No. You don't need to go. You stay and visit with Ellie, then get her and Maggie on their way to Seattle."

"Absolutely not," Josie said. "I'm going with you. I won't take no for an answer, so save your energy."

"I'm going too," said Ellie. "And neither one of you can talk me out of it. So, let's all get ready."

Their voices were grating on him, though Vic knew they were speaking out of love.

"Listen," Vic said, with what energy he could muster, "I'll probably be back by tomorrow or the next day. I'll call you and let you know what's happening. If I need you, you can drive down then."

"Vic, I don't want you going alone," Josie said. "You shouldn't be driving such a distance in your state. Think of the meds and lack of sleep. We'll all go, then. We can take turns driving."

Vic knew she was right, but a part of him just wanted to push Josie away. Her concern felt stifling at times.

"What about Maggie?" Ellie asked.

The dog, Ellie, Josie. He just wanted to focus on getting down there.

"See?" Vic said. "It's better if you stay and take care of things here."

"*I'll* take care of things here." His father spoke from the doorway. "As long as you need," he finished, with a sharp nod. They all turned in silence to face him.

Vic had forgotten about his father. Looking at him now, he saw the strain of this visit and wondered if it had been such a great idea after all. Sometimes things were better left alone.

"Oh, Dad," he said apologetically, "and you need to catch a bus on Tuesday. Jo, it'd be better if . . ."

"I said," Tony interrupted, stepping into the kitchen, "I can stay here and take care of things as long as you need me. There's no damn hurry for me to get back to Vegas. It'll be there Tuesday, Friday, next Wednesday, for chrissakes. The damn city never closes. Go do what you have to do, and I'll hold down the fort."

"But Maggie," Josie pleaded, "Maggie would be better with you, El. You should probably stay, too."

Vic knew Josie didn't trust leaving Maggie with their father, but there was no fight left in him to take any sides. He wished they'd all just step aside and let him go.

Ellie settled the issue with her emphatic statement, "Maggie will be just fine with Grandpa. I'm going with you. So, once again, let's get ready. We're just wasting time."

Josie hesitated, frowning at Maggie, who had stood protectively beside her during all of the commotion. Vic shrugged. Having Josie and Ellie along might be helpful, especially if he felt himself sinking again. After all, he'd be walking into a hospital—and he had no idea how he'd feel about that. Maybe having Josie there for support wasn't such a bad idea. As long as she and Ellie didn't start clashing.

Vic pushed himself up from the table. He'd let them work it out while he packed.

"Wait," Tony said, turning back toward the hallway. "Before you all go anywhere, I have something for you, Vic, something I'd like you to take along."

Vic sat back down as his father disappeared into Miguel's room. Josie got up and approached Ellie, who was standing by the sink, one hand on her hip and an annoyed look on her face. Vic could hear Josie mumbling something about Maggie.

They all looked toward the doorway as Tony returned. He walked with a slight limp, swaying slightly from side to side. Though he carried a bag in one hand, as he approached Vic, he reached into his pants pocket and pulled out a small white box.

Handing it to Vic, he said, "Sorry, it's not wrapped or anything, but I got it for your birthday."

Opening the box, Vic saw a silver chain and medal similar to the one his mother had always worn, only this one was larger, more masculine. His mother's, he remembered, was of the Virgin Mary. This one looked slightly different. A woman in a nun's habit, gazing at a crucifix in her hands.

"Saint Rita," Tony said, his eyes cast down. "She was an Italian saint who lost her husband and children—was left alone in the world." He paused, then looked into Vic's eyes as he said, "I thought maybe she might bring you some comfort. I don't know." He glanced nervously at Josie, then added, "Your mother believed in such things, and, of course, it's her name."

With trembling hands, Vic looped the long chain around his neck, then touched the medal that lay against his chest. "Dad, thank you. It means a great deal to me." He choked back the lump in his throat and wondered if the medal his mother wore had been a gift from his father as well.

"Hell," Tony said, with a forced, quick laugh, "I couldn't believe they actually sold these things in Vegas."

"Yes, in Vegas!" Ellie said. Stepping around the table, she lifted the medal from Vic's chest for a closer look.

Josie remained tight-lipped and silent at the sink, her arms crossed.

"And wait, just one more . . . for you, Ellie," Tony continued, holding forth the flat, thin paper bag, "this is something I wanted you to have, though you may not be able to actually use it nowadays, but anyway, here you go. Happy birthday, sweetheart."

Ellie pulled out a weathered 33 ⅓ record album of Gene Krupa. "Cool!" she exclaimed. "And it includes 'Sing, Sing, Sing'! I love it, Grandpa. Thank you." She flung her arms around his neck and kissed his cheek.

Vic was struck by the ease with which Ellie called him "Grandpa." Over Ellie's shoulder, Vic saw his father's surprised face relax into a smile as Ellie stepped back.

"I don't suppose you've got a record player?" Tony asked.

"No," she answered, "but there are tons of swap meets in Seattle. I'll find one."

Then, as Vic stood, he heard Josie say, "I have one. You can have my old record player—and all my albums and 45s, too."

"Thanks, Mom," Ellie said, still reading the cover.

"Well, let's get going," Vic said. "Pack for an overnight stay. He said there are a few motels near the hospital."

"But Maggie . . . ?" Josie asked, still lingering.

"Wait," Tony suddenly said. "Any reason we can't all go? I mean, me and the dog, too? You got a big van there. Plenty of room."

The three of them looked at each other, then at Tony with Maggie now sitting at his side. Josie turned to Vic and opened her mouth, but it froze in an 'O.' As if on cue, Maggie trotted up to Josie and stood before her, wagging her tail.

"Oh sweetie," Josie said, bending to pet her. Vic knew exactly what she was thinking: At least she wouldn't have to worry about Maggie if they all came. Dealing with her father would be a lesser evil.

What the hell, Vic thought. "Let's all go, then," he said, turning his thoughts toward Ernesto.

They settled into the Chevy van as if they traveled together regularly: Vic at the wheel despite Josie's protests, Tony in front beside him, Josie in the middle two-seater, and Ellie and Maggie sprawled in the back. In minutes, they were on the 101 Freeway heading east. Glancing in the rearview mirror, Vic saw Ellie bobbing to the sounds of whatever she was listening to on her Walkman. This constant movement in his periphery reminded him of the way Miguel would kick his leg up and down in the car seat until he fell asleep. He and Irma used to change radio stations to see if his leg would change with the beat. If he was fairly alert, it would; if he was close to sleep, it wouldn't. Vic smiled slightly at this treasured memory and considered sharing it, but the thought of saying it out loud was just too much.

The heat was oppressive. He'd cranked up the air conditioner, but the hot stale air within was holding its own. It'd be a while until the temperature would reach a comfortable level, and even then, Vic wasn't sure how long his engine could maintain this extra load. His hope was that as they approached San Diego and closed in on evening, it would cool off enough to open windows. It was now four-thirty; he figured they would make it to El Centro by eight-thirty or so, if traffic allowed—and so far, it did. But it *was* summer, and it *was* the weekend, and they *were* heading toward San Diego. All good reasons for traffic to slow down, and in Southern California, it often slowed for no reason at all. But so far, so good.

Vic eased onto the transition for the 405/5 south. A couple of hours on this freeway, then maybe two more east on the Interstate 8, and they'd be there. Moving to the far-left lane, he settled in with the flow and sighed. He used to like driving long distances; he'd listen to talk radio or just let his mind drift. It was the one time it was okay to do nothing. A kind of limbo in which you were suspended from life for a while, unreachable, unable to participate—but excused, of course, because you were on your way to something important.

Now Vic always felt in limbo, not sure where the hell he was headed. In fact, that's how he'd often felt—suspended from life—in Binghamton, in Vietnam certainly, even in Arizona. It wasn't until he'd come to LA with Santiago and started working at the law office that he began to feel he was participating—no, *getting ready* to participate in life, because then he'd met Irma, and that's when he felt like he really started to live. He'd been well into his thirties before he felt like a responsible adult, so when at thirty-nine he met Irma, Vic was eager to take on the responsibility of marriage and family. And Irma, at twenty-eight, had had her fill of irresponsible men. Their ten years together *were* his life as far as Vic was concerned.

"Ellie, please stop bumping my seat!" Josie shouted, interrupting the silence and startling Tony awake.

"Chrissakes!" Tony snapped, looking around with a dazed look.

"You kids settle down back there," Vic joked, "or do I have to pull this car over?"

Ellie pulled off her ear phones. "Huh? What? Somebody say something?"

"Ellie, you keep bumping my seat; please sit still."

"It's not just me. Maggie keeps scratching and thumping her leg."

Josie groaned and leaned her head against the window.

Tony pulled out his wrinkled handkerchief and blew long and hard. Vic caught Josie's look of desperation in the mirror and winked.

"Are we there yet?" Josie asked in a childlike voice.

"Almost. Only four more hours." Vic grinned, and though she stuck her tongue out at him, he saw her face soften into a tender smile. Josie always had a way of making him feel better.

They had no trouble finding Imperial Valley Medical Center, but once there, they were instructed to wait in the lobby for a supervisor. Restless and irritable from their long drive, the four of them paced, sighed, and took turns at the drinking fountain, until Josie finally said, "This is ridiculous," and headed for the elevator. She returned several minutes later, motioning to Vic to follow her and for Ellie and Tony to stay put.

Ever the competent nurse who knew her way around any hospital, Josie had a confident attitude that led her boldly through the doors of the Intensive Care Unit.

"He's in the ICU," Josie said, once they were in the elevator. "Still semi-comatose, rambling when conscious, was dehydrated, but recovering well."

Lowering her voice as if someone else might hear, she added, "The charge nurse is a young woman, in charge just for this evening, not very sure of herself. I told her it might be your relative and you were desperate to see him. Apparently, there's a Border Patrol agent on guard duty, but he went to the cafeteria. She'll let us come in once the agent returns."

Vic followed her out the elevator door and through the double doors marked "No Admittance: Intensive Care Unit." The whooshing sounds of machines and an antiseptic smell with a nauseating sweetness flooded Vic with memories of Irma's last days. He reached out to steady himself on Josie's shoulder, relieved that she was there.

A young woman in surgical scrubs met Josie at the door of the glass-enclosed nurses' station. She looked questioningly at Vic, then led them in silence toward one of several small cubicles. Sitting outside the door was the agent, in uniform, a cup of coffee in his hand.

He quickly stood, blocking the doorway, the cup held forward as if in offering.

Vic glanced over the shoulder of the stocky officer, who was at least four inches taller than Vic, and said, "I was called this afternoon. I'm the one whose phone number was found in his pocket. It might be my brother-in-law." Glimpsing the name on the tag above the right front pocket of his green shirt, he added, "Officer Muñoz."

"You'll have to give us some information, if it is. And you can only step in for a minute." His gray eyes held Vic's for several seconds before he stepped aside.

Lying in the bed was a thin, brown-skinned man with green tubing in his nose, wires on his chest, and an IV in his arm. Vic approached slowly to get a closer look. The man's face was turned slightly to the side, a white washcloth draped across his forehead. Vic saw that his lips were cracked and scabbed. Swollen eyes strained to open, but as his head rose up, the cloth slipped to the side and the lips curved into a slight smile.

"Vic," he murmured. *"¿Y Irma? ¿Mi hermana, está aquí?"*

Vic's heart raced at the sound of her name, Irma. Then as Vic was about to say that no, his sister wasn't here, Ernesto's inflamed eyes squeezed shut, and he shook his head back and forth, sobbing, "No. No. Irma . . . *recuerdo.*" He remembered.

Just as quickly, his eyes opened again, *"¿Y Claudia? ¿Dónde está, Claudia? ¿Dónde?"* He clutched Vic's hand.

Claudia, that was his wife's name. Vic had forgotten it.

"Ernesto," Vic said. *"No sé."* He didn't know where she was, so that was no lie.

The truth would come out soon enough if Claudia was the woman—the body—they had found.

They sat quietly for a moment, reading more in each other's eyes than either man needed to say in any language. Ernesto rested his head back onto the pillow. "Claudia, Claudia," he murmured.

Just what Ernesto remembered—his sister dead, his wife collapsed in the desert—Vic wasn't certain, but either way, it meant sorrow. He took the small, limp, calloused hand in both of his and bowed his head.

No Olvidado
Not Forgotten

August 2001

JOSIE

When Josie returned to the waiting area, only her father was sitting on the bland beige sofa. Ellie was nowhere in sight. Josie considered making a sharp turn toward the women's room, but Tony glanced up, catching her eye, and immediately struggled to stand. A wave of nausea descended upon her as Josie reluctantly approached him. It struck her that she had never disliked anyone with such intensity, and this disgust left her feeling hard and insensitive—something generally alien to her character. That made her feel even more resentful.

"Where's Ellie?" Josie asked, turning her eyes away as Tony stumbled slightly and then steadied himself on the sofa's arm.

"She's walking Maggie." He cleared his throat, and she prayed he wouldn't pull that disgusting hankie out again. "So, is it him? His brother-in-law?"

"Yes, it is. He doesn't know yet about his wife—if she's the one that they found. They wanted Vic to ID her, but he's only seen her once . . . at their wedding. He's talking with the Border Patrol agent now, trying to work something out."

"What the hell were they thinking?" Tony's voice rose as he

continued. "Crazy to walk through the damn desert. Why didn't they just stay in their own country?"

Josie felt the hairs on the back of her neck stand up as her anger flared again. "Perhaps," she began dryly, "because they felt a sense of responsibility toward their families, so they risked their lives to send money home to *their wives and children*." The last words she spoke sharply, hoping they'd slice through the air like arrows. He flinched.

As Tony lifted his chin and looked down at Josie through squinted eyes, she held his gaze. "But I suppose that's something *you* can't understand," she finished. Not giving him time to respond, she turned on her heel and exited to the parking lot to look for Ellie. Josie couldn't wait to get to a motel—with separate rooms—so she could finally get away from him.

"Sorry, no pets," or "Only *small* pets," had been the message everywhere they went after leaving the hospital. Since Josie had never traveled with a dog before, it hadn't occurred to her that they might have difficulty finding a room for the night. Ellie suggested sneaking Maggie in—if that was even possible—and then offered to sleep in the car with Maggie, which Josie opposed. But finally, they came upon a Desert Inn, where, for a substantial fee, Maggie could sleep with them.

It wasn't until close to midnight that the weary group finally claimed the last available room. "Peak season," the sleepy desk clerk had said with a shrug of his thin shoulders, adding, "Mariachi festival in Calexico." Josie looked questioningly at Vic, who shrugged as well.

Ellie and Josie sandwiched into a small concave mattress on a sofa bed, with Maggie on the floor beside Ellie. Vic and Tony shared a queen. Ellie fell asleep quickly and remained in the same position all night. Josie spent most of the night watching Vic and Tony roll from side to side, like a couple of Italian sausages on the grill, and, of course—of course!—Tony snored like a donkey's bray.

Josie drifted in and out of a light sleep until Vic's activities brought her fully awake. He had risen early, walked Maggie, showered, and then, after mouthing the words "I'll call you," he left—all with a focused energy reminiscent of the old Vic.

Later that morning in a nearby Applebee's restaurant, Josie, Ellie, and Tony slouched and yawned as they downed cups of coffee in dazed silence. Josie realized that she should have sat next to Tony in the booth rather than with Ellie—that way she wouldn't have to face him directly. Having finished breakfast and several cups of coffee, Josie no longer had anything with which to occupy herself, so she looked beyond Tony at the entrance door.

"If you're not gonna eat that last sausage, I'll take it for Maggie," Ellie said, reaching for the link even before Josie answered.

"Wait, El. It might not be a good idea. I always worry about how well sausage is cooked. And the last thing we need is a dog with the trots."

"The trots?" Ellie laughed, wrapping it in a napkin and standing. "She'll be fine. You ate it and you're okay. If you both get sick, you can trot together." With that she swept out the door, leaving Josie breathless at her unexpected departure—and alone with Tony. Josie fidgeted in the booth, anxiously looking for her waitress so she could get the check and leave herself.

Tony grunted through his nose. Josie watched him mop up the egg yolk with the remaining piece of toast. Glancing up, she saw that he had a slight smile on his lips. As he lifted the toast to his mouth, he said, "She's a caution, that one."

Her mother always used that phrase. "She's a caution. He's a caution." Did she get it from him? Or he from her? Or was it just a common idiom of their youth? Josie had never heard anyone else use it since.

"Mom used to say that," she said.

"Did she? Well, I'll bet Ellie was a spitfire when she was a little tyke." He set his empty dish aside and picked up his coffee mug. "And I'll bet your mom spoiled her rotten."

"Who? What are you talking about?" Josie asked, confused.

"Your daughter! Didn't you just say that your mother said the same thing about her—that Ellie was a caution?"

"No! Mom died when I was pregnant with Ellie. She never got a chance to know her." As she spoke those words, their meaning tugged at her heart and drew tears to her eyes. "I meant the phrase 'she's a caution.' She used that a lot. I haven't heard it since . . . she died." A tear escaped and rolled down her cheek. She quickly wiped it away.

"Christ!" Tony said.

Josie signaled to the waitress, who nodded but walked in the opposite direction.

Suddenly, the table shook as Tony slammed down the mug and leaned toward Josie. "You know, you're just like your mother in every way. You're a wonderful mom, so loving, so concerned about every little thing. But Christ, you know how to make me feel like a piece of shit."

Before Josie could answer, Tony leaned in even further and continued in what bordered between a whisper and a hiss. "And don't think I don't know what I am. I know all too well. But being around you rubs my face in it every second—every goddamn second. Just like her." He paused, then pushing back from the table, he added, "And that's why I left." With that, he stood, fumbled in his pockets, threw a ten-dollar bill next to his plate, and lumbered toward the door.

Trembling, Josie took a long drink from her ice water. She desperately wanted to get home—either home, Vic's or hers. Perhaps Vic had been right in suggesting he come alone. Their decision to accompany him had been impulsive, although she had to admit, his state of mind these last weeks had been worrisome. But so far, Vic was doing fine, and their presence was, perhaps, an inconvenience. Yet how she wanted to get away from Tony. Josie wasn't sure how much more she could take.

Just like your mother. Well, she considered that a compliment. The nicest thing he could have said. Tired of waiting, Josie walked to the cashier and asked for the check.

Ten minutes later, Josie entered the motel room to find herself, once again, alone with Tony. Ellie was still out walking Maggie.

"Any word from Vic?" she asked coldly.

No response except for a shake of his head.

"And let me make it simple for you." Josie took a few steps toward Tony before she continued. It was then that she noticed the beer bottle in his hand. "We have no relationship—you saw to that. So, let's leave it as is. No need to say anything—explain anything. No need to talk *at all.*" He stared at the floor, his shoulders hunched forward, his face void of emotion. He simply glanced up with dark, empty eyes, then back to the spot on the carpet.

As she turned away, the door swung open and Ellie, Maggie, and then Vic entered the small room.

"Sorry to keep you waiting," Vic said, sinking into the chair by the door and rubbing Maggie vigorously on the side.

Ellie threw herself on the bed and said, "Okay—now tell us, what's up? How's Ernesto?"

"He's being released from the hospital today. The Border Patrol has to process him, and if he's cleared, then he'll be deported—put on a van to Mexico. But first . . ." Vic looked around at each of them. "First, he has to identify the body—see if it is Claudia. And then, if it is, make arrangements for what they call repatriation of the body—returning it to its home country."

"He's being released from the hospital already?" Josie asked.

"Yeah, he is. The nurse said the young ones bounce back quickly if the dehydration hasn't caused what she called organ tissue damage. Actually, he's sitting up and can't keep still. He just wants to get to Claudia. He refuses to believe it's her. Christ, I know just how he feels." Leaning forward, his hands clasped between his knees, Vic paused, then continued. "They wanted him to ID a photo of her, but Ernesto refused, of course. Since it's not far, Muñoz said we can swing by the medical examiner's office before they take him to be processed. I can follow in my van. They'll let me be with him for support."

"Thank God," Josie said. "What a nightmare."

Vic's face was flushed and his eyes alert, yet sad. "Ernesto is about Ellie's age now, maybe twenty. Christ, he was just a kid—around nine or ten—when Irma and I met. After our wedding, we went to Mexico to celebrate with her family."

Josie remembered the limo drive together to the airport as Vic and Irma were heading for their honeymoon in Mexico, and Josie, Ben, and Ellie were flying home. How happy they'd all been that day. Drinking champagne and toasting each other in the limo. Josie now wondered if Vic had wanted to invite his father to the wedding.

"At that time, Ernesto was this skinny little kid running around in his bare feet," Vic said. "Then I saw him again about two years ago. We flew down to Veracruz when he married Claudia. Poor kids. They just wanted to earn a little money to build a house of their own. That's why Claudia came too. They figured if they both worked . . ." His voice trailed off.

"Isn't there any work where he lives?" Tony asked.

"Yes and no. He works on coffee and citrus plantations when there's work and makes about 35 pesos a day. That's about $4.00—*a day*. And no, that's not enough to live on in his village. His father and brothers have done migrant work in the US over the years and were able to build a small house with the money they earned. They add on to it as they can. Ernesto and Claudia wanted to do the same."

"Didn't you say they had a baby?" Josie asked. "Or was that Irma's sister?"

Vic's face softened. "Yeah, they do. He's about eighteen months old now. They left him with Claudia's mom. Their plan was to work about six months, see what they could make together—double what Ernesto would make alone—then head back. In their own country, they'd never be able to make enough money for a house. Just wouldn't happen. American dollars go a long way in Mexico."

Vic reached for the beer in Tony's hands. "Mind if I take a swig? Man, it's hot out there."

While he chugged a good portion of Tony's precious brew, Josie sat on the edge of the bed and asked, "Well, what do you want us to do? How can we be most helpful?"

"Well, I want to go with him to the mortuary, of course. And I've given this some thought." Vic stopped and looked tenderly at Josie. "I'm glad you all came. Knowing you're here—well, it comforts me. And the truth is, I don't know how I'll feel when we get to the mortuary. So, rather than have you hang out here, why don't we all go? I don't expect it will take very long."

"Of course," Josie said, relieved to hear he was glad they'd come along.

Ellie sat up on the bed. "Poor Ernesto. After all he's been through, now he has to identify his wife's body? What if it's not her?"

Vic took another long drink, then handed the bottle back to Tony. "Apparently the description of her clothes and the general area where she was found are a good indication. Ernesto said when Claudia couldn't go any further, he left her by a bush, draped a shirt to block the sun, and gave her the last of his water. Then he continued on, in search of a highway, hoping to find help. He got disoriented and wandered for a while before he was found."

The three sat in silence.

Josie ached at the thought of this poor young woman lying alone in the middle of the desert. How terrified Claudia must have been— hoping, praying, waiting . . .

Josie said, "We'll do whatever you need, Vic. Shall we leave our stuff here or pack up? What happens after he sees her?"

Vic stretched his legs in front of him and leaned back. "Afterwards, Muñoz takes him to Border Patrol, and if he doesn't have to be detained for any reason, in a few days, he's more or less dumped just past the border—a good two thousand miles from his home. That's another thing." Vic paused. "I want to take him home, eventually, to Veracruz. Once he's deported, I'd meet him on the other side of the border. I'm not sure of any details yet. There's no way to know right now. We'll discuss that later."

"Okay," Josie said hesitantly. Vic was in no condition to travel anywhere. Certainly not *a good two thousand miles from the border.* Josie bit her lower lip and asked instead, "Have you eaten anything?"

"No, but I'd love a burger. Could you get me one to go while I call Santiago? And let's pack up. We'll probably head back later today. If not, I'm sure there'll be plenty of rooms available since it's Monday. Mariachi weekend's over."

As Vic stood, Ellie leapt from the bed and threw her arms around him, giving him a big hug. "I love you, Uncle Vic. I'll go get the burger, Mom."

"*I'll* go," Josie said, determined to get away from Tony. "You can come if you want."

Vic turned to his father. "Dad, how are you doing? Is this too much for you? Would you prefer to rest here?"

Tony pursed his lips and seemed to give it some thought before replying, "No, I'd like to come along, lend some support, as you say." He spoke barely above a whisper.

Josie suppressed a groan and walked out the door.

A few hours later, with Josie at the wheel, the van followed the Border Patrol vehicle carrying Ernesto. Vic sat beside her, nervously tapping the armrest between them.

"What's the All-American Canal?" Ellie asked from the seat behind. "I saw a sign that said 'Food grows where water flows. All-American Canal.'"

Vic twisted toward the backseat. "Well, there's no river around here, so they built a man-made canal to bring water from the Colorado River to this entire area. Supplies homes and farms. Pretty amazing." He stopped tapping.

An electric sign flashed the temperature: 106 degrees. Josie noticed that El Centro was surrounded by farmland as far as the eye could see, but Vic had told them that just beyond was a stretch of desert encircling most of the county. They were in an oasis of sorts— an oasis that poor Ernesto and his wife hadn't been able to find.

Josie glanced over her shoulder at Tony, who was leaning his head against the window. His bloated face was bright red. She wondered what meds he was on and if he'd remembered to take them. This heat was taking its toll on him. Why on earth had he insisted on coming? *Probably to spite me* was Josie's first thought, but as soon as that entered her mind, Josie knew it wasn't true. Tony genuinely cared for Vic. He clearly wasn't well, and his drinking didn't help matters, yet he made the trip by bus from Vegas and then chose to come along on this one as well—all for Vic.

Josie could certainly understand why. Vic was probably the only person in Tony's life who didn't judge him. Vic had told her about the contents of that first letter Tony sent when Vic was in basic training. It was brief and focused on Tony's concerns about Vic possibly being sent to Vietnam and wishing him well. No apology or explanation for his years of no contact. When Vic later asked why he suddenly wrote, Tony had replied that he'd been worried Vic might get drafted, so when their mother sent word through an old friend that Vic had enlisted, he felt compelled to write. It had been their mother who set it in motion, but Tony could have ignored it. Remembering how anxious Vic had been at the time, Josie realized that his father's letter must have brought such comfort.

The Border Patrol vehicle ahead made a right turn, then changed lanes to get around a slow-moving truck. Josie sped up and eased in behind it again.

Ellie had pulled her new flute from her bag and began to play a few notes.

Maggie's collar jingled, but Tony didn't stir. After warming up a bit, Ellie paused, then began again, five notes—one long and low, then four ascending. She repeated it over and over. It was sad, yet soothing.

Josie glanced at her in the rearview mirror, wondering what Ellie was thinking about. "El?" she asked.

Ellie stopped playing, the flute still poised at her lips.

"Do you ever think about your . . ." Josie hesitated, then simply said, "Paul Reid?"

Ellie lowered the flute and looked out the side window. "Mom, no, not him, mostly I think about Dad." The tender way she referred to Ben made Josie's heart flutter. "I remember things he said, or I wish I could show him something or ask him a question. Like last year, I had so many medical questions about Lizzie's cancer and her chemo. I thought about him a lot then."

"Who's Lizzie?" Josie asked, suddenly confused.

Ellie sat forward. "You know Kelly, my roommate? It's her fourteen-year-old sister. And that's why . . . well . . . that's why we shaved our heads. Actually, we donated the hair to Loving Locks. They make wigs for kids with cancer."

Josie's eyes welled up. "Oh, honey! Why didn't you tell me? I thought you were being punk and rebellious! I would have reacted so differently if you'd only told me."

"I knew something was up there," said Vic, still focused on the back of the Border Patrol vehicle.

"I'm sorry, Mom." Ellie reached up and gently touched her shoulder. "I should have. I was going to, but I don't know. I got in that stubborn mind-set, I guess, and just let it keep going."

"Honey, *I'm* sorry. What an unselfish thing to do, especially for a young woman. My God, our hair is such an important part of our appearance and self-esteem. That was a lovely act."

"No big deal considering what Lizzie was going through."

Meeting her gaze in the mirror, Josie smiled. "The truth was, Ellie—you looked stunning. You really did. I think it kind of frightened me how exotic my little girl looked! And now, well, you look so cool and stylish."

Ellie struck a pose in the mirror.

"How's Lizzie now?" Josie asked, noticing the turn signal ahead and putting hers on as well.

"I think she's going back to school this fall. She gets checked every six months or something. But so far, okay."

Josie followed the vehicle into the driveway and pulled up before a long, white, windowless building. Easing into a spot beside the vehicle, she put the car in park, but kept the motor—and air—running. Tony stirred, then cleared his throat. Vic opened the door. The blast of heat made Josie catch her breath. The thought of Ernesto and his wife walking for miles in this was unimaginable.

"You guys wait here a sec," Vic said. He grimaced as he closed the door and turned away.

Josie watched as Officer Muñoz signaled for Vic to stay back. Ernesto inched his way out of the back seat. As he struggled to stand, Josie saw that his hands were cuffed and his legs shackled.

Tony's "What the fuck?" echoed her thoughts exactly.

Finally, assisted by the officer, Ernesto stood up and looked anxiously at the building. His eyes were wide with fear—and hope.

Josie remembered that feeling—the mad dash to the ER the first time for Ben, and then running into the house the second time to find the paramedics working on him. The fear and the hope. At this moment, as frightened as he was, Ernesto could still hope that it wasn't Claudia, that she was somewhere else, alive and safe. But soon, he would know, and if it was her, he'd have to live with that truth forever.

After talking briefly to the officer, Vic turned back toward the car. Josie lowered the window.

Leaning in, Vic said, "I guess there's a small waiting area that's air-conditioned. You could check it out if you want or wait here."

"Do you want me to come in with you?"

"Muñoz said just me, but you can wait inside, close by."

"I need to use the john," Tony grunted.

Josie glowered toward the back, then said, "You go ahead, Vic. We'll be in shortly." Then after rolling up the window, she turned to Ellie and said, "Let's give it a minute." Nodding toward Ernesto, who was shuffling awkwardly toward the door with Vic and Muñoz on either side, Josie said to Tony, "Can you wait just a bit? Let's let him get inside first."

Tony nodded, but his tight lips conveyed otherwise. Josie wondered if his prostate left him any choice. She considered asking about his health and any meds, but instead, she said, "Just a few quick seconds and we'll go."

The waiting room was no more than two black metal chairs against one wall and a water cooler and fire extinguisher on the other. An unmanned counter was a few feet beyond, with a door marked "Restroom" to the left and a hallway that led to windowless double doors and a large white sign with red letters denoting "No Admittance."

Tony headed for the bathroom. Josie sat down, while Ellie filled a paper cup with water and offered it to Maggie, who lapped it up.

The double doors suddenly swung open and a tall, thin woman with short salt-and-pepper hair appeared. Her thick glasses magnified her eyes, giving her an air of being startled. "Can I help . . ." she began, then immediately changed her tone. "I'm sorry! No dogs are allowed in here!" She hung back, clearly frightened by Maggie.

"We won't be long, I don't think." Josie stood and approached the woman, who stepped behind the counter. "We're here with the gentleman that was just brought in to identify . . . to see if it's his wife."

The woman seemed puzzled. "Gentleman?"

"Yes, with Border Patrol," Josie said.

"Oh, I see." The owl-eyed woman glanced at Ellie and Maggie. "Well, you may certainly wait, but the dog is not allowed." Then flatly, "I'm sorry."

"But it's 106 degrees out there!"

"Sorry," the woman responded.

"*Sure don't sound sorry,*" Josie mumbled under her breath as she walked back toward Ellie. Reaching into her handbag, she pulled out the keys. "Here you go. I want to be here for Vic. Get the air conditioning cranked up. If it takes longer than expected, I'll come check on you."

Ellie nodded, then rolling her eyes at the woman, she and Maggie headed for the van.

Turning back toward the counter, Josie was about to ask if she could join Vic and Ernesto, but the woman had already shoved open the doors and disappeared behind them as they swung shut.

Josie and Tony sat sipping cold water from small paper cups. At least ten minutes had passed since he had sat down beside her with a long sigh. After establishing that Ellie had taken Maggie to the car and that, no, she hadn't yet heard from Vic, they sat in silence. A clock on the wall ticked loudly.

Tony balled up his empty cup and tossed it into a small trash can beside the cooler. Then stretching his legs, he cleared his throat a few times—each time getting louder. Clearly a sinus issue, Josie thought, maybe aggravated by the air conditioner, which had a stale smell to it. She noticed his brown wingtips were scuffed and weathered. One shoelace was loosely tied.

Leaning her head back against the wall, Josie closed her eyes.

"Vic said you lost your husband a few years back." Tony's unexpected words jolted her eyes open. "Must've been tough on you." He rubbed a swollen joint at the base of his thumb.

Josie swallowed the lump in her throat and nodded, unable to speak.

"Vic says he was a good man. A doctor?"

"Yes."

"Must've been hell, with Ellie and all."

"Yes, it was." Josie glanced sideways. Tony's head was lowered, chin to chest, and his hands clasped as if in prayer.

She knew so little about this man, his childhood, his dreams. She certainly knew his disappointments.

"Have you ever lost someone," Josie asked, "someone dear to you?"

He didn't answer at first—the clock filling the silence—until, finally, he said, "My mother. Lost her when Vic was a little guy—before you," he added. "July 8, 1957. Heart attack. Happened quickly."

Tony fidgeted in his chair. "I'd been meaning to visit her, especially when I knew she was living alone—after the prick she shacked up with died. Then one day, I got a phone call that she was gone. Knocked me for a loop. Guess I didn't realize how much she meant to me. I just fell apart." He tugged at a cuticle on his thumb. "Actually . . . your mother helped me through that. We'd separated, but after that, she took me back, took pity on me, I guess. And I . . . I really wanted to make things work." He looked nervously at Josie, then away. "I wanted to change. Vic was such a lively little guy, curious, full of questions. Everything seemed clear, for a while. Then, I don't know . . . I just fucked it all up again."

Suddenly, Josie could see them, her mother and father in the living room—dancing in the dark. That's what her mother had told her. How they would dance in that small space to no music or to a song he'd sing to her.

"You used to dance," Josie said haltingly, "in the living room. Mom told me."

Tony turned to her, his face suddenly animated. "Yes, yes. Oh, she was the best dancer. Could follow my lead like no one else. God, yes." He paused with his mouth open and his eyes moving as if following a memory. "She told you, did she?"

"She did," Josie said. "Mom used to sit in the living room after work in the dark, smoking. Usually, I left her alone. But one night, I fell asleep on the sofa. She came home and sat down at the other end. Lit up, of course." She mimicked holding a cigarette. "We started to talk, first, about Vic in Vietnam, and then, I don't know . . . I started asking about you."

Josie remembered how her mother took a deep draw on her cigarette and let it out in one long sigh, then, setting the cigarette down, she had turned and stretched out her legs, overlapping Josie's. They were both reclined on the sofa, facing each other—like two girlfriends.

Turning her attention back to Tony, Josie said, "I wanted to know what you were like. That's when she told me—how you'd dance together."

Tony was smiling into her eyes, and for a moment, Josie could see traces of that handsome man in the photographs—that warm, inviting smile. "You asked about me?" His face softened. "And she told you we danced."

Tony was still smiling when Josie said, not with anger, but with an earnest heart, "So, that's around the time I would have been conceived, right?"

The smile faded, and his head gave the slightest of nods as he said, "Yes."

"Why did you deny *me*?" Josie asked. "I mean, I understand when a marriage fails, but you connected with Vic later, why not me?" Her voice tightened with those last few words, sounding high-pitched.

Tony pressed his lips together. Then after a heavy exhale, he said, "Sweetheart, I've never been good for no woman."

Woman? But I was just a child, Josie was thinking, when the double doors flung open and the sounds of wailing echoed from the hall beyond.

The same woman from earlier approached, but this time a softened brow made her eyes appear tender behind her thick lenses. She asked them to follow her. They were led down the hall toward the plaintive cries.

Ernesto was sitting in a chair, clutching a backpack and rocking back and forth, his animal-like moans piercing the walls. Vic squatted by his side, murmuring or praying—Josie wasn't sure which. She ached for them both, remembering Santiago's description of Vic, how he refused to leave his babies' bodies and had to be led away, calling their names.

Vic glanced up as they entered, then slowly stood and made his way to them. "It's her," he whispered, confirming the obvious.

"Are you okay?" Josie asked, reaching up and rubbing Vic's back.

He nodded. "Yeah."

She glanced in the direction of Agent Muñoz who stood behind Ernesto, his arms crossed, head down. Josie wondered if he had a wife, maybe even children. Ernesto continued rocking, the wail now low and long, chillingly similar to Maggie's nighttime howl.

"Poor Ernesto," Josie whispered. "So, what happens next?"

Vic frowned. "I tried to see if we could arrange a flight for him and the body, or at the very least, see if he could just be taken back across the border right now. I could follow and get him on a bus home. But they won't budge. Insist they have to follow protocol. Ernesto has to be taken in to be processed."

Tony, standing behind her, suddenly bellowed, "Christ, he's not a god-damned criminal. He's just a kid who lost his wife!"

Muñoz stepped forward, hands on his gun belt. "I'm afraid you'll need to wait outside. Now, sir."

Vic shook his head, then with an arm around them both, he walked them toward the lobby.

"Sorry," Tony said. "Sometimes I just can't keep my damn mouth shut."

Josie couldn't help but say, "You just said exactly what we were all thinking."

Despite Vic's persistent pleas, a despondent Ernesto was led away by Agent Muñoz, who promised Vic he would keep him updated. Santiago was also in the loop, making sure there were no legal problems. They were to be notified when Ernesto was actually deported so that Vic could help him return to his village in Veracruz. Meanwhile, Vic and Ernesto had spoken with an official to arrange for Claudia's body to be returned home, and Vic had made the heartbreaking call to Claudia's family, sparing them the impersonal voice of the deputy coroner.

Once the Border Patrol vehicle had pulled away, Vic joined the others in the van, only this time, Vic insisted on driving. "I want to take you somewhere, show you something," he said, turning to Josie beside him. He looked pale and disheveled, but although his eyes were full of sorrow, there was a keen focus about them that gave Josie some relief. Still, she wondered how he was really holding up. Had he taken his medication? Was he reliving his own nightmare? Josie couldn't help asking once again, "You sure you're okay?"

Vic held her gaze. "I am. Don't worry."

Then, turning onto the interstate highway, he settled back into the seat and said, "The deputy coroner kept saying how relieved he was to be able to identify Claudia, that so often the bodies they find have no identification on them at all. Last week, they had to bury an unidentified kid. They guessed him to be maybe fourteen."

"Fourteen? Dear God," Josie said.

"The problem is they often travel without any papers. If they did have a wallet, it may have been stolen or lost in the journey. No identity means no way to contact family. He said they work with the Mexican Consulate to try to make an ID. They check missing persons reports, even track down bus ticket stubs or labels on their clothes. Then after two months, if no ID is made, they bury them in a pauper's grave. No family. No ceremony."

"Their families never know what happened to them?" Ellie asked.

"They never know."

"Oh, that's so sad," Ellie sighed.

Tony leaned forward, pulling on the back of Josie's seat. "I don't understand why they come through this blazing desert. I thought they just walked across from Tijuana?"

Vic glanced back. "At one time it was that simple, but a few years ago the government began building a massive wall from the beach in Tijuana stretching east for miles. Operation Gatekeeper they called it. 'Prevention through deterrence' was the plan. But it didn't stop them. Instead, it pushed them further east, through the desert."

"Don't they hear about that back in Mexico, about the desert and the deaths?" Tony asked, letting go of her seat, making it vibrate. She gritted her teeth but held her tongue.

"Sure, but most people make it, so they keep coming. The jobs are here. Plenty of jobs and money—even some family."

"A shame," she heard Tony say. "A god-awful shame."

Farmland, sectioned in varying shades of green, stretched on both sides of the highway. A sign on the side of the road read "Holtville: Carrot Capital of the World." They drove in silence until Vic exited on Orchard Road; then they all stirred in their seats, each looking out their windows. Even Maggie moved back and forth between windows in the rear of the van. They passed a Family Dollar store on the left and began to approach a stretch of small shops ahead, when Vic, muttering to himself and squinting to read street signs, suddenly took a sharp left.

After a series of turns that took them around an industrial area and then to a stretch of barren land, the van slowed as they approached a cemetery. Signs on the chain-link fence declared: "Caution: Do Not Drink This Water / *Precaución: No Tomar de Esta Agua*" and another warning that the headstones were loose and could cause injury. As they pulled into the driveway, Josie glanced up at the metal arch decorated with maple leaves, white doves in flight, and the words "Terrace Park Cemetery."

Once Vic parked the van, they all stepped out into the intense, dry heat. Maggie hopped out last and immediately gave her entire body a good shake.

Tony reached down to pet her. "Hardly a peep out of her. Does she ever bark?"

"She howls," both Ellie and Josie said at the same time.

"I'd like to hear that sometime," Tony answered.

Josie and Ellie exchanged a look. Maggie had howled both nights since he'd been there.

As they began to walk up the cemetery path, Vic said, "We're going straight through to the back. Maybe no one will pay attention to us and Maggie can come along."

It was a small cemetery, nicely maintained, with grass and trees and a few wooden benches. Josie wondered whose grave they were going to visit. A relative of Irma's, perhaps? But once they had walked beyond all headstones to another section of the cemetery, there was no green grass. No trees. No benches. Only a plot of dirt with rows and rows of small brick markers.

"These are the paupers' graves," Vic said, "the unidentified migrants who died crossing. Irma and I came here with her church once. We put paper flowers on every grave and even hand-painted wooden crosses, with words like *No olvidado* / Not forgotten and *El alma no tiene papeles* / The soul has no papers." As he spoke, it was as if he were saying a prayer.

Ellie stepped up closer and read, "Row 4-10 John Doe. Row 4-14 Jane Doe."

"John and Jane Doe, huh? Like on detective shows?" Tony asked, wiping the beads of perspiration off his forehead with the back of his hand.

The sun was merciless. Josie could feel it burning her shoulders and wished she'd worn a shirt over her tank top. She decided to keep a close eye on Tony in case he passed out in this heat.

"Yep, just like on TV," Vic said. "In this case, their families never know if they made it across. They just never hear from them again. Since there's no family burial or ceremony, local churches and human rights groups—in place of their loved ones—honor those buried here."

Josie watched Ellie as she walked along the rows, pausing at each brick. She thought of the few days after Ellie had left last summer, when Josie had no idea where Ellie was or what she was doing—and no way of contacting her either. The unknown could be agonizing.

And yet, there was something to be said for not knowing: You could still hold on to hope. She wondered how many of these families still held on to the belief that their loved one was alive somewhere.

Vic knelt down and wiped dirt from a marker. His fingers lingered on the name, Jane Doe. "Irma and I talked about bringing the kids this November for Día de los Muertos, the Day of the Dead. Isabel was excited about decorating the graves with marigolds and sugar skulls. It's a Mexican tradition." He stood, then turning to Josie, he said, "I guess I'll be decorating theirs instead. Maybe we can do that together?"

Barely able to speak, Josie managed to say "Of course. Absolutely."

Behind her, she heard Tony blow his nose. When she turned, he was wiping his eyes as well.

Once back in the van, they rode in silence, each lost in a separate sadness, yet bound by the day's grace. As they drove beyond the farmland to stretches of barren land, Josie glanced up to see in the distance what looked like a blue flag. It hung limply until caught up in gust of wind, then fluttered for a few brief moments.

"What's that?" Josie asked. "Why's there a flag in the midst of that god-forsaken land?"

Vic looked in the direction that Josie pointed. "Ah, a blue flag. That's an aid station. They're located at random points in the mountains and deserts. Volunteers set out boxes with water, sometimes even blankets and canned food—whatever provisions meet the needs of the season—and they mark them with blue flags."

Josie strained to see the base of the flag as she heard Vic say, "Some men build fences; others erect blue flags."

"Amen," Ellie said from the back seat.

"Does it help at all?' Josie asked, thinking of Claudia and Ernesto.

"I don't know. When you consider how vast the area is and how random their routes, it's hard to say. The stations get some use and are restocked, but whether they save a significant number of lives, well, folks figure they have to do something, and if they save a few lives, then it's worth it."

"I should think so. It's a wonderful act of compassion," Josie said, craning her neck to get a final glimpse of the flag.

Turning to Josie, Vic said, "That's something else Irma and I wanted to do one day. Through the church, we donated stuff, but we kept meaning to volunteer with the group and help replace the water. They're called Water Stations Project. They go out once a month, I think. It's a strenuous day and requires a bit of hiking. But with the kids and work, we never got around to it." His voice faded at the end, and Josie reached out and touched his arm.

"Hiking?" Tony interrupted, pulling on her seatback again. "Sounds like something you might do, huh? Don't you hike a lot?" His voice was right in her ear.

Josie paused, startled at his question and uncertain how to answer.

Suddenly, Ellie was beside him, saying, "Mom, I'd go with you!"

Josie's heart jolted with the sound of Ellie's voice, so warm and eager, just like that treasured phone message. *Mom, you should see the mountain here. You'd love it!* Only, Ellie was here, now, speaking directly to her. Choked with emotion, Josie couldn't answer right away, so she nodded.

Vic chimed in, "I know someone you could call. One weekend a month, they have a bus that leaves from downtown LA early in the morning and then returns in the evening."

Her seat shook as Tony let go and both he and Ellie sat back into their seats.

Clearing her throat, Josie managed to speak. "Sounds like a plan.

We'll look into it El, okay?" When she glanced back and their eyes met, she felt that intimate connection again. Josie's first thought was she couldn't wait to tell Lucas. The last time they'd talked, he'd been sad about his son moving into his own place, but said they'd had a few beers together on the deck. A special moment. He would definitely understand about her and Ellie. So much to tell him tonight when she got home.

Beside her, Vic said, "I can't imagine what Ernesto is going through at the detention center. He must be out of his mind. Muñoz said processing could take a couple of days. I wish they had just let me take him back today, instead of keeping him at that fucking prison." He slammed his hand on the steering wheel.

"Want me to drive for a while?" Josie asked.

"No," Vic answered. "I'm fine for now. I'll let you know if I get tired. I just want to go home and get organized for the next step."

The next step? Josie wondered just how much of the next step Vic could really handle.

Ellie reached into the cooler and passed around water bottles. The cold water eased Josie's dry throat. A collective sigh seemed to release as they each settled into their spots.

Josie leaned her head against the glass and closed her eyes. She could still see the blue flag flapping briefly in the breeze. Certainly, it was a marker of sustenance in the midst of a barren landscape. But there was something more about the flag that lifted Josie's spirits and filled her with a sense of hope. She thought of all those who set out on their journey north, carrying with them that promise of possibility and a fierce belief that life held endless opportunities for those who try, risk, and persevere—though sometimes at great cost. Hope, yes, and something even greater, for there were also those kind souls who trekked out to the desolate desert to restock the water—an act done out of love and compassion for complete strangers. Like the cool water on Josie's own parched throat, that touching thought alone brought her comfort after this heart-wrenching day.

With a quick glance at Vic, who was focused on the road ahead, Josie closed her eyes again and let herself drift off as they headed home—to whatever the next steps would be.

About-face

August 2001

VIC

As soon as Vic pulled into his driveway and stepped out of the van, he felt like he was walking through water. Each step, each movement of his legs, was an effort. The energy that had carried him through the past two days was suddenly depleted. Without a word, Vic went straight to his room and collapsed onto his bed. He could hear voices in the hallway, toilets flushing, doors closing, then silence. Soon, Vic was deep asleep.

It was close to noon the next day when he walked into the kitchen to find Josie and Ellie, both groggy-eyed, making a grocery list.

"Where's Dad?" Vic asked, then suddenly remembering, he added, "Oh, no! It's Tuesday, isn't it? Doesn't he need to get to the bus station?"

Josie poured a cup of coffee that she handed to Vic. "I sent Tony back to bed," she said. "He looked as exhausted as you do. There's no way he's riding in a Greyhound bus all the way back to Vegas today. In fact, I'm booking him a flight for tomorrow."

"Does he know?" Vic asked, looking from Josie to a grinning Ellie.

It was Ellie who answered. "He sure does. Mom didn't give him much of a choice. She told him he wasn't taking any damn bus today. Then she told him to get some more sleep, and they'd discuss a flight to Vegas when he woke up."

"And he agreed?"

"He looked kinda surprised. Then just nodded and shuffled back to his room," Ellie said, adding, "He may have been half-asleep. Might have to remind him when he comes out again." She reached for a banana on the counter and began peeling it.

To Josie, Vic asked, "How's he doing? Do you think he's okay? Maybe this was too much for him."

Josie motioned him to sit down. As the three of them shifted their stools around the island, Josie described how the night before, she had insisted on checking Tony's pulse and asking him a few medical questions before they all turned in for the night. As if she were giving a shift report to other nurses, Josie said, "His skin was warm and dry, his pulse was regular, and I found out he takes meds for arthritis, cholesterol, and gout." To Vic's widened eyes, Josie said defensively, "Well, I had to be sure he was okay before we all went to bed."

"Hell, Jo, I'm glad you did," Vic said. "Shit, I should have checked on him, too." Glancing at Ellie, he noticed she was smiling at her mother with what appeared to be genuine affection. Vic wondered what had happened between Tony and Josie, and even with Ellie, in the past two days. There'd been plenty of tension at first, but then something else that he couldn't quite put his finger on. Now wasn't the time to ask. Maybe later, when he and Josie were alone.

The coffee was strong, just the way he liked it. After a few sips, Vic said, "The flight idea is thoughtful, too. I doubt he can afford it, so—"

Josie interrupted. "I'll take care of it. No problem." She kept her eyes averted.

Vic was about to say a simple, "Okay," and leave it at that for now, when Tony suddenly appeared in the hallway.

"Morning," Tony said. "Christ, it's noon already? Sorry I slept so long." Short wisps of gray hair stood up straight on Tony's pink scalp, reminding Vic of an old-fashioned crewcut. He doubted his father ever embraced that style. Not as dashing as his slicked-back look.

As Tony walked slowly to the island, Ellie jumped up and offered him her stool, then poured Tony a cup of coffee.

"Thanks, sweetheart," Tony said, sitting next to Josie, who kept her eyes on her own mug. "So, Vic, how you doing? Any word yet on the kid?" Tony asked, as he scooped three heaping teaspoons of sugar into his coffee and stirred.

"Not yet. No phone messages. I'm about to check in. Just got up myself. You feeling okay, Dad?"

Tony shot a quick look at Josie. "Me? I'm fine. Ask Doctor Jo over here," he said with a curt laugh. "Practically gave me a physical last night." His smiling eyes suggested he was pleased with the interaction.

Josie didn't respond, then clearing her throat, she said, "Well, how about some breakfast—or I guess lunch? Anyone hungry?"

Vic watched as Josie and Ellie worked together making sandwiches with the leftover meatballs from their Sunday meal. There was a definite dynamic going on between mother and daughter, a subtle change for the better, Vic hoped, although Josie still seemed very cool toward Tony.

Once they were seated and everyone was eating, Josie said in a matter-of-fact tone, "So I'll book you a flight for tomorrow. Then I'll let you know what time it arrives in Vegas, so your wife can pick you up at the airport." While she was clearly talking to Tony, she still kept her eyes on her plate as she pushed a few escaping meatballs back between the slices of Italian bread.

Despite a mouthful of food, Tony answered, "My wife? Hell no! I'd rather catch a goddamn cab home."

At that, Josie finally turned and looked Tony full in the face.

Wiping his mouth, Tony did a double-take and said, "What? What?"

Pressing her lips together, Josie raised one eyebrow—Vic was sure of it—and then went back to her sandwich.

As Josie took a bite, Tony asked, "Any idea how much this is gonna run me?"

Josie froze, then tearing through the bread with her teeth and yanking the sandwich away, she slowly chewed and swallowed. Setting the sandwich down, she reached for her glass of water and said, "Not a cent, Tony. We'll take care of it." She nodded toward Vic, though she didn't meet his eye.

Tony paused, looking at Vic, and said, "That's mighty nice of you. Appreciate it. Yeah, I can cover the cost of the cab." Then he stuffed the remainder of his sandwich into his mouth.

Vic watched Josie for a while, hoping to catch a hint of what might be going on in her mind, but she busied herself with dishes and the grocery list. That's when Vic reached for his phone to call Officer Muñoz. He'd leave the inner workings of Josie's mind for later.

But that opportunity never came, for Vic was busy packing again, trying to figure out what he would need for a couple of weeks in Veracruz. Ernesto was being transported to the Mexican border town of Mexicali later that afternoon. Santiago had offered to drive Vic down and across the border to meet up with Ernesto. From there, Vic and Ernesto would get a flight to Veracruz —in plenty of time for Claudia's funeral that week.

Meanwhile Josie was frantic with worry. One minute she was questioning his decision, and the next she was organizing his medications. It was finally Ellie and Tony that managed to calm her down.

From his bedroom, Vic could hear Josie's high thin voice, "Who's going to look after him? Maybe I should go, too. He's not ready for this. Not yet."

Then Ellie's reassurance. "Mom, he's done just fine these past few days. And he won't be alone. He'll be with Irma's family."

Vic couldn't make out what Josie said in response, but what he did hear was his father's deeper tone. "It's not a matter of being ready. It's just what he has to do. Just like you dropped everything and came to help your brother—Vic's gotta do the same for the kid."

There was a silence after that. Vic stopped and listened, wishing he could see Josie's face, read her eyes, but by the time Vic joined them in the living room, all three sets of eyes—full of tenderness and concern—were focused entirely on him.

"I'll be fine," Vic said to Josie, "just fine. I'll call you as soon as I meet up with Ernesto. Don't worry." With that, Vic walked out the door and strode down the driveway toward Santiago's waiting van.

Lost Fathers
September 2001

JOSIE

Josie hummed as she buttered the toast, then flipped the eggs onto the plate beside the bacon. "Vic, they're ready!" she called toward the hallway.

Vic had arrived home from Veracruz quite late the night before, unshaven and greasy-haired, but there was a light in his bloodshot, travel-weary eyes that put Josie at ease. He'd collapsed into bed with a promise that he'd tell Josie everything over breakfast. Vic had been gone almost three weeks, with one brief call to reassure Josie that he and Ernesto had made it to Veracruz, another after Claudia's funeral, and then a call two nights before to say he was heading back. His voice sounded upbeat as he said, "I've got some ideas brewing, Jo, that I can't wait to tell you about. Let Santiago know I'll be home, and I'd like to talk to him, too."

Those weeks had been like a roller coaster ride for Josie. The joy of spending a special week with Ellie eventually came to an end, and Ellie and Maggie had gotten into a rental car and headed north for Seattle. With the two of them gone, Josie felt staggeringly lonely. She tried to keep busy in the weeks that followed. She met Rae for dinner twice, catching her up on the latest about Vic, Tony, Ellie—and of course, Lucas. Whenever they talked about Josie's latest phone call with Lucas, Rae would ask, "And then what did *he* say?" and together they'd analyze what it might or might not mean.

Though Josie filled her days with hikes and other small trips in Los Angeles, she was anxious about Vic and also just plain restless. Without Vic's presence—without a reason to be there—she no longer felt at home. In fact, her nightly talks with Lucas also pulled her thoughts toward getting back to her horses and her own life—whatever that would be. While Vic's return the night before seemed to smooth the edges a bit, Josie still felt unsettled. A lot depended on how Vic was—and just what plan was brewing.

"The toast is getting cold!" Josie warned, just as Vic stepped into the kitchen, freshly-shaven, towel-drying his curls.

"Smells great," he said, sliding onto the stool, tossing the towel aside, and immediately digging in. As she handed him a cup of coffee, Josie noticed his face was tanned, but he had deeper creases across his forehead and down his cheeks.

"Well, tell me. How's Ernesto?"

Vic grimaced. "What can I say? He blames himself—literally every day—but he's trying to be strong for his son." Vic paused, then said, "There's a lot to tell you, Jo, but first, while I eat, you tell me about Ellie and Maggie—and Dad." He looked up, pointed the fork at her, and commanded, "Everything. Especially about Tony."

Josie gave him a sideways glance. "Well, I prefer to start with Ellie." Just saying her name brought a flood of emotions that Josie knew lit up her face, for Vic was smiling at her in response.

"Oh Vic, it was such a nice week," Josie began. "We cooked together, painted our nails, watched chick-flicks, and hiked. It was nice. I don't know. She is who she is, you know? I have to respect her dreams. And she's so much fun to be with when I stop being pushy. I realized that."

Vic nodded in agreement, watching her face closely, as he continued to eat.

"I'm proud of her," Josie continued, "and I think she felt that. She seems so sure of herself. I don't know where she'll go with her music, but she wants to give it a try. And who knows? She might end up going to college at some point. Look at me—I had one plan and ended up going in an entirely different direction that brought me a great deal of happiness."

"I'm glad to see you two are close again. I saw it happening gradually—especially through Maggie. They got off okay?"

Josie thought of the moment when Ellie drove off—Maggie's nose poking out through the small opening Ellie had allowed in the rear window. Afterwards, Josie cried with such force, her chest hurt. "Yep, and they made it safely to Seattle," she said. "I only called her once, and she wasn't too irritated. Heck, I'd have called you every day if you were reachable by cell. Anyway, they're settled in their new place. She sounds happy. I plan to visit her at some point soon."

"And Dad?" Vic asked. "How'd that go? I'm sure glad he agreed to the flight."

Josie fidgeted on her stool, twisting side to side. "I don't know. It was such an emotional few days, we were both too worn out to fight anymore. But when I drove him to the airport, I found myself telling him how you and I used to listen to the cars at night and wait for one to stop, hoping he'd come home."

"What did he say?" Vic put down his fork and sat up.

"Well, he said he wasn't good for anyone then, that we were better off without him. That he just brought misery to Mom's life, and it made him feel worse being around her, knowing he was ruining her life. Then he . . . sort of . . . apologized. Said he never meant to hurt us." Josie didn't mention how Tony kept glancing out the side window as he talked, unable to make eye contact, even when they stopped in the parking lot.

"That's pretty much the kind of thing I heard from him—except for the sort-of-apology," Vic said.

Sitting still now, Josie asked, "Did he ever tell you that he sent money now and then, but Mom would forward it to his sister and her five kids living in Rochester?"

Vic shook his head. "No, don't ever remember anything about a sister with kids. So that means we have an aunt and cousins?"

"And . . . did you know that after *his* mom died, Mom and Dad got back together for a while? This was about a year before I was born. Tony said he tried to make it work, but, eventually, things fell apart. He was probably drinking and screwing around again. Anyway, when he left, he said he didn't know she was pregnant. He told me this while we were waiting at the gate."

Vic had picked up his fork again, but held it in mid-air as he asked, "You walked him to the gate? You parked at LAX and actually walked him in?" His incredulous grin bordered on a smirk. "You didn't just dump him off—I mean drop him off?"

Josie lifted her chin and set her shoulders back. "Well, he seemed so fragile after El Centro that I felt I had to walk him in. I mean it's LAX—a crazy, crowded mess. He'd never find his way. I'm a nurse, for cryin' out loud. I had to make sure he got on the plane okay."

"All right, all right," Vic said, raising his hands in surrender. "Sorry, I couldn't resist. So, you were at the gate, and he said . . ."

"Well," Josie continued, "he was just about to board when he turned to me, out of the blue, and said, 'I didn't know your mother was pregnant when I left. I took off for Florida and came back about a year and a half later—after you were born—so I thought . . . maybe . . . you weren't mine.'"

Josie paused, listening to herself imitate Tony's voice. He'd been defensive, but at the same time desperate to explain himself. She continued. "He went on to say that a part of him suspected I was his daughter, but he led Mom to think he wasn't sure, and that really put up a wall between them—can you imagine? Mom must have been out of her mind with frustration. Then, when he left for good, he said he convinced himself she'd been with someone else because it made it easier." Josie rubbed her temples. "Easier for him, of course."

"That's for sure," Vic agreed.

"But you know what I keep wondering? If Mom knew she was pregnant before Tony left for Florida, did she keep it from him, fearing how he'd react? Did she think it might drive him away? Or did she worry he'd stay out of guilt?" Josie had been thinking about this since Tony left. It felt good talking about it with Vic.

"There's so much about Mom we'll never know," Vic said.

"I know," Josie said, "but I'll bet if I'd been able to talk to Mom about Paul and *my* pregnancy, she might have shared that part of her life with me. She certainly would have understood my predicament. God, I wish I'd talked to her then. If only I'd told her!"

Vic reached across and squeezed her arm. They sat in silence for a while, then, tilting his head, Vic said, "Sounds like a ceasefire was declared between you and Dad?"

Josie thought of the way Tony looked at her after a couple hugged goodbye beside them. A quick nervous look, then away. They had stood there in silence until Josie simply said, "Have a good flight," and Tony said, "Take care," and hobbled away toward the boarding gate.

"I don't know, Vic. I can't forget who he was, no matter what he is now," Josie said.

Vic raised his eyebrows. "Maybe not, but you can, on some level, forgive the past and take him on whatever terms seem acceptable now. He doesn't have to be your long-lost daddy, but he is your father. Plus, Ellie seems to have formed a relationship with him."

Josie didn't answer right away because her first thought was, *I'm not you, Vic*, but then she realized it wasn't about her. "You know what it is," she said, startled by the sudden thought. "I don't trust his motives. I feel like he wants something more from me than he wants to give. And a father should be giving, not taking."

"Maybe he needs your acceptance before he can give. Or maybe he *was* giving when he opened up about his failure as a husband and father."

Josie rested her chin in her hand, thinking of Lucas's similar words on the topic of Tony. Lucas had said, "Sounds like your father is trying to find his way back to you, but he doesn't exactly have a lot of practice. Might be doing the best he can right now." Josie hadn't responded to Lucas then beyond a scornful grunt, but she'd thought about it afterwards, and she'd most likely give Vic's words some thought, too. But not now.

"All right, Mr. Peacemaker, enough of this talk. Now tell me about Ernesto and this 'idea' that's brewing."

Vic carried his dish to the sink and refilled his coffee. Then sitting at the small island again, he began to describe the poverty and simplicity of the village, the crudely assembled house that was filled with color, children's laughter, and tears. How Irma's mother—so thankful that her son, Ernesto, had survived—would not let him out of her sight, had clung to him weeping and stroking his face, begging Ernesto to promise that he would never attempt the journey again. "Your son needs a father more than he needs the American dollars," she scolded. And then she turned to Vic, saying she did not know how he did it. She couldn't survive the loss of two children in one year. One—her precious Irma—was unbearable enough.

"The funeral was beautiful," Vic said wistfully, "made me wonder if Irma should have been buried there. Votive candles flickering, wreaths of flowers, a procession through the village to the cemetery. I carried little Juan Manuel on my shoulders in the procession." Vic's face softened and some of the harsh lines disappeared. "He was so good—wide-eyed, curious, fascinated with the lights and colors around him—poor little guy was oblivious to what it was all about."

Vic seemed lost in thought until his eyes brightened a bit and he said, "Josie, I plan to go back and see if Ernesto and I can start a business."

He sat up and began speaking excitedly about villages that were creating their own businesses in an attempt to keep their young from migrating north. "One village weaves hand-woven wool carpets. Another has built a greenhouse where they grow flowers for local markets. That's what we're thinking of doing. I've done some research and found out that there's a program at UCLA that provides technical support and training, and I read about a community of immigrants in San Diego that have helped fund a greenhouse back in their village. I want to do the same, see if I can get some funding here with Santiago's help—maybe local churches and immigrants might contribute. But I want to sell the house, take my savings, and just give it try."

As surprised and concerned as Josie was, she was also moved by his energy. Vic had come alive again. He had a plan. Though she worried about him being so far away, she couldn't deny that this might be good for him. In fact, she could already see him in a sweat-soaked T-shirt, erecting a greenhouse in a small Mexican village.

Josie smiled into his hope-filled eyes and said, "That sounds wonderful, Vic." At the same time, she wanted to ask, "Are you sure you're up for this?" but she held back. He didn't need to hear that right now. Better to give it some time. Let the reality sink in. What mattered now was forward movement—a purpose for him to keep going.

Just as quickly, the light in Vic's eyes faded as he said, "I can't stay here anymore. This house is empty now." Then, accentuating each word, he said, "They're not here."

"I understand."

"And yet, strangely, there in Irma's village, I felt somehow close to Irma and the kids—connected, even comforted."

"I can imagine. Especially being with her family and little Juan Manuel."

The sound of a neighboring lawnmower disrupted the silence that followed. Vic cleared his throat. "Some of these businesses that I spoke of, well, they're not doing that great. They end up employing mostly women, since many of the men still go north to make significant money quicker than they could in Mexico. But it's believed that these businesses often struggle because they lack effective marketing and sales skills. And that's where I want to focus and find out all I can. See if we can really make it work."

Vic's face eased into a genuine smile as he said, "Ernesto wants to call it *Las Flores de Juan Manuel*—Juan Manuel's Flowers. He sees this as his son's future. Ernesto went to town, bought a shovel, put it in the corner, and said, 'I'm ready whenever you are. I wait with my shovel. You, me, and Juan Manuel, we'll dig the foundation together.'"

Josie couldn't deny that Ernesto and Vic needed each other, and the little tyke needed them both. Maybe this *was* where Vic belonged—the next part of his journey.

That evening, when Lucas called, Josie was so excited to tell him about Vic, she almost missed his first words.

Speaking in a hushed tone, Lucas said, "I thought about you all day."

Josie's heart seemed to stop for a moment as she took in not just the words, but the sound of his voice. Warm, intimate, genuine.

She responded at first with a simple "Oh!" Then added, "How lovely . . . and I couldn't wait to tell you about my day."

A tender silence followed.

Then Lucas spoke. "Me too. Jacob came for his last load today. He's all moved into Jenny's apartment now and ready for vet school next week. I'm officially an empty nester. I'm looking at his room right now, which is too neat for words. Bed made, no clothes on the floor."

Josie knew Lucas's son was moving in with his girlfriend in Ithaca, near the university. "He's still close enough for you to see often, don't you think?" she asked.

"He'll be pretty overwhelmed with the program. It's intense," Lucas said. "But, yeah, I'm sure I'll see him now and then, especially if I'm in the area on a call." His subdued tone lifted as he asked, "So, have you heard from Vic yet? What's the latest?"

"Yes! He's home!" Josie exclaimed, telling him about Vic's current plan to move to Veracruz and start a business with Ernesto. She ended with what she really needed to talk about. "I hope Vic's well enough to take this on. I mean, he looks tired, but, at the same time, he seems energized—if that makes any sense." Josie paused, then, with a heavy heart, she added, "And he says that this house holds too many memories now. That Irma, Isa, and Miguel aren't here anymore."

"Yeah, that's how I felt about six months after Kate died. Maybe this is what Vic needs right now."

"I know. I just wish he wasn't going so far away. I feel like someone needs to keep an eye on him."

"If you consider all he's done in these past weeks, sounds like he's managing okay," Lucas said, echoing Ellie, Tony, and even Josie's own inner voice.

"I suppose," Josie said, her mind whirling with all sorts of questions—saying one out loud to herself really. "I wonder if I need a passport to go to Mexico—in case I need to get to him quickly?"

Josie was still distracted as she and Lucas finally said their good nights. She was thinking if it didn't work out for Vic—if it all fell apart—she would just insist that he come live with her back east.

Hanging up the phone, Josie suddenly remembered Lucas's first words, "I thought about you all day." Smiling, Josie lay back on her comforter, her arms crossed behind her head. A calm descended, like a flock of geese that had ventured far and finally lighted upon a placid lake to rest. She closed her eyes. A new journey was waiting for her as well. Where it led, Josie didn't know, but one thing was certain: she was ready.

But some things no one can be ready for. A few days later, Josie returned from a hike to find Vic on his knees in front of the TV.

"Oh, Christ, Josie, sit down, sit down. This is terrible, unimaginable. I still can't believe it's real."

Josie sank onto the sofa where she stayed the remainder of the morning, watching over and over again, as fully fueled jets exploded into two giant buildings, tumbling them to earth in breathtaking horror, crushing innocent lives within. The Twin Towers, the

Pentagon, a field in Pennsylvania, four hijacked jets. Vic wept openly. For more than an hour, they sat together shocked and speechless— listening, watching, until the ringing of the phone startled them both.

Vic seemed paralyzed, weighed down, Josie imagined, by the all too familiar burden of great loss, so she rose and reached for the phone.

"Josie? Is that you?" a deep voice asked, all in one breath.

"Yes. Tony? Right?" Though she knew it was him.

She heard a long exhale on the other end, then, "You watching New York?" he asked.

"Yes, it's terrible, isn't it?"

"Know anyone there?"

Josie hesitated, for it hadn't entered her mind that she might know someone on a plane or perhaps in New York that morning. And she wouldn't know until names were listed or word spread among friends and relatives. "I don't know," she answered. "Not that I know of. How about you?"

Tony responded with an awkward sound, like a nervous chuckle, then said, "No, I don't think so."

An uncomfortable silence followed.

"Well, I'm sure you called to talk to Vic. Let me get him," Josie began. But Tony cut her off with a sharp, "No."

"What?"

"I mean . . . I called . . . because . . . I was worried about *you*. I thought you might be flying somewhere or in New York. Vic mentioned you might be going back at some point." Tony hesitated, then added firmly, "I called about *you*, not Vic."

"I see," was all Josie could bring herself to say.

"So . . . I'm glad you're safe and okay."

"Thank you," she managed to reply.

"Though, of course, if Vic's there, back from Mexico, I'd like to talk to him."

"Sure," Josie said, then handed the phone to a puzzled Vic.

As Vic talked solemnly into the phone, Josie watched the replay of the building collapse and the thick, billowing dark clouds that chased terrified, ash-covered people down the street. She began to sob for all of the victims and their devastated loved ones—and for the little girl that lost a father many years ago, but this morning, he called to say he cared.

Heading South
October 2001

VIC

Within three weeks, Vic had finalized his plans, packed up his van, and was ready to leave. It would take five days to get to Veracruz, maybe more, depending on his stamina. Despite the concerns of Josie—and just about everyone else—Vic was confident that he'd be just fine. While some days he still felt like he'd been flattened by an 18-wheeler, he now had a reason to get up and get moving. The problem was, if he stopped, even briefly, he feared he'd be knocked down again. So Vic kept going—and he was on a roll. He'd successfully mobilized Santiago, Irma's cousins and their extended family, and four local churches. All were going to raise funds for his venture. He'd made contact with the head of the department at UCLA involved in start-ups in Mexico, and they were going to stay in touch as things progressed. Santiago and Rodrigo were planning to visit Veracruz in the months ahead—Rodrigo, as soon as he finished a kitchen remodel scheduled for November, and Santiago, once he felt comfortable enough to leave the new associate that he had just hired to replace Vic. So far, everything seemed to be coming together.

But Vic knew that none of this would be happening without the unwavering support of Josie. Clearly, she was concerned about him, but she'd taken all of her pent-up worries and put them into excessive planning. Josie insisted that Vic leave her with a detailed map of his intended route. He was to check in daily during his drive and once a week after arriving—even more, if possible. And Josie had renewed her passport, since travel restrictions were changing post-9/11, and she wanted to be able to reach him if needed. Vic had agreed to anything and everything that might lessen his sister's fears. Josie deserved nothing less.

The house was going on the market shortly. Santiago would oversee the details. The plan was to pack up and put everything in storage for now—a task Rodrigo and Josie insisted on doing so Vic could get on his way. If the house didn't move in due time, it would be rented to cover his mortgage. But Vic was not in the least concerned. He felt a deep-seated calm that it would all work out. Josie would stay through mid-November, deal with any final issues, and then, after a visit with Ellie in Seattle, she'd head home to Binghamton.

Vic couldn't believe Josie had spent close to a year with him. He could never thank her enough, though he had tried several times these past few weeks. Now it was time for him to say his goodbyes to Josie—and his house.

Both had risen early that morning. Vic tried to eat some of the massive breakfast that Josie had prepared, but his stomach was clamped so tight, he feared that whatever went down would just come back up. He didn't want to disappoint her on this final morning together, so he did his best, moving the food around on his plate and taking a few bites. Vic even managed to find a spot in his packed van for a box labeled "Road Food" that Josie had prepared and held forth while delivering a swift kick to Vic's shin after his "Road Kill?" comment.

Now they were standing in the living room, suddenly subdued.

"Walk with me, Josie," Vic said. At first, she seemed confused until he led her slowly down the hallway—toward the kids' bed-rooms. He stopped first in Isa's, which was now cluttered with Josie's belongings—but that's not what Vic saw as he gazed in. He still saw a Strawberry Shortcake comforter on a twin bed, with a father and daughter curled up, reading books together. He swallowed hard as he glanced tenderly at the embroidered wall-hanging of the tree and worry dolls that Irma had worked on for months.

Next, Miguel's room, now piled high with boxes. But sitting in the corner, as if leaning on each other, were Miguel's soccer ball and yellow dump truck. Vic gathered both up gently, then, returning to Isa's room, he took down the wall hanging. These would go with him to Veracruz, of course.

"You don't mind, do you?' Vic asked Josie, as he neatly smoothed out the embroidered fabric on the bed, then rolled it up, securing the stitching and worry dolls inside.

"Of course not. It should be with you—on her mother's wall."

"Exactly what I was thinking." Vic shifted the soccer ball to his hip, trying to secure it under his arm.

Josie reached out and took the wall hanging. "But let me wrap this in plastic, so it doesn't get soiled."

Vic paused at his own bedroom, already emptied. The previous week he'd invited Irma's cousins to take some of her belongings; others he had packed to bring to her mother.

With Josie following solemnly behind him, Vic walked through the kitchen. He stood at the sliding glass door, taking in the small yard with the swing set. He'd already said his goodbyes to this yard and each room—and their many memories—over these past weeks. They would always be with him.

It was in the garage that Vic began to weep.

Josie sat beside him on the bench. In her hand was a shopping bag with the truck, soccer ball, and carefully wrapped wall hanging. She was still wearing her green plaid flannel pajamas.

"I was thinking," Vic began, struggling to speak, "of giving all this to Rodrigo."

He motioned to the exercise equipment. "But . . . if it's a family . . . if a young family moves in—and they want it—I'd like to leave it for them. You know?"

Josie nodded. "I'll tell Rodrigo and Santiago."

"Good," Vic said, then stood and took one last look around. "Well . . ."

They walked arm in arm through the living room to the front door. "Don't worry," Josie said. "We'll take care of everything."

"I know you will. I'm not worried. And I know you'll be fine, too." Vic turned, and grasping both of her arms, looked into her dark, wet eyes. "I've never worried about you, Jo," he said. "You've taken care of yourself since you were a kid—and me and Mom, and Ben and Ellie. Hell, one of these days you have to let someone take care of you for a while."

Her lower lip trembled and a few tears dripped down her cheeks. Josie wiped them away with her flannel sleeve and gave him a weak smile. Then handing him the shopping bag, she reached up and squeezed his face tightly between both hands, saying, "I'm sure gonna miss seeing this ugly mug every day!" With that, Vic tilted back his head and let out a laugh so full it released even that tightness in his stomach.

As he drove away, Vic forced himself not to look back. Ten minutes later, a block before the freeway entrance, he pulled the van over, opened the back, and reached for the Road Food box. Suddenly, he was starving.

Blue Flags

October 2001

JOSIE

J osie wept inconsolably that morning. Missing Vic. Worrying. Draining herself of all the heartbreak that this house—this year— had held. Then she remembered Vic's comment. "I've never worried about you, Jo. You've taken care of yourself since you were a kid." Josie had always seen herself as leaning on Vic, but perhaps those were the memories and muddled emotions of a little girl, and she had been standing on her own all along.

Vic's house felt empty now. Josie sensed it as soon as he drove away and she wandered aimlessly from the living room, to the kitchen, to the bedroom. He wasn't just gone for a few weeks—he wouldn't be coming back—leaving Josie all the more anxious to return home.

Fortunately for Josie—though not for her friend Amir—her house would be vacant mid-November. Amir had called a few weeks after 9/11 to say his wife had moved back home—to Syria—and he would be joining her in six weeks. They just wanted to be with their family. At the time, Amir offered to pay through December, but Josie reassured him that it wasn't necessary, for she'd hoped to be heading home herself by year's end.

Now, Josie actually was. Once Vic's house was packed and

cleaned—maybe even sold—she would visit Ellie in Seattle and then—home sweet home.

It wasn't until later in the afternoon that Josie felt strong enough to call Ellie without breaking down—she hoped. They'd begun twice a week phone calls since 9/11. The need to stay connected and say the things that should be said rose to the surface in Josie's mind when the dust settled on that immense tragedy.

"So, Uncle Vic got off okay?" Ellie asked immediately.

Josie told her about the heartbreaking walk through the house, but to keep them both from crying, Josie ended on a high note. "Oh, Ellie, right before Vic left, I told him how much I was going to miss seeing his ugly mug, and he let out that laugh of his—that boomerang laugh." Josie paused, hearing it again as if it were still bouncing off the walls. "I swear, if I hadn't heard that, I wouldn't have let him go."

"Mom, don't worry. He'll be okay."

"He better be, or I'll be down there faster than Maggie can catch a lizard."

They both laughed, and Ellie filled Josie in on Maggie's latest cute trick: balancing a treat on her nose until she was given permission to eat it. The signal was "Yum!"

Josie could hear the jangling of Maggie's collar and tags, meaning she was probably at Ellie's feet.

"Mom, I wish I could go with you this weekend. If we didn't have this amazing opportunity at the recording studio to cut a demo of a few of our songs, I'd be on a plane," Ellie said, referring to Josie's plans to join the Water Stations Project in the desert that Saturday.

"Oh honey, don't worry. I prefer our plan for November—Day of the Dead—like we promised Vic," Josie said. "We'll decorate their graves for him. If I wasn't running out of time, I'd wait for another month to join Water Stations, but I really want to take part in a water drop and see a blue flag up close."

"I know. I can't wait to hear about it."

"And I can't wait to hear your recorded songs! Sounds like things are coming together with your new band. Have you settled on a name yet?"

"No! I swear it's as difficult as naming a baby. We're pinning it down by Friday."

Just talking to Ellie had eased Josie's heartache. She felt energized now and ready to take on her milelong to-do list. "I can't wait to see you here in November," Josie said, "and then in Seattle before I head back east. How's my Maggie? I miss her so much, especially when I'm hiking. Is she adjusting to her new home?"

"Maggie's good," Ellie said. "She loves it here. Has her favorite spot under the tree in the front yard. No attempts to escape like huskies often do. Neighbors all know her, even call her by name as they pass. And we've met so many people just because of Maggie. No complaints yet about her occasional howling at night."

Josie smiled. "You sound great, honey. I miss you." It was easy to say those words now.

"I miss you too, Mom." Josie knew Ellie didn't miss her in the same way, but her voice was rich and warm.

"Oh, you know what?" Ellie asked. "I found out that one of my friends had an aunt on the plane that hit the Pentagon. Can you imagine? It's all so awful. I can't stop thinking about it, you know?"

"I know, I feel the same way."

"I want to do something, but I don't know what," Ellie said.

Josie and Vic had had that same conversation—wanting to do something in the aftermath of that unforgettable day.

Josie eased down onto the sofa, looking out toward Vic's yard—now a deep green. In the far corner, the lemon tree she'd planted months ago looked promising and the new fall annuals were starting to open. The purple primrose caught her eye.

"You know what I've been thinking? We each need to erect our own blue flag," Josie said. "But in our own way. Like when you cut your hair for Loving Locks. Or say you write a song—maybe about 9/11 or something else that comes from your heart. And Vic and Ernesto build a greenhouse. You see? Our own individual blue flag."

Josie thought of the brochure for Doctors Without Borders that she'd seen at a conference at UCLA. Maybe she could do something like that—spend a month or two somewhere, using her nursing skills where they might be needed.

"I like that, Mom. You're right. Our own blue flag. Actually, I've been working on a song about . . ." Suddenly Ellie stopped, and Josie could hear voices in the background. Someone called Ellie's name.

"Well, I'll let you go, honey," Josie said, already planning another trip to the nursery for more flowers—to plant in front for curb appeal.

"Yeah, a couple friends just came over. Let me know when you hear from Uncle Vic."

"I will."

"And Mom?" Ellie paused. "I love you—and Maggie sends tons of licks all over your face."

The tears came again after Josie hung up the phone—except these left her heart feeling light and hopeful.

That Saturday, Josie met the bus downtown at Our Lady Queen of Angels, a historic church known as *La Placita*. From there, she rode from LA to San Diego in the company of a diverse group of humble folks—about a dozen college students, four middle-aged women wearing matching blue T-shirts, a few senior citizens, and a number of Spanish-speaking church members. Once they arrived at a church parking lot in San Diego, they joined local volunteers and together loaded pick-ups and SUVs with jugs of water and canned goods. Since Josie was a first-timer, she was directed to a specific group. Only experienced members would head to more treacherous areas that involved boulders and narrow canyon passes.

About an hour later, Josie emerged from a van, hoisted a pack with supplies onto her back, and grabbed two jugs of water, as instructed by a young man about Ellie's age. "One for each hand—helps with balance," he said. Two men took the lead, as the rest of the group followed in single file. Josie glanced back to see the young man at the very end. There were nine of them total. Four women, five men.

Josie had imagined a desert landscape with towering saguaros, but on this particular trail, there was nothing but sand and brush as far as the eye could see. She'd been advised to wear pants and hiking boots—not shorts, which would leave her legs exposed to bugs, snakes, and sharp, spiky plants. Josie kept her eyes on her boots as she walked along, kicking up dust of decomposed granite and sand, stumbling over small rocks, and skirting the brittle brush that dotted the landscape. They were told to watch for snakes and scorpions, but the greatest danger was clearly the burning sun that kept sweat running down her back. And yet, Josie thought, this was October, with a high today of 90 degrees—not August and 109 degrees, when Ernesto and Claudia had struggled along, confused and alone.

Finally, in the distance, Josie saw it—her first blue flag. Would she have noticed if the leaders hadn't pointed it out? The thin pole was invisible at such a distance, and the tattered flag a mere shadow against the sky. But as they got closer, the blue flag materialized in all its battered glory. The thin white pole and the fraying, flapping canvas, as a hot wind brought it suddenly to life.

The group gathered around two large cardboard boxes at its base. The young man removed empty items, placing them in a large black trash bag that he would carry back to the van. Everyone took turns placing their jugs of water into the boxes. Josie wondered whose hands would touch hers, as she sent out a silent prayer to those hopeful travelers, wherever they were. Large stones were then placed on top of each box.

The group stood back in silence.

The blue flag towered above Josie, at least twenty feet or more. In her hand, she held half of a Mexican bus ticket that the young man found inside the box beside empty jugs. He'd handed it to her with a gentle smile. Printed in large letters was the word *"Gracias."* Josie's heart ached for Ernesto and Claudia—whose story could have ended so differently—but, at the same time, there was something about that simple "thank you" that stirred in Josie an overwhelming sense of gratitude.

A sudden gust of swirling sand forced Josie's eyes shut, and she could hear the rustling of the blue flag above. As the warm wind and sand tickled her cheeks, she felt Maggie's licks all over her face and Ellie's fierce hug just before she left for Seattle. She heard Tony's voice say, "I was worried. I called about *you*," and Lucas's words, "I thought about you all day." And echoing throughout that god-forsaken desert, Vic's boomerang laugh filled her ears. How deeply fortunate she was. To love and be loved. To be healthy and safe. To be alive.

After a long, grueling, yet rewarding day, Josie finally made it home, took a quick shower, and dove into bed. Lucas had said to call even if it was 3 a.m. his time. He was a restless sleeper most nights and curious to hear about her experience. Utterly exhausted, Josie just wanted to go to sleep, but she put the call through anyway—an act she would later regret.

It happened at the end of their conversation. Between yawns and her own sleepily slurred words, Josie had told him about her unforgettable day and then about her phone message from Vic, who had arrived safely at his destination. Lucas sounded equally drowsy but his voice was warm.

As she and Lucas said their goodnights, Josie said, "Yep, I'll be home before you know it. Just a matter of weeks."

Lucas responded quickly. "I'd be happy to pick you up at the airport."

Josie hesitated.

She didn't respond with "That'd be great," or "I'd like that," or "That would be wonderful!" She hesitated—confused by her uncertainty and thinking that maybe it'd be better to get settled back home first, before they met up in person, face to face.

After an extended silence, Josie said, "Uh . . . well . . . maybe . . . I'll think about it." She tried to sound upbeat, but her voice was shaky and high-pitched.

No response from Lucas. Dead quiet.

"So . . . goodnight. Talk to you tomorrow?" Josie held her breath and listened.

On the other end, she thought she heard a "Yeah" or some other one-syllable, murmured sound before the line went dead.

Exhausted as she was, Josie lay in her bed, saucer-eyed, heart pounding—wondering what she had just done.

So Close

Ellie's Songbook: October 2001

So Close
Words and Music by Eleanor Serafini
*Open with piano.

Verse 1
From Chihuahua, black bears swim
the Rio Grande on a whim
Coral snakes from Sonora
ease their way to Arizona.
Crested Caracaras, Spotted Owls
glide over the border at all hours

Chorus
On both sides of the border
city lights are just as bright.
Las luces de la ciudad
glow the same at night
Tijuana, San Diego,
Mexicali, Calexico
Arizona, California, Texas,
and Mexico
So close

Verse 2
So young, in love, with an infant son
Their life together has just begun
In their village, they keep trying
But work is scarce, farms are dying
They make a choice to head north together
Work hard, save money, for a life that's better

Chorus
On both sides of the border
city lights are just as bright
Las luces de la ciudad
glow the same at night
Tijuana, San Diego,
Mexicali, Calexico
Arizona, California, Texas,
and Mexico
So close

Verse 3
Their searing thirst, the scorching heat
the bleeding blisters on their feet
A swarm of velvet ants crawls
He reaches for her hand and calls
Hurry! Hide! Dive for cover
—the whirling iron bird hovers
Stay close

Chorus
On both sides of the border
city lights are just as bright
Las luces de la ciudad

glow the same at night
Tijuana, San Diego
Mexicali, Calexico
Arizona, California, Texas
and Mexico
So close

Verse 4
From a rugged ridge, they see below
just a few more merciless miles to go.
Despite his pleas, she begs, "No more!"
then lies down on the desert floor
He runs for help to save their fate
Despite his hope, it's too late

Bridge:
On both sides of the border, there's darkness and there's light
There has to be an answer, none of this is right
We must find common ground, where all can stand together
Hand in hand, across our lands, with open hearts unfettered

Chorus
On both sides of the border
city lights are just as bright
Las luces de la ciudad
glow the same at night
Tijuana, San Diego
Mexicali, Calexico
Arizona, California, Texas
and Mexico
So close, so close

Amazing Grace

November 2001

JOSIE

Once again, Josie found herself in the Applebee's restaurant in El Centro, but instead of sitting across from Tony, she was facing a man named Jim that she had met the previous month while volunteering with Water Stations Project. Same booth, same seating as with Tony months before, so Josie assumed that was why she felt uncomfortable. It was Jim who had told her about the group's *Día de los Muertos* celebration at the cemetery in Holtville in November. When Josie mentioned it to Ellie, they decided to do both. November 1st in Holtville with Water Stations Project and November 2nd in LA to decorate the graves of Irma and the kids—as they'd promised Vic.

Ellie had flown in the afternoon before, and the two of them had set out at dawn in a rental car that smelled of Armor All. The plan was to meet the group at Applebee's for breakfast at ten, then head out to Terrace Park Cemetery for the noon ceremony. When they arrived, Jim had signaled them to his booth. It wasn't until she sat down that Josie realized it was the déjà vu scene with Tony. Only this discomfort felt different. Something in the way Jim was looking at her—the warmth in his eyes when he smiled—made her feel very ill at ease. Josie hoped he hadn't gotten the wrong idea. He'd given her his number in case she wanted to join them, and she'd called him only to verify the details of the ceremony. Did he think her call meant otherwise?

After introducing him to Ellie, who reached across the table and gave him a hearty handshake, they opened their menus and sat in silence until Jim set his down and asked Josie, "So, what's new?"

She ended up talking, rather rapidly she realized, about Vic and his plans in Veracruz.

"Your brother sounds like a great guy," Jim said, adjusting his San Diego Padres cap, "and what he's doing now, well, that's truly admirable. Unfortunately, it won't put a dent in this problem. Three hundred and eighty-four migrants died while crossing last year, and with factories moving overseas and small farms in Mexico failing, well, they're going to keep coming. As a result, we can expect an average of a death a day in the coming year."

Josie frowned at the heartbreaking statistic. A death a day! She had talked about this with Santiago and was surprised to hear that little was being done to help those dying in the desert. In fact, she'd discovered that most people were more concerned with the large influx of undocumented immigrants, not the migrant deaths. The whole thing was so confusing to her, but all she could see was Ernesto, clutching his wife's backpack and howling.

"A death a day?" Josie repeated the words. "And with our fear of terrorists now, the crackdown at the borders will probably be worse, won't it?"

"It certainly stalls any progress in human rights at the border." Then Jim turned to Ellie and said, "At least there are good folks like you. It was sure kind of you to join your mom today. She told me about the couple that tried to cross—the wife that died."

Ellie sat up. "Yes, it was heartbreaking. I never knew any of this until we came down here with my uncle. Actually, I'm working on a song about them . . . about Ernesto and Claudia. I've got most of the lyrics, but I'm struggling with the melody. I want it to have just the right feel. I'm calling it 'So Close,' and I'm trying to tie in both how close they were to making it and how physically close the US and Mexico are. I thought maybe this trip would help."

Josie smiled with pride at her daughter who today looked like a grown-up version of ten-year-old Ellie. Her chin-length hair was covered with a red bandana, tied at the back of her neck, and she was wearing a denim jacket and black jeans—dressed almost like she did when she was getting ready for a trail ride all those years ago.

"Maybe we'll hear one of your songs on the radio someday," Jim said. "I have a daughter just graduated from UA—Arizona. She's determined to be an FBI agent." Then looking directly at Josie, he added, "You women today are something else."

Ellie gently elbowed Josie. When Josie glanced at her daughter, Ellie quickly raised her eyebrows, then turned back to Jim.

"Do you have any other kids?" Ellie asked, a polite tone to her voice.

"My younger daughter lives with her mother in San Diego. But my son . . ." Jim chuckled sarcastically and said, "he's with me in La Mesa, and he's quite a handful. Sixteen going on twelve, if you know what I mean."

"Wow, three kids. That's not easy nowadays," Josie said. As he started to respond, someone called his name, and Jim excused himself to talk with a group seated at another table.

Josie was about to ask Ellie why she had nudged her. Had she noticed something about Jim, too? But Ellie suddenly turned to her and asked, "Mom, how come you never had more kids?"

Josie hesitated for a moment. That had been an issue for Ben since he'd had a vasectomy when his first wife was forced to go off birth control pills and they decided not to have children. Ben's ambitions as a struggling cardiologist were in tune with his wife's wishes not to be a mother. Yet once Ben fell in love with Josie, he was concerned because she was so young. Before they married, Ben explained the possibility of reversing the procedure. The truth was, Josie didn't mind. Ellie was her focus at the time, and later, Josie was intent on returning to college.

Looking at Ellie now, Josie said, "You were enough. You and Ben. I was content with the three of us—and then the horses. I was happy."

"You were, Mom, weren't you?" Ellie frowned, then said, "I'm sorry I made things so difficult when Dad was sick."

"Oh honey, don't worry about that. You had your own problems back then, and I should have been there for you more. It was a tough time for both of us."

Jim had returned and sat back down, smiling into Josie's eyes. She blushed but was relieved when Ellie spoke to him, forcing him to take his eyes off Josie again.

"I was a real pain in the ass when I was sixteen," Ellie said. "Man, I could give your son lessons."

Jim laughed, tipping his head back and adjusting his cap again. "Well, if he grows out of it and ends up like you, I feel better already." He winked at Ellie, then turned his twinkling eyes back to Josie, who quickly looked away.

Josie was relieved to leave the restaurant and board the bus with other group members. She and Ellie sat near the back, and soon she lost sight of the San Diego Padres cap. Once they arrived at the entrance to the cemetery, their group joined another fifty or more.

Josie was struck by the diverse faces, young and old. She noticed a young man wearing a turban and two women with colorful head-coverings—an interfaith gathering, she had been told. Many were carrying traditional *Día de los Muertos* decorations: colorful, decorative paper called *papel picado*, candy skulls, and marigolds. Josie and Ellie each carried bags of clipped orange marigolds that Josie had brought at Vic's suggestion.

A priest led the group in prayer in both English and Spanish, speaking of the anguished families who would never know of their loved one's passing and of the many who had been buried without being mourned. Then he walked amongst the crowd, blessing their decorations and reminding everyone why they were there.

"In the Mexican tradition, there are three deaths," he said. "The first is when we draw our last breath. The second death is when we are buried. But the third death—the most final of all—is the day we are forgotten. So, we are gathered here today to remember the souls buried in the back of this cemetery. They will not be forgotten."

Slowly they walked to the barren field in the rear of the cemetery where just a couple of months before Josie had stood with Vic. A young woman was speaking to the group as they arrived. "Approximately 175 unidentified migrants are buried here," she concluded, then pointed at three freshly dug graves.

People began decorating the brick markers, as a few sang traditional Mexican songs of *despedida*—farewell.

Ellie and Josie knelt at their first chosen site. Josie placed three marigolds on a brick marker that read "Row 10-24, Jane Doe." Sitting back on her heels, Josie tried to think of a prayer or something special to say. As she searched for just the right words, Ellie began to sing "Amazing Grace."

Her voice began low and timid, but then Ellie closed her eyes and lifted her face to the sky. In a moving crescendo, her voice rose in tender mourning, as first one person, and then another, joined in, singing with a mix of heartfelt joy and sadness.

A little girl with large brown eyes knelt beside Ellie and watched intently while Ellie sang. Her tiny hands placed a candy skull and a piece of the punctured paper in front of the trio of marigolds.

"Everything means something," Jim said, as he approached and squatted beside Josie. "The marigolds and the *papel picado* remind us that life is fragile . . . and ephemeral."

"What's that mean?" Ellie asked, as the little girl's eyes followed Ellie's words to Jim's reply.

"Ephemeral? Means . . . fleeting. Short-lived. Brief," he replied.

And suddenly Josie saw Ben's face, so vivid and clear. How it softened when he would look at her with a boyish shyness. How completely happy he'd been with her. "I can just be myself when I'm with you," he would say—something he'd never felt with his first wife.

If we'd only had more time, Josie thought. *If only we'd made it to now, with Ellie on her own, with time to focus on each other.*

Wiping a tear, Josie offered the little girl a few marigolds in exchange for some papers and sugar skulls. These she placed gently in her empty bag, for tomorrow—for Irma, Isa, and Miguel. And she'd take one home—for Ben.

As she gazed across the sea of faces lovingly tending each grave, Josie thought of the family members in New York City waiting for word of their loved ones, hoping remains would be found to bury, to honor, to put to rest. For them as well, Josie placed one more trio of marigolds, between markers, humming softly to herself "Amazing Grace."

It was on the drive home, later that afternoon, that Ellie finally commented on Jim's attentiveness.

"That old dude had eyes on you, Mom!" Ellie had her bare feet up on the dashboard and her seat tilted partway back.

Josie laughed at her daughter's blunt words. "He made me so uncomfortable," Josie said with a visible cringe. "I guess when I asked him tons of questions that weekend in October—questions about Water Stations, not him—and then called him to ask about today, well, he might have gotten the wrong idea."

"And he may not have been so happy to see *me* this morning," Ellie said, nudging her mother's arm again. "Wanted you all to himself!"

Josie glanced at her daughter and with a half-laugh said, "I feel like a teenager again, making a mad dash to leave without thanking him or saying goodbye. I just wanted to get away!"

Ellie took a long swig from her water bottle. "He was a little creepy. I'm sure he was bald under that cap the way he kept pressing it down for fear it'd slip back or something," she said, quickly adding, "I know. I know. You're gonna say he's probably a very nice man."

"I'm sure he is—but I wasn't going to say it."

Josie heard Ellie chuckle.

"But seriously, Mom, you should consider dating again." Ellie stretched her legs until they almost touched the windshield. "You're still young enough. How old was Dad when he met you? Close to your age now, right?"

"Point taken."

"There's on-line dating sites, you know, for people your age, where you can try to connect with someone with similar interests. Or you could go on a cruise, maybe find some romance." Ellie lingered on the word 'romance' and elbowed her again.

Josie gave her a sly smile.

Then, after a moment of silence, Josie said, "Actually . . ."

Ellie snapped upright, bringing her feet down onto the car mat.

"What? *Actually* what? Who?" She leaned forward, trying to see Josie's flushed face. "Mom! Tell me! Are you dating someone? Did you meet someone in LA?"

Josie cast her eyes to the heavens and shook her head. "Not LA and not exactly dating, but . . ."

"Well?"

Josie bit her lip. She knew talking about it with Ellie would change everything. Make it more real. It was one thing to talk with Rae—hear her own thoughts take form while getting her friend's perspective. But Rae wasn't a part of Josie's past life—with Ben. That's why she hadn't discussed it with Vic either.

To speak of Lucas to Vic or Ellie was like saying it in front of Ben.

Hesitantly, Josie began to tell Ellie a little about Lucas, some of their conversations and emails, about their growing friendship that might be on the border of something more. Unlike Rae's frequent question about Lucas's responses, Ellie repeatedly asked, "So then, what did *you* say?" Clearly, Ellie was trying to get to the heart of her mother's feelings—something Josie wasn't so certain of herself.

Finally, Josie told Ellie what she'd said—or more to the point, *not said*—when Lucas had offered to pick her up at the airport, and how, even though they still called each other and talked about their day, it wasn't the same. Their conversations now lacked that spark. She didn't add that neither had brought up the topic of airport pickup again.

When Josie finished talking, Ellie remained silent. Josie wondered if, perhaps, she'd said too much, but then Ellie began to speak, shifting to a deeper tone that left Josie stunned by the realization—it was the voice of a woman.

"Well, Mom, you said you don't remember what Lucas looks like exactly, 'just a vague memory' you said. Not that looks are necessarily that important, but there has to be some kind of physical attraction—some kind of connection when you're actually together—or else the relationship just stays as friends."

Ellie turned toward her and, touching her mother's arm, said with great tenderness, "Maybe you're worried you won't *feel* that connection? Or maybe *he* won't? And when that happens, the friendship is never the same. I know that one well."

Josie was speechless. Not only did Ellie understand, but she helped Josie see exactly what was at the heart of this. *Of course* she was afraid of losing this new friendship, and she was equally uncertain what she wanted it to be. It was safer at a distance—less confusing.

That's when their conversation shifted to Ellie's relationships: one heartbreak last fall; one guy friend who wanted more, so their friendship had ended; and currently, a possible budding romance with one of the band members, Ian, who played keyboard.

The way Ellie said his name, Josie knew this one was important.

As they pulled to a stop in the driveway of Vic's house and Josie turned off the engine, Ellie said, "I hope it works out with Lucas, Mom. But if it doesn't, there will be someone, when you're ready. Dad would want you to be happy. I know he would."

Josie's heart fluttered. In the darkness of the rental car, they squeezed hands.

The next day, as requested by Vic, Josie and Ellie brought their decorations to Oak Park Cemetery in Chatsworth, under the magnificent Simi Hills boulders that Josie loved so much. They spread a blanket over the resting place of Irma, Isabel, and Miguel, its earth now settled and covered in rich green grass. Each knelt before the large bronze marker, embedded in the ground, with "Serafini" across the top, then Vic and Irma's names below. Josie flinched at the sight of Vic's name with a blank space beside his birth year. On each side of the marker, etched angels floated above "Isabel" on the left and "Miguel" on the right.

Josie wiped the marker tenderly with a paper towel and pulled a few weeds; then, in silence, she and Ellie arranged the marigolds, colored paper, and candy skulls beneath the marker. Ellie began singing, "You are my sunshine, my only sunshine . . ." but she broke down before she finished, "please don't take my sunshine away."

Ellie was wearing a pink Strawberry Shortcake T-shirt that she bought especially for this day—for Isa. Looking at her daughter, Josie no longer saw Ellie as her little girl. She was not a dependent branch from Josie's tree anymore. Ellie was her own strong trunk, ready to spread unique branches into the sky. Josie knew they would always be bound by their intertwining roots—just like the two maple trees beside their house back home. The thought of this image brought a smile to Josie's lips as she reached up and wiped a tear dripping down her daughter's face. Instead of pulling away, like she might have the year before, Ellie had simply smiled. Then they each sat back, Josie cross-legged, Ellie hugging her knees, as they took in the multitude of colors that now brightened the cemetery.

Several families had come to celebrate *Día de los Muertos*. Children were laughing and chasing each other. Adults—some on lawn chairs, others seated on the grass—were gesturing and talking, a few even eating from a feast set out on blankets before them. What a beautiful tradition, Josie thought, truly a celebration of love and remembrance, not a ritual of mourning. No wonder Vic had asked them to do this. She would tell him every detail when he called.

They sat in silence for a while, then gathering up their belongings, each gently touched the marker and headed back to Vic's. Ellie was flying home early the next morning, anxious to get back to Maggie—and probably Ian, too, Josie thought. And Josie was finishing up last-minute details for Vic before she headed to Seattle for a short visit and then back to her own home—and whatever her life would be. Like Vic, Josie had a few ideas brewing that left her feeling an excitement she hadn't felt in a very long time.

A few weeks later, Josie sat on Ellie's soft futon in Seattle with Maggie's nose buried in her lap. The rain poured down at a steady rate, precluding any outdoor activities, but it was soothing nonetheless to someone as content as Josie.

Everything had been settled for Vic—his belongings safely in storage, his house potentially sold—and Josie was on her way home. After six days in Seattle, with four young women, loud live music, and the endless drone of the TV or stereo, Josie was ready to head to an empty, quiet house.

Today, however, was an anomaly. With all four girls gone—Ellie out on some mysterious mission—Josie and Maggie had the house to themselves for a while. Josie had nestled in with a cup of Seattle's best brew and the morning paper, but so far, all she'd done was stare out at the rain and revel in the silence.

Josie was thrilled to see the home the girls had made. Expecting clutter and chaos, she was immediately humbled. In just a few months, they had created a lovely home. On the walls, a Dave Matthews poster, of course, but also some original earth-toned landscape paintings done by one of the roommates. In the living room, a beige futon, three large, colorful floor pillows, and a selection of scented candles placed on high shelves, well out of reach of Maggie's ever-wagging tail. The décor invited a sense of calm and reflection when there weren't four girls chattering, singing, or playing the myriad instruments along the far wall—three guitars, Ellie's handmade conga and flute, a box-like drum called a cajón that Josie tried out one night when the band got together, and an electric keyboard sitting on top of an ironing board. All of it made her smile.

But what Josie loved the most—what had caught her eye the minute she entered their house—was the centerpiece on their rustic dining table. It was hypnotizing. A mass of vibrant, multi-colored tubes of glass, twisting and branching in a Medusa-like display, an original work of art made by their next-door neighbors and given as a house-warming gift for the girls. Wherever you sat, in either room, it was like gazing into a blazing fireplace in the midst of a rustic cabin. You couldn't take your eyes off the swirling colors that captured the incoming light.

Perhaps that explained this artwork's success in Seattle. Despite the rain and overcast skies, such glass art sculptures brought color and light into any room. *Kind of like Ellie,* Josie thought.

Picturing Ellie within these walls made it easier for Josie to leave. There was order and serenity in the physical surroundings that balanced the bounding energy of their music and youth. And there was also the fact that Ellie was in love with a very nice young man. Josie had met Ian, a talented musician himself, who taught piano and guitar at a local studio. He was humble and kind and had treated Josie with the utmost respect. Taller than Ellie (even in her thickest-soled shoes), Ian was rail thin, despite a voracious appetite. He wore his brown hair short, often topped with a black beanie, which seemed to be the style. When Ellie walked into the room, Ian's dark brown eyes lit up as bright as the glass centerpiece.

Tomorrow they were planning a week-early Thanksgiving dinner, since Josie was leaving on Friday. Despite Ellie's vegetarian lifestyle, Josie was going to show Ellie how to make turkey with sausage dressing, something she had imagined doing several times over the years, and now that Ian was drooling at the prospect, Josie was overjoyed. Life was certainly ephemeral, but Josie intended to savor each moment before it passed.

Maggie's startled jerk to attention, followed by the sound of footsteps at the front door, disrupted the peace of the rain-soaked afternoon. Ellie burst in, her long, olive-green, over-sized raincoat dripping as she passed quickly by, hunched over and carrying a bundle into the kitchen.

"Hi, Mom, just a sec," she said, Maggie at her heels. "Stay there," she called over her shoulder to her mother.

Puzzled, Josie sat on the edge of the futon and strained to hear what Ellie might be doing. She heard her scold Maggie to stay down, then the beep of the phone pad as Ellie placed a call, followed by muffled sounds as she stepped into the pantry off the kitchen.

Suddenly, in a whirl of excitement, Ellie was back in the living room, handing her the phone, and saying, "Say hi. I'll be right back."

"Hello?" Josie said into the phone.

"Hey, Jo-Jo, how's Seattle? Have you tackled every mountain peak yet?" Vic's voice was vibrant and warm.

"Vic! What a surprise. What's going on? Why is Ellie acting so strange?"

"Oh, you'll find out in a minute. You see, I had to be a witness to this. So, tell me, did you conquer any mountain ranges?"

"More like the mud conquered me, but the view from Hurricane Ridge was worth the struggle. Witness to what?" Just as Josie finished asking, Ellie walked in carrying in her arms a tiny Siberian husky puppy. She held its wiggling body out to Josie.

"Here Mom, she's all yours. Isn't she adorable?"

"Oh my god, she's precious!" Josie squealed, dropping the phone as she took the pup into her arms.

"Look at those markings. Maggie, what do you think?"

Maggie had nosed her way back to Josie's lap, sniffing the puppy curiously. Ellie held the retrieved phone so Vic could hear her response.

"I love her!" Josie shouted, then grabbed the phone back. "Oh Vic, you should see her. She's beautiful."

Ellie knelt, one arm hooked around Maggie and her other hand stroking the puppy. "Oh Mom, I looked at three litters, all over the city. I wanted a female who looked sort of like Maggie—or who had her own unique style. And she's it, definitely."

"Aren't they expensive?" Josie asked, knowing husky puppies could cost around five hundred dollars because she'd done some research after Maggie left.

"There are tons of them here, husky rescues, so just two-fifty. She's had her initial shots and all. Uncle Vic paid for her. Thank him."

"Oh Vic, thank you! But that's money that I'm sure you can use," Josie said, clutching the phone.

"Listen. We both know I owe you my life, truly. I can't do enough to thank you, Jo. I only hope this little mutt brings you half as much happiness as Maggie did."

Josie wished he was there so she could hug him. "Oh Vic, I didn't do anything that you wouldn't have done. So, what's the latest there?" He sounded upbeat, but Josie worried he might be hiding any difficulties.

"Well, I visited a village in Oaxaca where a small group started a greenhouse about a year ago. I wanted to learn from any mistakes, too, so I focused on weaknesses, as well as their success. Learned a lot. And oh, yeah . . . Rodrigo will be arriving the end of the month!"

Before he comes, he's gonna visit a friend who manages a nursery in Carpinteria. See what he can pick up from him."

Then Vic's voice softened as he spoke of Irma's family. "Ernesto's doing okay, considering. I still hear his stifled weeping at night, but during the day, he keeps it together and does the best he can. And the little one—Juan Manuel—Irma's mother keeps saying that Juanito will end up bow-legged like a *vaquero*, a cowboy, since he rides on my shoulders most of his waking hours." Vic's laugh was light and genuine.

Josie sighed with relief. Vic was always the first thing on her mind when she woke at 2 a.m. and couldn't get back to sleep.

"Well, I have to say, this is going to be the happiest Thanksgiving I can remember in a very long time," Josie said, as she squeezed Ellie's chin with her free hand. "Thank you, both of you. This is a wonderful surprise."

Josie couldn't help but wonder how she would manage a puppy on a cross-country flight, not to mention once she got her home, but she figured, with so much up in the air, why not add a mischievous husky puppy into the mix?

The puppy nestled deeper into Josie's lap, its little heart beating rapidly against her stomach. The rain came down steadily outside. Stroking the puppy, Josie suddenly felt an overwhelming sense of déjà vu. Just like that ice-cold morning sitting in her car outside the Women's Clinic years ago, Josie realized she wouldn't be returning to an empty house alone. She'd be taking another "foxy lady" with her.

"That's it! Foxy Lady!" Josie shouted into the phone. "That's her name. But we can call her Foxy or Lady for short, whichever feels natural."

Ellie beamed, and across the miles, Josie heard Vic say with his characteristic flair, "Foxy Lady!"

Dad's Song—for Ian

Ellie's Songbook: December 2001

Dad's Song—for Ian
Words and Music by Eleanor Serafini

Verse 1
I wish that you could meet him
The man that was my dad
He was kind and patient
Only once did he get mad
But I deserved it. Really earned it
'cause I didn't call him Dad
—I called him Ben

Chorus
Oh!
If I could have that day back again
Back again
Oh!
If I could have that day once again

Verse 2
Don't ever want to see the man

that is my real father
Long ago I reached out
Sent a tearstained letter
begging him to meet me
His long-lost daughter
But he just said

Chorus
"No!"
I never want to have that day back again
Back again
No!
Never want that day back again

Verse 3
How I wish that you could meet him
The dad that loved me so
Gave me anything I wanted
And always let me know
That he loved me, he'd be there
I'd never be alone
And he'd listen

Bridge
Oh!
Like *you* listen, and love me. You always let me know
That you'll be there, forever, I'll never be alone
You love me so—like he loved me so

Final Chorus

Oh!

Feels like those days are back again

Back again.

Oh!

Feeling loved once again

Home

December 2001

JOSIE

Josie woke to yelps from Lady, imprisoned in her crate. Stumbling quickly in response to her call, Josie said a silent prayer and then bent to peek in: *No mess, still dry!* Quickly she scooped her up, slid open the bedroom's sliding glass door that led to the deck, and then hurried down the steps to the grass. The cold air cut through her flannel pajamas as she set the puppy down.

"Don't you complain about being cold, you little mutt. You've got a Siberian fur coat. Now do your thing and we can both get warm."

Shuffling from one slippered foot to the other and rubbing her arms, Josie smiled with satisfaction as Lady squatted and let out a long, steady stream. If this kept up, she could soon let Lady sleep on her bed at night. Following orders for house training was as painful for Josie as for the pup, but it looked like they were getting close.

Once inside, Josie set the coffee brewing, fed Lady, and opened the white shutters to let the sun soak through the family room. Then, curling up with her new Washington Huskies coffee mug, she watched Lady scurry back and forth, growling and tearing at her few toys scattered on the floor. Josie had already blocked off the doorway beyond the kitchen, limiting the pup to these two rooms, as Lady had already chewed on one oak dining room chair leg and scratched the leather sofa in the living room.

The family room had always been a comfort zone—the blue and white sectional sofa was well-worn, the throw rugs old and stained, and the pillow that Lady had torn to shreds was worthless anyway. The kitchen was even safer. Besides the tile floor, there was the retro kitchen dining set, just like the one she and Vic had grown up with, only not in red and white. She'd chosen teal and white to match her teal stand mixer on the white granite counter. These kitchen chairs had chrome-plated steel legs, impervious to chew marks—she hoped. With newly installed pet gates, Lady now could be safely kept in the good-sized kitchen, when needed.

Glancing out the side window, Josie could see part of the empty barn, badly in need of fresh red paint. It would have to wait until spring or summer, depending on the rain.

Stretching out her legs on the ottoman, Josie sighed. She was home. She had felt it as soon as she looked out the plane's window and saw the gentle rolling hills that surrounded Binghamton Regional Airport, their colors subdued post-autumn, awaiting that blanket of snow that would later lead to spring's lush green. And she had known it as soon as the cab pulled up to the old-style colonial brick home with slate blue shutters and a small pillared portico. Glancing up, first at the vacant second floor, and then above, at the roof's three dormers—once Ellie's attic music studio—Josie felt the enormity and the emptiness of their family home. But as she walked up the driveway, the two leafless maples seemed to stretch out their branches in greeting. The creak of the door that Ben had oiled a million times also made her smile, reminding her of the can of WD-40 they always kept in a basket in the corner of the foyer.

As she pulled her luggage through the doorway, Josie was greeted by the scent of an unfamiliar spice, as well as an arrangement of exotic flowers on the console table, left by Amir with a simple note: "Many thanks. Your home was our haven for a brief time."

She hoped that he and his wife would also find peace back home, whatever the future might hold.

This morning the house smelled of coffee, fresh-baked bread that she'd toasted for breakfast, and hints of garlic from last night's dinner. She'd made herself pesto pasta with Caesar salad and drank close to a whole bottle of Chianti all by herself.

It was Lucas who suggested she give herself some time to settle in before she worried about the horses, and perhaps he meant about the two of them as well, but she couldn't be sure. They hadn't had a real talk in several weeks. She'd been busy packing up Vic's house, then visiting Ellie, so when they did talk, it was mostly superficial. She found herself wondering if maybe all there had ever been was friend-ship—like Ben's friendship with her mom. Maybe it was like that?

But then she would remember Lucas's voice in September when he'd said, "I've been thinking about you all day," in a tone that made her feel an excitement she hadn't felt in years. Neither had brought up the topic of airport pick-up at all. They'd left it that Josie would call once she got home, and that's when he had encouraged her to give herself some time.

"The horses are no bother. Get your bearings first," he'd said, while she was in Seattle. In fact, he'd suggested that when Josie was ready, she could drive up for lunch on a Sunday, meet his mom, visit with the horses, and they could discuss everything then. He'd been friendly, but there was something in his voice that was a little off. She couldn't put her finger on it. But he had finished with, "Give your-self a few days before you start thinking about taking on the horses. You've had a pretty intense year." Then his voice had been tender.

It was true. As much as she couldn't wait to see the horses, there was a lot to think about and to plan. Preparing their stalls, mending fences, checking the pastures, and getting hay delivered and unloaded. Fortunately, with no snow in the immediate forecast, there was time.

So Josie had given herself a few days to unpack, restock the kitchen, take inventory in the barn, and Lady-proof the house. Next week, she would stop by the hospital to check out the cardiac rehab center and make some plans about getting back to work. She figured with part-time hours at the rehab center, plus occasional per diem in the Coronary Care Unit, she could live comfortably this year while she decided what came next.

Josie knew the house was too much for her now. She could already see that she and Lady would be living in just these few rooms. When she and Ben had first bought the house, they'd added the master bedroom and bathroom on the first floor and the family room that opened to the updated kitchen. This was all she needed. In fact, after Ellie left, there had been no reason to even climb the stairs. The second-floor bedrooms and the refurbished attic where Ellie had played her music and entertained friends were deserted. Josie knew it was silly to continue living in a house that was crying out for a big family.

But there was no hurry to make that decision yet. Financially, Josie had a solid foundation: there was the house, which was paid for, and substantial savings and investments, thanks to Ben's life insurance. She could take her time making decisions.

Setting down her coffee, Josie reached for the phone to call Lucas. She was ready to drive up on Sunday.

Josie didn't expect rattled nerves and butterflies as she eased onto the highway, so she tried to focus on the horses. She couldn't believe it had been almost an entire year since she last saw them. The time had sped by in so many ways. The horses would certainly remember her, but most likely, they'd appear indifferent, especially after having settled into their new surroundings for so long.

Her decision to leave yipping, furious Lady behind in the kitchen had been a good one. Josie wanted to be able to focus all of her attention on the horses, as well as Lucas's mom Alice—and, of course, Lucas. On her many walks with Lady, she'd reconnected with her closest neighbors, including fourteen-year-old twins, Calvin and Max, who had sprouted a good five inches. They'd eagerly agreed to check on Lady and walk her a couple of times during the few hours Josie would be gone.

Josie had felt like a teenager herself as she agonized over what to wear. Tossing so many rejections on the bed, she had to put Lady in her crate when one blouse fell on the floor and was immediately attacked. In the end, she wore her nicest jeans, black ankle boots, and a black turtleneck under her favorite denim jacket with an Aztec design on the front pocket and back panel. Her hair was another matter. Always an unruly mass of curls and waves, it needed taming, so she wound it up in a neat knot and secured it with a silver barrette with turquoise stones. A touch of blush. Light on the mascara. No perfume. She felt comfortable.

It was warm for a December morning, fifty-five degrees when she set out at eleven. There was nothing more lovely than the country roads of Upstate New York, even at this least dramatic point in the season. No lush green, nor autumn splendor, and no blanket of white just yet. Just the rush of trees on either side: leafless maples, oaks, and elms, stunning in their starkness, and the imperious pines and spruces, always leaving Josie eager to wander into their deepest shadows. She lowered both windows to feel the cool air on her face and inhale the fresh earthy scent.

Her jittery nerves left her needing to use the bathroom halfway there, so she stopped at a service station, took care of business, and was able to relax and focus on directions once she exited the highway.

Right at the post office, then drive a good five miles to a large red barn with two silos on your left, where you take another right. About three miles up, our place will be on your left just as you round the curve.

And just as Josie rounded that curve, she saw them—her horses Jack and Luke—and her heart leapt. They were grazing about a yard apart in a pasture surrounded by white post and rail fencing. Turning up the gravel drive, Josie wondered if they'd recognize her silver Jeep Grand Cherokee. At home, they'd spot it half a block away and head to the rails to follow her along the driveway. Now, each horse turned and paused, necks bent in her direction. She pulled over and came to a stop, but before she could fling open the door and step out, they were on their way to greet her. Not a wild dash, by any means, but a steady trot.

The tears that came erased any trace of light mascara, and the touch of blush disappeared as well as she repeatedly wiped her wet checks with the back of her hand. As always, Luke kept snapping at Jack, interrupting the love fest as she stroked Luke's neck and Jack's favorite spot on his forehead.

"I should have come with carrots and treats. What was I thinking? It's been too long. I'm sorry, boys." Then, realizing that they were leaning against the wooden rail as they nosed her pockets for treats, she stepped back. Glancing up toward the property, Josie could see the side of a barn in the distance with only one empty horse run visible. No Fire Mountain yet. "Okay, boys, I'm gonna go see your brother now. Follow if you want. But I promise, I'll find you some carrots."

As Josie drove further up, the house, which had been hidden by a row of pine trees, came into view—a two-story farmhouse, pale yellow with white trim, and a covered porch the entire length of the front with a swing and a couple of chairs. The drive came to a fork: curve left to the house and a carport on the far side; turn right, straight to the barn. Josie paused for only a second and headed toward the barn. Just a glimpse of Fire and then she'd politely announce her arrival—if they hadn't already heard her car. She hoped Lucas and Alice would understand.

Stained in a light wood finish with dark green trim, the barn appeared to have six stalls—a center aisle with three on either side— each with good-sized runouts. Josie glanced at the row visible on the right side of the barn—no Fire. Her heart racing, she got out of the car and approached the partially opened barn door.

"Hello?" Josie called out and was immediately answered by the frantic braying of Spartacus. Sliding open the barn door, she entered the center aisle. To her left, she could see, through the first stall, another pasture where Spartacus and two bay quarter horses were turned out. Spartacus was heehawing at the fence, his nose reaching between the rails. That's when Josie heard, to her right in the furthest stall, a deep, familiar nicker. As she hurried to greet him, Fire slowly approached the Dutch door and lifted his muzzle to her face. As her arms wrapped around his neck, he rested his head on her right shoulder. Josie held him in a tight embrace. Fire wasn't well. She knew. But he'd waited for her. That she felt deeply.

As Josie stepped back to take him in—his dull coat, dull eyes, significant weight loss—she saw movement to her right. Lucas stood quietly in the doorway.

"I wanted to talk to you before you saw him," he said, his voice deep but soft. *Almost like Fire's nicker,* Josie thought. "But not on the phone, not with you so far away. I wanted to tell you about him in person . . . prepare you." Lucas paused, then added, "That's why I offered to pick you up."

Josie nodded and swallowed the lump in her throat as he approached.

Lucas was taller than she remembered, with light brown hair slicked back, some gray at the temples, dark eyes behind wire-rimmed glasses, and a youthful face, reminding her of an older John-Boy Walton. Freshly shaven and showered, his hair still damp, he smelled like Dove soap. She realized now that she'd never seen him without a baseball cap of some sort, his face always shaded.

"I hoped he'd hang on until you got back," Lucas was saying, "especially after telling you to wait a few days before coming up. But I just thought you'd be wiped out. Too much too soon. Of course, I would have called if he took a sudden turn." His hand had found Fire's sweet spot under his mane. Her treasured horse closed his eyes and rested his chin on her shoulder again—his head between the two of them.

Josie closed her eyes as well and leaned her head against Fire's. "So, are you saying it's time to . . . ?" She couldn't say the words.

She felt Lucas's other arm circle around and briefly touch her back as he said gently, "Soon."

After a moment of quiet—aside from the distant snorts of horses beyond the barn—Lucas added, "Once we sit down in the house, I'll go over the details, and we'll take it from there."

Josie couldn't hold back any longer. The tears fell and her shoulders shook as she sobbed softly. Lucas stepped back, then turning toward Josie, he slipped both arms around her—and she buried her face in his chest.

His mother Alice, a slim, petite woman with a short silver bob and lively blue eyes, greeted Josie at the side door with a firm handshake and a "So nice to finally meet you." Then, seeing Josie's tear-streaked face, Alice took both hands in hers and said, "I'm so sorry about Fire. Lucas has practically slept out there lately."

Lucas mumbled something that Josie didn't quite hear as he disappeared back out the door.

Dressed in jeans and a green sweatshirt with two cardinals perched in a tree, Alice tenderly squeezed Josie's hands again and said, "Well, welcome to our home. I've got a pot roast in the oven, some appetizers for now. Why don't you freshen up, and then I'll show you a bit of the house, if you'd like?" Alice led her by the hand through the mudroom, where flannel shirts and denim jackets hung on the wall above a bench, and weathered boots lay beneath at odd angles. Alice motioned toward a small bathroom and let go of her hand.

Once Josie pulled herself together and gave up on the make-up-less face in the mirror, she stepped out and followed Alice, who began recounting the house's history.

"Built in the 1880's, this farmhouse has been in our family for three generations—and Lucas and Jacob have pledged to carry that on." Alice led Josie first through the sun-filled kitchen, with white cabinets, a large pine-top island—its base painted mint-green—and, in the corner, a pine breakfast nook with dark green cushions and sunflower pillows. Turning briefly, Alice said with pride, "Lucas and my husband updated the kitchen and the bathrooms themselves."

On to the dining room and its long, rectangular pine table beside sliding glass doors with a view Josie ached to see—but the tour kept

HOME 245

moving. So, she followed Alice to the living room with its white beamed ceiling, hardwood floors, and an immense white brick fireplace with two inviting cushioned rockers on either side. A formal white sofa with light gray throw pillows and gray and white area rug added an elegance to the cozy room.

On the walls were two paintings of flowers with the signature "Alice" in the lower right corner. When Josie asked about the paintings, Alice scoffed and said, "Oh, I did those a long time ago. I never even notice them anymore." As Alice motioned onward, Josie glanced toward a small alcove to the right and saw a rolltop oak desk, with a black phone and steno pad, beside oak file cabinets. Josie smiled, picturing Alice there, taking Lucas's vet calls.

The far side of the house consisted of a family room with a large TV, an old desk with a computer, and a well-worn dark green sofa with a horse-print quilt draped along the seat back. Framed photographs lined one wall, some black and white, some sepia.

Josie paused and pointed to one. "Lucas?" she asked.

Alice smiled. "Yes, with Jacob, of course." A younger Lucas on horseback beside Jacob, at perhaps nine or ten, seated on a palomino pony.

Alice then pointed to a photo that was clearly her—the same bright eyes, even in black and white—and her husband, whom Lucas definitely favored. "Lucas's dad, Steve," she said, gently touching the face of a man whose arm draped comfortably around her shoulders.

Josie's eyes then traveled to a silver-framed photo in the center. A family photo of Lucas, with toddler Jacob sitting on the lap of a pretty young woman—her long dark hair parted down the middle and her arms securely wrapped around her son. Clearly, Lucas's beloved Kate.

"Jacob developed these," Alice said, beaming. "He's quite the photographer. Has a dark room in the cellar. Took the old negatives and made a few look old-fashioned."

She paused for a moment, and then motioned toward a bedroom just off of the family room, where Josie could see a four-poster bed with a log cabin quilt and matching pillows neatly placed against the headboard. Alice explained that it used to be Jacob's room, but now that he had moved out, she wanted Lucas to take over the space. "He's always falling asleep down here on the sofa anyway," she said, nodding toward the one with the horse quilt.

That's when Josie noticed the phone on the end table and smiled, realizing that that's where he called from late at night, down here— so his mother couldn't hear.

"After lunch, I'll show you the upstairs," Alice said, as she guided Josie back toward the kitchen. Touching Josie's arm, she added, "Wait until you see my quilting room." Her blue eyes sparkled. "Do you quilt?"

Josie shook her head, but Alice had turned away as Lucas stepped out of the bathroom, wiping his hands on a towel.

"I brought your guys around back," he said to Josie, referring to Jack and Luke.

His face looked soft and boyish.

From the pine dining table, where Josie sat with Lucas and Alice, the view of the back was stunning. Beyond the deck was a sweeping lawn that led down to a picturesque pond and inviting woods in the distance. To the left, several raised beds, now empty, waiting for spring. To the right, two pastures, divided by wire post fences. In one, Spartacus and two bays grazed. In the other, Jack and Luke rolled and ran. Josie's heart warmed at their sight, but ached for sweet Fire, though Lucas had said that they'd check on him again shortly.

For the third time, Josie said to Alice, "This place is just heavenly."

"It's come a long way over the years," Alice repeated. "But it's been our sanctuary, that's for sure." She had put out a cheese and cracker platter and glasses of iced tea, insisting they not eat too much since the pot roast would be done in about an hour. Then standing, Alice excused herself, saying to Lucas, "I promise I'll keep it short, plus, I'm sure the two of you have lots to talk about." And like a humming-bird, she darted away.

"Her sister?" Josie asked, remembering that every Sunday at one o'clock, his mother called her sister who lived in Florida. Sometimes they talked for an hour. There'd been a few times that Josie had tried to call him on Sunday mornings from LA, unable to get through, and he'd say, "The girls were yapping," followed by an affectionate laugh.

Lucas nodded. "She goes down every winter for a visit, usually spends two weeks. I think they're planning that today."

Their eyes met for a moment, and Josie felt her heart flutter. Ellie had been right about that in-person connection. Lucas seemed to feel it too, although Josie couldn't be sure.

Then Josie remembered Fire, and she knew the light in her eyes had faded.

Lucas looked away and cleared his throat. "So . . ." and he began to talk about Fire's compromised immune system after years of battling Cushing's disease, as well as frequent respiratory infections the past six months. Then, gently, Lucas spoke of impending cardiac problems. "As you well know, when the lungs are struggling, it puts added stress on the heart and can lead to the decline of other major functions." He took a deep breath, then added, "I've been focusing on supportive care and keeping him comfortable, but his blood work isn't stabilizing and his appetite is poor." He paused, then reaching for her hand, he squeezed it briefly and said, "I'm glad he's made it this long."

"Oh God, I'm just not ready." Josie barely got the words out. "And I can't bear to leave him now. I can't just go home and leave him here—and he's not in any condition to be trailered."

"You can certainly stay here. Spend time with him. A day or two, depending . . ."

She nodded, then shook her head. "Lady! I have to get back. I should've brought her with me."

Lucas sat back. "I guess I should have told you. I realize that now. I'm sorry. I just thought it'd be easier in person and to give you a chance to catch your breath."

This time, it was Josie who reached out and touched his hand. "No, I appreciate your thoughtfulness. I do."

His dark eyes softened and his thumb stroked the back of her hand. "How about after dinner, I drive you back to pick up Lady and pack a few things. Come back and spend time with Fire."

"Your mom said you've practically been sleeping out there with him lately."

"Yeah, well, not the first time. Did it with my old guy, General, and with my dad's horse, Tex. We've been through this a few times before. Last year, it was one of our dogs." Lucas sighed. "We tend to hang on too long. It's so hard to let them go."

Startled by the sudden footsteps down the stairs, they both released hands and almost simultaneously reached for their iced tea to take a sip. Alice appeared with a slight smile on her face.

"See, kept it short and sweet, although I told her I might call back later." She looked from Lucas to Josie. "We decided on a date. I'll visit in February—around Valentine's Day. Thought that might be a good time to give you the house to yourself for a few weeks. I'd have gone sooner, but she's got a houseful over the holidays and into part of winter break with her grandkids. Everyone flocks to Florida in winter. And we girls like it to be just us when I visit. Hope that's okay? February?"

"Sure, Ma, whatever works for you."

"Okay then," she said, then turned on her heel. "Gonna check on the roast."

Later that evening, Lucas set Josie up in the far corner of Fire's stall with a bale of hay covered with a thick comforter, another quilt neatly folded beside it, and a thermos of hot chamomile tea. He'd given Fire a bran mash that he barely touched, cleaned his stall, then scooped up Lady, who had been running back and forth the length of the center aisle, looking for the barn cat who had mysteriously disappeared.

"You okay?" he asked gently.

Josie nodded.

Lady was licking the side of his face, then as Lucas turned his head, she started in on his nose and lips. Lucas chuckled. "My mom will be in heaven looking after this little one. It's been pretty quiet since we lost Thor last year, and then Jacob took *his* dog Buck with him to Jenny's apartment."

Scratching Lady under the chin, Lucas added, "We've always had dogs running around the house, so it's been mighty empty with both Thor and Buck gone—and Jacob, of course."

"But you've sure had your hands full with my horses."

"They honestly weren't any trouble at all."

Their eyes locked, and Josie's heart raced at the thought of the one kiss they'd shared at her house just a few hours before. They had loaded up the back seat of his truck with her small suitcase, Lady's crate, food and a few toys, then had come back to the house to get

Lady and lock up. Josie paused in the foyer and placed her hand on Lucas's arm. She was about to thank him again for everything he'd done, but when he turned, Josie found herself stepping forward and lifting her face to his. And they kissed—a long, slow kiss that left Josie lightheaded. She pressed her forehead against his chest to steady herself. Lucas held her for a few seconds more, his lips brushing the top of her head, and then they both stepped back and turned toward the yelping pup behind bars in the kitchen.

That's what most filled Josie with a quiet joy. The silence between them was both comfortable and comforting. No need to discuss, question, or explain. No need to wonder what was happening or what might happen next. Even the ride back through the dark country roads had been soothing, with Lady curled up on Josie's lap, the heater buzzing its white noise, and the gentle peace between them that warmed her aching heart.

Once back to his place, Lucas had kindly set her up in the barn to have some quiet time with Fire.

"Hey!" Lucas cried out as Lady nipped at his ear. Nodding toward Josie's jacket pocket where she'd put her cellphone, he said, "If you need anything, just call. Even if you just want company. Otherwise, I'll leave you alone."

Josie blinked back tears. That was exactly what she needed. To be alone with Fire. Lucas said he'd been through this before, so perhaps that's how he knew. Grateful, Josie managed to mouth the words, "Thank you."

Once the barn door slid shut, Josie stepped up, facing Fire. He lifted his head slightly and opened his soft, brown eyes. Stroking under his mane where the fur felt like velvet, Josie rested her forehead against his. Fire leaned into her, and the two stood quietly. Josie wished this moment could last forever.

As her first horse, Fire had certainly changed Josie's life, but he'd also had a powerful effect on Ben and Ellie's as well. While they all learned the basics of horse care and horsemanship with him, they'd also discovered the special peace that comes in the presence of a horse—especially Fire. Whether it was his years of experience or some inner wisdom, Fire had a serenity about him that enveloped those close by in a cocoon of tranquility. Josie had witnessed this many times, but two in particular stayed etched in her heart. One was when Ben came home stressed after losing a young patient; the other was when Ellie returned from school dejected because she'd been shunned by a group of popular girls. Each time—after spending just a few moments with Fire—they'd relaxed a bit, eased up on themselves, and settled into an acceptance of life's disappointments.

"Fire," Josie said, just above a whisper, "you are a treasure. One of the greatest joys of my life. You, more than anyone, helped me when Ben died. What will I do without you? Oh Fire . . . you'll be forever and ever in my heart." Then Josie began humming, then singing, "Home, Home on the Range," a song Ellie used to sing when they made a campfire out back and the horses would gather by the fence and listen. Fire pulled his head away from hers and stepped back slightly—so he could watch her as she sang.

After kissing him on the forehead, Josie settled back in her corner, pulling the quilt up around her shoulders. Fire lowered his head and closed his eyes. She knew she had to make a decision tomorrow. How much pain and discomfort he was in was impossible to gauge. Unlike most humans, horses hid their suffering stoically.

Jack, in the stall beside Fire's, had been watching them closely the whole time. His eyes were fixed on Josie now.

"Mama's home now, Jack, for good. We'll be heading back together very soon."

Together. She couldn't picture the pasture without Fire's blazing coat, gleaming in the sun.

With a deep, long sigh, Josie leaned her head back against the wall, closed her eyes, and listened to the munching of hay, the occasional snorting and blowing of the horses, and the shuffling of hooves. It was peaceful and surprisingly warm, and though Josie's mind was swirling like a dust storm on a California trail—thoughts of losing Fire, kissing Lucas, worrying about Vic—she was utterly exhausted and, finally, fell asleep.

Startled awake by a sudden jolt, Josie opened her eyes to what appeared to be an empty stall—until she realized that Fire had collapsed and fallen over. He lay on his right side, his legs jutting out, stiff and straight. As she jumped up and knelt at his head, she saw his eyes were open, staring blankly ahead—glassy and lifeless. Josie let out a short, sharp cry, like the crack of a gun in the woods. Trembling, she placed her hand on his belly—no respiratory movement. She laid her head on the left side of his chest. No heart sounds. As expected, his heart could only take so much stress and struggle—and then it had had enough.

Just like that, Fire was gone.

Reaching into her pocket for her cell phone to call Lucas, Josie suddenly stopped. Sitting back on her heels, she looked at her Fire's face, the crooked white stripe down his nose that she had traced with her finger so many times. Josie bent and kissed his muzzle, then closed his eyes.

She'd let him be—let him rest in much-deserved peace.

Bless your heart, you waited for me—and you spared me from making that difficult decision. One of a kind to the end.

Then, reaching for the quilt, Josie stretched herself across Fire's still warm body and covered them both. Burying her face in his neck, she let the tears fall, washing over them both.

She was still there when Lucas found them just before dawn.

That week, Josie accepted Lucas's offer to lay Fire to rest on his family's property with all of their beloved animals that had passed. Whether her own future involved this land wasn't the point. Yes, she sensed she was going to be spending a great deal of time here, but where their relationship would lead, she didn't know. What she did know was that eventually she would be selling her own home, so there was no point in putting Fire there. More importantly, she liked the fact that this land would stay in Lucas's family to be loved and tended to for a very long time by Lucas, and, ultimately, his son Jacob.

But what Josie loved the most was that Fire would be in a peaceful spot, graced by an array of different trees, for each horse or dog's burial was followed by the planting of a tree of choice. Josie hadn't decided yet what tree she wanted for Fire—perhaps a flaming red maple—but it brought her great comfort to think that Fire would be held forever within the arms of a tree's protective roots—in an eternal embrace.

Their Letter

December 2001

VIC

Dear Isa and Miguel,

My little angels. I miss you so much my heart hurts. Like the time at the park when you picked up that hard ball you found, Isa, and threw it at me with all of your might, and it thwacked my chest so hard I fell back, stunned. Man, that sucker hurt, and you cried so hard, and I kept telling you I was okay, but your mom made me go to the emergency room to be checked out. Yeah, sweethearts, it hurts like that. And I know it always will. But that's okay. I can handle it. You know how strong your daddy is. Remember how you'd each hold on to my biceps, one of you on each side, and I'd lift you off the ground, and your mom would count to see how long? That's how strong your dad is. I can carry this pain. I can.

Sometimes when I'm sitting on your abuela's slanted stoop, watching kids run and play here in Veracruz, I see you both. Isa, your hair is braided down your back with pink and white ribbons woven through, and you're skipping, like you do, happy and dreamlike. Miguel, you're wearing that Spider-Man T-shirt that your mom had to wash practically every night because you just had to wear it every day, and you're kicking your soccer ball. I hope you don't mind, but

I gave it to Juan Manuel. Well, he's borrowing it, until I can bring it to you one day.

I talk about both of you all the time—to Juan Manuel. He's too little to understand. He barely talks himself, but he listens with his big brown eyes open wide. I ramble on and on. I want him to know everything about you. As he grows up, it will be like he's always known you—his American cousins, Isa and Miguel—played with you and learned all your secrets.

That's how I keep you with me.

Tell your mom I'm doing okay, as okay as I can—although she probably knows. She must be so happy to see I'm surrounded by her family, *su familia*. We're all working together to grow flowers, to make a business. We've met lots of really good people who want to help us, so it just might work. I like working outside, digging and building, but I also like meeting new people, groups of people, and telling them about this special plan and asking them for money. I remember how clever you were, Isa, convincing your mom and me to let you pierce your ears. How you explained that it would help us save money because the earrings wouldn't fall off easily and get lost—so we wouldn't have to buy more earrings. So very clever! I think of that when I tell people how our flower business will help the village, the state, the country. Just like it worked for you, Isa, it's working for us here, too.

Oh, my little monkeys, how I miss you! There are times I wish that one of you stayed with me, but then I realize, no, I'm glad you're together. Wherever that is, you're with your mommy, waiting for me. And that thought—that picture in my mind that one day we'll *all* be together again—that keeps me going. That fills me with hope.

Pangaea Still

December 2001

JOSIE

Dressed in her pastel blue scrubs, Josie slid onto a seat by the window in the hospital cafeteria. It felt good to be back to work—one day this week and two the next, before heading back to Seattle for a hastily planned family Christmas with Ellie and Vic. It had been Ellie's idea that they should try to meet on Christmas every year, starting with this one. Despite the fact that Josie had just settled in at home, she was overjoyed that Ellie wanted the family to be together for the holiday. Since Maggie was an important part of that family, it made the most sense to meet at Ellie's, and since Vic was planning a short trip to LA to visit the cemetery on December 18th—and also to speak to a local church that was raising funds for his project—the arrangement worked for him as well. He'd stay with Santiago for a few days and head to Seattle for Christmas. Josie's heart was full.

Nodding to two nurses that were leaving, she noticed at the next table a young woman—a new ER doctor—who had responded to a potential problem that morning. A patient, exercising while monitored by telemetry, had experienced chest pain and threw a few PVC's. Josie had been impressed with this doctor's ability to effectively evaluate the situation and act on it, all with a calm, soft-spoken manner. Josie motioned for her to sit at her table.

"Kristen, right?" Josie asked, as they had spoken briefly in the unit.

"Yes. Thanks for asking me to join you. I haven't entirely regained my social skills yet. Actually, I'm still experiencing culture shock," Kristen said, with a slight laugh.

Kristen went on to tell Josie that, though originally from Pittsburgh, she had spent the last few years working for Doctors Without Borders, traveling to developing nations, treating diseases barely covered in medical school, as well as machete wounds and omnipresent malnutrition.

"I was fighting compassion fatigue and dysentery, so I knew it was time to come back to the States. My third day here was September 11th. Set me back a bit, but I'm beginning to feel like myself again." Her short blond hair was tucked behind her ears, and with her smattering of freckles and upturned nose, she looked younger than her thirty-five years.

Josie was thrilled to meet someone who had firsthand experience with Doctors Without Borders. After telling Kristen of her own interest in the program, Josie peppered her with questions.

After talking at length, Kristen had suddenly paused, glanced around the cafeteria, and leaned forward. "Actually, I hope you don't mind me asking." She blushed as she asked, "Do you know Dr. Neilson, Tom Neilson?"

"Yes," Josie said. "He's a pulmonary doc." Josie knew that he went through a nasty divorce a couple of years before, but didn't mention it. While she refused to take part in hospital gossip, she always soaked up whatever she heard.

"Well, he asked me out this morning," Kristen said. Her reddened cheeks and wide eyes held the innocent excitement of a young girl, which made Josie like her even more. "It's been a while since I've been on a date," she continued. "What do you think?"

"I think that's great! Tom's a nice guy. I think you should go."
Josie thought of her innocent first dinners with Ben, when she hadn't
even known they were on a date. Sitting back in her chair, Josie told
Kristen a bit of her and Ben's story.

Kristen listened intently, smiling, then frowning as the story
reached its sad end. "Do you think you'll ever fall in love again—get
married?" Kristen asked softly.

Josie traced the lip of her cup with her finger. "I don't know," she
began, then continued. "Actually, I'm seeing someone now, and it's
really nice. But where it's headed, who knows? One thing I've learned,
life has a way of turning things upside down and inside out. When
your head stops spinning, you just get your bearings and see where
you fit, where you belong."

"Have you stopped spinning yet?" Kristen asked with a wink.

Josie felt her own cheeks flush, thinking of the previous weekend.
Lucas had helped move Jack and Luke back home. Then, after dinner
and a few glasses of wine, they made love for the first time. It was a bit
awkward, yet tender. Afterwards, Lucas whispered, "Next time will
be better. We'll take our time." In the morning, before he left, they
did—and it was.

"Still spinning," Josie had to admit, with a light laugh.

Then Josie began talking about her lifelong dream to travel, learn
about other cultures, and explore diverse geography. "That part of
me is still spinning, too."

Kristen laughed. "God, and all I want is to stay put for a while.
I've been to Angola, Somalia, El Salvador, and Sri Lanka. In fact,
tonight I'm giving a talk at Binghamton University and showing
some film footage of my experiences. Would you like to come?"

"I'd love to," Josie said, curious about this glimpse into another
part of the world and also pleased to have met such an interesting

woman. In fact, she looked forward to telling her about Vic, and Ernesto and Claudia, and the Water Stations Project. Josie sensed that Kristen would understand. When Josie had spoken of her experiences at the border to others at the hospital, they'd simply nodded in sympathy, but didn't seem to *feel* the impact of her words. Perhaps it was something people had to experience first-hand.

While Josie was pleased at the prospect of a new friendship with someone who could relate to her experiences on a deeper level, she also had to admit it'd be nice to have a new friend who didn't know her as Ben's wife—but as Josie today. A nurse, horse-lover, hiker, traveler—with a new love in her life, and a family scattered to different corners of the hemisphere, yet still very much connected.

Later that evening, standing in the lobby of the lecture hall, Josie played with the idea of working for Doctors Without Borders. As a nurse, she could sign on for six months to a year, live amongst the people of a foreign land, and contribute her skills where they were desperately needed. But, of course, she had the horses to consider, and Lady—and especially Lucas. Perhaps she could do a month clinic somewhere. That sounded more realistic for now. Although if Josie mentioned any of this to Lucas, bless his heart, he'd probably tell her to go and he'd look after her animals. Not that she wanted to travel anywhere quite yet. But there was a comfort in his easy-going attitude and in his pleasure in seeing her happy.

Recently, Josie had discovered the university's extension catalog and opened up to a "Weekend of Learning." One was to explore the flora and fauna of the Finger Lakes region, and another one involved a backpacking trip in the Appalachian Mountains. When she told Lucas about them during their nightly phone call, he had immediately said, "You should go!" Then, laughing, he'd added, "I'll stay home and watch the kids."

"Or you could join me?"

"I could," he said, leaving the choice in her hands.

It was clear that Lucas was deeply pleased to have Josie in his life, but there was no pressure. He was neither needy nor demanding, but more of a "We'll take our time" kind of guy, and that was precisely what Josie needed at this point. They'd meandered the trails in his neighborhood on horseback and hiked her favorite trail behind her house. While there was a quiet comfort between them, whenever their fingers touched or their eyes met and lingered, there was also an undeniable spark. Josie looked forward to the months ahead, for there was still so much to learn about each other.

Josie watched Kristen greet people in the lobby, shaking hands and answering questions. The two were planning to go out for drinks as soon as she was finished. While waiting, Josie overheard a woman beside her discussing the crisis of AIDS in Africa. She was the director of a local project raising funds and awareness throughout New York State. *Another erector of blue flags,* Josie thought with respect, until the woman's cell phone rang and Josie watched her turn away, her face contorted, her voice harsh. Then, the woman slipped the phone into her bag and turned back to her friend and said, "My mother! Won't leave me a minute's peace. Pay for the best nursing home money can buy and she still complains. Says she's not feeling well, says she wants me to stop by. Like I have all the time in the world!"

That's what stayed with Josie after she got home and curled up in bed with Lady. How easy it was to erect blue flags for the faceless and nameless souls of an honorable cause. But what about those familiar faces we know all too well, voices we don't want to listen to or can't hear clearly because they're muffled behind walls that we build to keep them away? Josie knew she was guilty of this herself. That woman's bitter tone, her ugly sneer—Josie could have been looking in a mirror.

So, when Vic called the next day, Josie's response was immediate. No hesitation on her part.

"It's Dad . . . um, Tony," Vic said awkwardly. "He was hospitalized for a few days, but he's out now. I talked to him briefly, and to Sally, and I insisted she notify us of any health issues no matter what he says. I hope you don't mind, but I gave her your number. It's kind of complicated for her to reach me here."

"No problem, of course," Josie said. "What is it? What happened?"

"I'm still not sure. He said it's nothing serious, just his stomach or liver. 'Not gonna croak tomorrow, nothing like that,' he said to me. He didn't sound too bad, but I don't know," Vic said, concern heavy in his voice. "Anyway, he certainly can't travel, so I guess he won't be able to join us in Seattle for Christmas." His voice trailed off at the end, sounding sad and wistful.

Josie knew there'd been talk of including Tony, but whether he'd agreed, she hadn't heard.

"No," Josie said, "he certainly can't travel." Then, without even the slightest pause, she added, "But we can. What do you think of Christmas in Las Vegas?"

Dead silence was followed by Vic's incredulous, "Are you serious?"

"Well, Vegas was never on my travel list, especially for Christmas. Sounds like an Elvis TV special, doesn't it? "Christmas in Las Vegas!" But I've heard of Red Rock Canyon—contains incredible geological formations that reveal the contrast between layers of gray limestone and red sandstone. Bet you've always wanted to see that, haven't you? Come on, admit it." She smiled just imagining his face.

"You are serious, aren't you?" He was clearly overcome. "Ellie too? All of us?"

"Yes, of course. I'll call her right away and see if she can make it, then I'll call the airline and change our flight destinations."

Josie had been looking forward to Christmas in Seattle. She was even going to bring Lady along since they'd survived their flight home unscathed. But a Vegas motel wasn't the same as the comfort of Ellie's house, so she'd best leave Lady with Alice, who adored the pup. She hoped Ellie would be okay with leaving Maggie with the girls.

"Where will we stay?" Vic asked. "He lives in a trailer park."

"We'll find something. Maybe outside the craziness of the city. I'm sure they have a Best Western there. We can pretend it's a cozy cabin in Colorado, surrounded by snow."

Vic laughed. "Josie, I love you. God, that's fantastic. Should I call Dad? What should I tell him?"

"Let me check it all out first. We'll take it from there." Her mind was on Ellie and what she would think of this change in plans. She hoped it wouldn't disrupt the current ease between them.

Hearing Vic say something in Spanish, apparently to someone nearby, Josie asked, "Things still going well there?"

"Yeah, Jo, they are. Everything's moving forward. So much to tell you. We even plan to grow some of our own food as well—tomatoes, peppers, zucchini." His voice sounded hopeful. That alone lifted her spirits.

Later that evening, unable to reach her daughter, Josie went ahead and booked their flights to Vegas. She'd be careful not to pressure Ellie when she called back. She'd let *her* make the decision, but Josie felt certain that Ellie would make it work for Vic, and especially Tony, once she heard he was ill.

After talking with a travel agent about finding a place for them to stay in Vegas, Josie then called Alice to confirm arrangements for Lady. Lucas was planning to bring the horses to his place that week, for they'd already worked out their holiday plans. Josie would stay with Lucas on her return, so they could celebrate a late Christmas—and spend New Year's Eve together. They both agreed that this was the most important holiday for them—looking ahead to their first new year together.

The next day, with an excited "Yes!" from Ellie, who declared she'd always wanted to see Las Vegas, Josie once again reached for the phone. Not Vic. She'd call him after everything was set, especially after this particular call.

Three rings.

"Hello," a deep, raspy voice answered.

Josie hesitated, just for a second, then said with as much levity in her voice as she could muster, "Hi … Dad? This is Josie. So, what's this about you being sick?"

A light snow had fallen the night before, leaving a dusting of white that would disappear by noon, but as Josie drove to the cemetery early that morning, she thrilled at the thought of the winter ahead. She loved all the seasons and the inevitable change that their arrival and departure implied.

Josie brought with her, not marigolds, but three poinsettia plants in festive Christmas pots. Their family plot was on the edge of the cemetery, just yards from a stretch of woods. She and Vic had chosen this plot for three since, at the time of their mother's death, neither of them was married—and they hated the thought of her being buried alone. This was where Josie had buried Ben, and this was where she would one day rest, between her mother and Ben.

Dressed for her plane trip later that afternoon, Josie wore her favorite stretch jeans, burgundy sweater, and short brown boots. Not wanting to get her jeans wet from the cold, damp earth, she pulled the floor mat from the car, knelt on that, and then arranged the flowers at the base of the two headstones that sat side by side, almost touching.

Margherita "Rita" Serafini, 1930–1981, Beloved Mother. Only fifty-one when she died, with so much of life ahead of her. The immensity of this tragedy bore new meaning to Josie, who at forty-three looked forward with excitement to the years ahead. Tenderly touching her mother's name, Josie said, "Vic's going to be all right, Mom."

Benjamin O'Neill, 1939–1997, Devoted Husband, Loving Father. Just the thought of Ben brought such comfort. She'd be forever grateful for the life they had shared. To Ben, she said, "Ellie sends her love, but I suppose you know that."

Reaching into her jacket pocket, Josie pulled out the candy skull and punctured paper that she had saved from *Día de los Muertos*, and also strands of Fire's tail hair. After securing them gently within stems of the center plant, she sat back on her boots.

Even after great loss, the world still held such promise. There was Christmas in Las Vegas and Las Flores de Juan Manuel. There was Maggie and Foxy Lady, and Jack and Luke. There was Ellie, flying home next summer so the two of them could drive to New York City, visit Ground Zero, and maybe catch a Broadway play. There was Tony, who choked up when she called with their Christmas plans, until he managed to say, "Bless you, sweetheart." There was Vic, always Vic, who seemed to be finding his way back to the light. And now, there was Lucas, with his quiet, gentle way.

Standing, Josie brushed her fingertips along the top of each gravestone. Then looking up above the stretch of dense forest at the cloudless blue sky, she realized it was the same blue as the flags in

the desert. A soft yet vivid azure. Closing her eyes, Josie remembered the kindness and compassion of those who walked beside her
with the Water Stations Project and those who tended the graves in
Holtville. She could almost hear Ellie's voice, sweet and strong, singing "Amazing Grace."

That's when she saw it—Pangaea—in her mind's eye. The continents, that were once connected and always a part of a whole, had
drifted apart all those years—yet the Earth *was* a sphere. At some
point, those same landforms were no longer pulling apart, but
moving toward each other—coming together again in a new form.
Pangaea still, Josie thought.

Picking up the floor mat, she headed toward her car—toward
Vic and Ellie, toward Tony and Christmas in Las Vegas. As she eased
onto the two-lane highway, Josie kept her eyes on the horizon ahead
and smiled at this new image of Pangaea—one of constant movement
and change, but also reconnection and hope.

Epilogue
The Promise of Pangaea

Ellie's Songbook
December 10, 2002: Human Rights Day

Performed by Common Ground at the Seattle Human Rights Commission Celebration, honoring the memory of Eleanor Roosevelt, Chairperson of the Drafting Committee for The Universal Declaration of Human Rights, adopted 1948.

The Promise of Pangaea
Words by Eleanor Serafini and Josephine Serafini
Music by Eleanor Serafini and Ian Holmes

Verse 1
A world connected, long ago
When Pangaea was one
No separation, segregation
Demarcations—none
A land united, people derived from
One world under the sun
Can we ever return
To where we all came from?

Chorus

One planet, one people, Pangaea

Till division and difference came

One planet, one people, Pangaea

Honor that sacred name

Verse 2

Kept apart by invisible borders

And too many manmade walls

Different language, religion, and culture

The unfamiliar only stalls

A chance to connect and converse

To remember and recall

This world was once undivided

A land for one and all

Chorus

One planet, one people, Pangaea

Will discord and conflict remain?

One planet, one people, Pangaea

At our core, we're all the same

Bridge

Yet the pieces of Pangaea that drifted apart long ago

Continue their constant movement as they slide, collide, and flow

Moving toward each other as they glide around our globe

Will reconnect—Pangaea Still—reborn in a new form

Chorus

One planet, one people, Pangaea

Fulfill our hope to proclaim

One planet, one people—Pangaea

One humanity. All the same.

Acknowledgments

Alone we can do so little: together we can do so much.
—Helen Keller

With an abundance of gratitude, I'd like to acknowledge all those who contributed to this novel in distinct yet valuable ways. Nothing is accomplished alone.

First and foremost, the RBGs, Radical Badass Gals (Who Write): Shelley Blanton-Stroud, Gretchen Cherington, and Ashley Sweeney, my writing critique group extraordinaire. I learned so much about writing through your thoughtful and perceptive eyes. I hope by the time this book is in print, we will have met in person for a long group hug.

To my early readers: Romalyn Tilghman, Rae Cook, and Amanda Banks, thank you for your helpful insights; Patricia Daniels, for your broad view, as well as your razor-sharp copyediting and proofreading skills; and Elizabeth McKenzie, for your valuable input and final stamp of approval. Each of you helped immensely.

I am forever grateful to my mentors, Gayle Brandeis, who lit the flame many years ago, and Alma Luz Villanueva, who helped keep that flame burning at a most difficult time.

I'm grateful to the Vietnam Veterans who answered questions while I was developing Vic's character. A huge thank you to Michael arclay, who shared a few amazing stories that he should put in writing himself; to Dean Gotham, President of Vietnam Veterans of America, California; and to Steve Mackey, who answered my questions with unfettered honesty. The words "Thank you for your service" never feel adequate enough to convey the deep sentiment intended.

Always my heartfelt gratitude to Father Richard Estrada, who, in 2002, introduced me to Water Stations Project (now called Border Angels), a group of volunteers that leave water in the desert, hoping to prevent deaths from dehydration. There are no words to express my admiration for Father Estrada. A tireless human rights activist, he has devoted his life to helping those in need, most notably founding Jovenes, Inc., for homeless immigrant youth.

I'd also like to thank Bradley D. Perdue, DVM for his advice regarding equine veterinary issues discussed in the novel—and for taking such good care of my own treasured horses, Fire, Jack, and Luke.

Thank you to visionary Brooke Warner, who saw a need for more women's voices to be heard and created award-winning She Writes Press. I am proud to have both of my novels published with the SWP logo. To my production team, project manager Samantha Strom, as well as Chris Dumas, Kiran Spees, and the entire team who create such polished and professional books, I thank you from the bottom of my heart. For the gorgeous cover design, I'd like to thank Rebecca Lown, Hoffman California Fabrics, and my dear friend, quilt artist Barbara Craig. To Krista Soukup and Janell Madison of Blue Cottage Agency, thank you for your most helpful advice and enthusiastic support of *Josie and Vic*.

To all of my family, who support, encourage, listen patiently, cheer me on, and always surround me with endless love, no words can thank you enough. Claire, Dean, Megan, Calvin, Max, and Dee. Mom and Dad, I know you are with me in spirit.

And finally, to my best friend and forever love, my husband, Bruce. With you, all the pieces came together. With you, I found my Pangaea.

Reading Guide
Topics and Questions for Discussion

1. How does the metaphor of Pangaea relate to the family through-
    out the novel?

2. In what way did Tony's abandoning his family affect both Vic
    and Josie's developing personalities? How might their lives have
    been different if he had stayed?

3. Discuss Josie and Ellie's relationship. How did it change over
    time? What led to this change?

4. What role does Maggie play in the novel, beyond just being a
    loving pet?

5. Discuss Josie and Vic's relationship. Has it changed over the
    years? If so, how?

6. What did Josie learn about love with Ben?

7. Discuss the relationship between Josie and Lucas. On what levels
    do they connect? What do you think will happen after the novel
    ends?

8. After Vietnam, Vic wandered from state to state looking for where he belonged. Why do you think he never returned to his hometown of Binghamton? What did he find in Arizona, then in LA, and finally at novel's end?

9. Discuss Ellie's songbook. In what way do her lyrics convey aspects of her personality?

10. Discuss Vic's letter to Irma and, in the end, to Isabel and Miguel. What did they reveal about Vic?

11. What key moments led to Josie softening toward Tony? Would you be able to forgive and reconnect in her situation?

12. Consider Ernesto and Claudia's tragic dilemma. The moment Ernesto went on alone, looking for help, what do you think was going through Claudia's mind?

13. How did the experience at the border affect each of the characters—Josie, Vic, Ellie, and Tony?

14. Discuss Josie's comment to Ellie about everyone erecting their own blue flag.

15. Which character did you connect with the most in the novel? Explain.

16. What role do the animals play—the horses, Maggie, and even the new puppy?

17. Discuss the meaning of the song *The Promise of Pangaea*.

About the Author

photo credit: Bruce Thomas

Debra Thomas is a Sarton Award winner for her debut novel, *Luz*. *Josie and Vic* is her second novel. Originally from Binghamton, New York, she has lived in Southern California most of her adult life. After working a decade as a registered nurse, Debra returned to college to pursue her passion for literature and writing. She is a former English teacher at a Los Angeles public high school, as well as English as a Second Language (ESL) instructor to adults from all over the world. Her experience as an immigrant rights advocate influences much of her writing. She currently lives with her husband and little dog in Simi Valley, California, just minutes away from her two horses. For more information, visit her website is http://www.debrathomasauthor.com

SELECTED TITLES FROM SHE WRITES PRESS

She Writes Press is an independent publishing company founded to serve women writers everywhere. Visit us at www.shewritespress.com.

Luz by Debra Thomas. $16.95, 978-1-63152-870-5
When Alma Cruz, a young Mexican woman, journeys across the US border to look for her missing migrant father, she encounters love—but also encounters profound cruelty—along the way.

The Lockhart Women by Mary Camarillo. $16.95, 978-1-64742-100-7
After Brenda Lockhart's husband announces he's leaving her for an older, less attractive woman, she—devastated and lonely—becomes addicted to the media frenzy surrounding the murder of Nicole Brown, which took place the same night her husband dropped his bombshell. In the ensuing months, her whole family falls apart—but ultimately comes together again in unexpected ways.

The Best Part of Us by Sally Cole-Misch. $16.95, 978-1-63152-741-8
Beth cherished her childhood summers on her family's beautiful northern Canadian island—until their ownership was questioned and a horrible storm forced them to leave. Fourteen years later, after she's created a new life in urban Chicago, far from the natural world, her grandfather asks her to return to the island to see if what was lost still remains.

Bittersweet Manor by Tory McCagg. $16.95, 978-1-93831-456-8
A chronicle of three generations of love, manipulation, entitlement, and disappointed expectations in an upper-middle-class New England family.

Don't Put the Boats Away by Ames Sheldon. $16.95, 978-1-63152-602-2
In the aftermath of World War II, the members of the Sutton family are reeling from the death of their "golden boy," Eddie. Over the next twenty-five years, they all struggle with loss, grief, and mourning—and pay high prices, including divorce and alcoholism.